His Hellion Countess

Lustful Lords, Book Two

SORCHA MOWBRAY

Published by Amour Press 2020, Second Edition

ISBN eBook: 978-1-955615-02-0

ISBN Print: 978-1-955615-20-4

Cover design from Fiona Jayde Media

Chapter Images from Illustration 13209099 / Victorian Vines © Freeskyblue | Dreamstime.com

Chapter One

June 1861

Robert Cooper, the Earl of Brougham, twined his cravat around the redhead's wrists at the small of her back and smacked her ass. The woman cooed her approval as she lay bent over the edge of the bed.

"Do keep the racket down, love."

He opened his trousers and pulled out his cock. He liked an enthusiastic lover, just not a noisy one. And having her restrained made his balls throb and his cock stiffen. Though, if he were forthright, not as much as it once had.

"Let the girl be, Cooper." Marion Thomas, Baron Lincolnshire, was balls-deep in a brunette's mouth as he made his suggestion. "Some of us enjoy the sounds of passion."

A low moan of pleasure interrupted them as Grayson Powell, Viscount Wolfington, smacked the backside of the woman he currently had strapped to the spanking bench. The raven-haired beauty he was treating to a stout spanking sounded as excited as Wolf seemed to be, if his rather impressive cockstand was any indication.

Cooper ignored his friend and refocused on the woman he was about to fuck. Reaching down, he slid two fingers into her wet slit and pumped in and out. She moaned softly when he added a third finger. While not the tallest or the stoutest man amongst his set, his cock had proven intimidating to a woman on more than one occasion, so he worked his fingers in and out to ensure the sexy redhead would enjoy taking him.

Once her hips bucked against his hand, he slipped free and notched his cock at her opening. As he slid inside her pussy, the door of their room opened, and Flint—Matthew Derby, Marquess of Flintshire—entered. His face was bloody and bruised, but he tossed everyone a grin.

"Anyone mind if I jump in?" he asked as he opened the front flap of his trousers.

Wolf waved him over. "I think Millie has a hankering for a lobcock."

Flint grabbed his shaft by the base and slapped it against his other hand, making a thick smacking sound. "Nothing soft here." He moved over to Millie and nudged her lips with his erection. "Open up, sweetheart."

The woman stared at Flint's cock for a moment and then eagerly swallowed him whole.

Cooper shook his head at his friends, though watching the eager girl sucking his friend's rather impressive cock helped bring his excitement up another notch. Then he returned once more to riding his way to ecstasy. He laid one hand on the redhead's hip and grabbed her bound wrists with the other as he pounded into her generous curves. He'd come to enjoy the carnal delights of a well-endowed woman, and at the moment, he planned to avail himself of hers. What was her name? Mary? He didn't remember precisely, not that it mattered.

All around him, the sensual sounds of sex filled the room. The slap of flesh, the slurping noise of a well-sucked cock, and the low groans of the participants climbing toward their climaxes. Sliding his hand from her hip to reach under her, he sought out his partner's small nub. As he stroked her clit, she wailed and heaved against him, increasing their tempo. He kept up the bruising pace even as his balls tightened. The redhead crashed over the edge of bliss, crying out her pleasure as he continued to stroke into her. Then, with one last thrust, he exploded inside her with a groan of fulfilment.

All around him, his friends were reaching their satisfying ends. But he needed to tend to the woman beneath him. He rose from the bed and withdrew from her body. Immediately, he released her wrists. "Stay still, love." Then he fastened up his trousers and inspected her wrists to ensure her skin was not overly abused.

"Thank you, my lord," she said as she sat up.

"Think nothing of it. I appreciate your eagerness. Now off with you."

He smacked her on the bum once more, eliciting a giggle from her as she departed. The other girls were either following suit or just finishing up with his friends. Was that a strange feeling of disappointment? Longing? No, it was envy that welled within him and had him feeling just the smallest bit jealous of what Stone had found with Theo.

Pushing aside the wayward thought, Cooper settled down in a nearby chair and waited for the rest of his friends to join him.

Flint sat down first, his trousers still hanging open a bit. "Hell of a night."

"It would seem so." Cooper took in his friend's blood-spattered shirt, split lip, and black eye. "I hope the other fellow looks worse."

"Never doubt it." Flint winked and poured himself a brandy from the decanter that sat nearby.

Wolf joined them then, his clothing set to rights. "Has anyone heard from Stone?"

Cooper laughed. "I believe he is still madly in love with his wife, however unfashionable that may be."

Linc finally joined them, sitting on the bed with his legs up. "I'm beginning to think he has the right of it."

Cooper looked at his friend, curious. "How do you see that?"

Granted, he had seen Stone and Theo's relationship up close in a way none of the others had. He understood the bond between them, even if he didn't wish to emulate it for himself.

"Why not? We all have titles to continue. Why not find a willing woman to do that with? Why strive for a typical *ton* marriage? Lifeless. Practical. Cold. When I must marry, I hope to follow his lead." Linc shrugged.

"Not I," Cooper averred. "I'm pressing on with the original plan. I'll find a suitable wife, one who is scandal-free, an heiress in her own right, and content to settle down to a regular *ton* marriage. We'll do our duty to the title and go our own ways most of the time."

He could picture quiet evenings at home sitting by the fireplace, a drink in his hand, and his favorite dog, Sally, asleep at his feet. His wife would be appropriately occupied tending to his household.

Flint snorted. "Cooper, have you gone soft in the head? No woman will let you have your dog in the house."

The others chuckled, but Cooper knew better. He'd already identified his prospective bride, and it would be a solid arrangement once he was certain there were no deep, dark family secrets lurking in the proverbial closet. His man of affairs had assured him that the investigation he was conducting would be wrapped up in a matter of days. Then he could approach her brother and make a formal agreement, as soon as he was ready.

Lady Emmaline Winterburn would be both docile and accommodating of his demands. Fortunately for her, he was of a mind to pluck her from the obscurity of spinsterhood and set her up as his countess. He fully expected her to all but fall at his feet in gratitude.

Chapter Two

Lady Emmaline Winterburn's heart felt as though it might burst from her chest at any moment. Considering she was attending a ball, some would count that as reason enough.

Double damn. Someone—a maid, likely—was trundling down the Harringtons' hall. She dashed into the first unlocked door she discovered and waited. The plodding footsteps came closer, and closer still. All the while, Emily was certain she was doomed. But then, the steps continued on past the room where she stood, back plastered to the wall as though that might somehow save her wretched hide.

Once she was certain the hall was clear and a quick peek confirmed it, she straightened up to find she had darted into the very room she sought. Moonlight spilled in through the bedroom window, illuminating the space just enough to help her with her task. The faint sparkle of gems caught her eye, drawing her to Lady Harrington's dressing table.

Clearly, the lady of the house had been indecisive on which pieces to wear this evening, much to Emily's benefit. With so many jewels strewn about, it occurred to her that nipping two items would likely be as equally unnoticed as one. With a careful eye, she selected the two pieces she thought were of a good size, but not so large as to be quickly noticed as missing.

Lifting the skirt of her ball gown, she found the hidden seam in her petticoats and tucked the first piece into place. She repeated the process on the other side.

Satisfied with her selection of baubles, she moved to the door and listened for movement. Hearing none, she whipped out into the hall and quickly made her way back to the cacophony of the ball.

As the noise and odors of the utter crush the Harringtons hosted every year swept over her, Emily considered leaving. Between the weight of the jewels in her skirts and the pounding of her pulse, it seemed departure was her most reasonable option. With her great-aunt Hortense home in bed—the poor dear's joints were too inflamed to allow her to attend the ball—Emily was left to her brother's dubious care and the good graces of their family friend, Lady Vardy. Focused as her brother likely was on his gaming, he would barely notice if she left. But good conscience had her stopping a footman to send a quick note.

"Please see that Lord Dunmere receives this as soon as possible."

The servant nodded and set off toward her brother's last known location.

Despite the scandalous nature of doing so alone, she was ready to depart the soiree. Emily turned to head toward the front entry; however, the foyer was so crowded that it prevented any forward progress. Much to her dismay, it appeared she would be forced to remain where she was for the moment.

Then her plight took a turn for the worse.

"Ah, Lady Emmaline, there you are." Lord Brougham bowed. "I searched all over for you. I believe the last waltz of the evening is about to be played."

"How perfectly lovely for you." Emily glanced back over her shoulder in hopes an escape route might emerge.

Seeing no such opportunity, she faced her unwanted suitor.

Taking her hand and tucking it into the crook of his arm, he quirked one brow up. "I believe we are engaged for this dance, if you will merely peruse your dance card."

She was well aware, without looking, that he was two of four names on her dance card. The previous two agonizing dances with men who were poor conversationalists and even poorer dancers made her wish she could avoid yet another. However, Lord Brougham was an acquaintance, which had made his earlier request for a dance both annoying and impossible to refuse. Emily had hoped to avoid the too-handsome man, with his golden-blond hair, darkly intense brown eyes, and chiseled jawline. He embodied the Corinthian style, which she had never found appealing.

Unable to deny the man his rightful dance—no matter how suspect she found his interest—she relented with as much good grace as she could muster under the circumstances. "Please excuse my forgetful nature, my lord. You are, of course, correct."

As the warning refrain sounded, he led her onto the dance floor, where they assumed their positions. When the music commenced, Lord Brougham swept her into his arms, and the too-familiar feel of masculine strength surrounded her in the most disconcerting fashion.

"You are looking quite fetching this evening, Lady Emmaline, if I may be so bold." His low rumble proved just loud enough to carry over the orchestra.

"Thank you, my lord. You too are in fine fettle this evening." She carefully pinned her gaze to the midpoint of his chest, somewhere below his chin.

The weight of the jewels seemed to grow heavier in her skirts with each sweep around the floor. The guilt tried to seep in, but she refused to surrender to it. Her dead parents would have been horrified to see how low she and her brother had fallen under the weight of his unstoppable gambling. It was up to her to salvage the family name and save her brother from certain ruin. If only she had learned the truth sooner, she might have had a chance to do so without resorting to nefarious means. Her only consolation? She chose her victims carefully, only stealing from those members of her set who were either known to be awful people, or who had personally treated her poorly. Sadly, there were victims aplenty, and with a new social season starting up, she would have an abundance of opportunities to turn her brother's—and, more importantly, her own—financial tides.

"Why, thank you, my lady." Lord Brougham pulled her ever so slightly closer. While the ladies of Almack's might have noticed the minute shift, Lady Harrington was certain to be too busy preening over her apparent crush to notice such a minor impropriety.

"Tell me, Lady Emmaline, when you are not attending social events, how do you entertain yourself?"

The man offered the most dashing smile she'd encountered since the Wilton Incident, and surprisingly, she believed for a moment that he truly cared about her answer. But then she reminded herself that men of his ilk, particularly a member of the Lustful Lords, would have only one interest in a woman such as herself. Certainly, marriage wasn't on the man's mind.

Worried about what his interest signified, she mustered up as vapid a reply as she could in hopes it would put him off. "Why, I shop, my lord."

"Indeed? Surely not all the time?" he queried with a small crease between his brows.

Emily felt her cheeks heat a little as a denial fought to make its way past her sealed lips. "Well, of course, one must eat and sleep."

The man coughed, though he somehow managed to retain his composure enough to keep time with the music. "Certainly. And do you attend any salons, perhaps something artistically inclined?"

Again, Emily fought the urge to allow her true intellectual pursuits to surface. Though perhaps her love of Wollstonecraft would be more off-putting than being a spendthrift nincompoop? No, his reaction so far indicated that her portrayal was effective. She summoned the kind of simpering tripe she had frequently heard spill from the mouths of the debutantes she came out with years ago. "How perfectly gauche, my lord. Of course, I sing adequately enough, but truly, a lady should not strain herself. We are the more delicate sex."

A faint pink dusted Lord Brougham's cheeks as he swept her about one more circuit. "How silly of me. You are, of course, correct. A woman would be taxed by intellectual pursuits. Why, I was just saying the other day to a chum that I appreciated nothing more than a woman who can keep herself occupied with appropriate pursuits. It is so tiresome to see these bluestockings gadding about, behaving in such a ridiculous fashion."

Emily ground her teeth and closed her eyes. She must remember that she wanted nothing more than to lead him to believe she was not worth his time. The derision in his tone confirmed her ploy was working, even if it made her wish to stamp on his toe and march off.

"My lord, I find it tiresome that you would speak of any woman in such a fashion." She pressed her lips together again and glared at the man as the music ended.

As the other dancers bowed and made their way off the floor to make way for the next dance, Lord Brougham grabbed her by the arm and led her out on the terrace overlooking the garden. "Lady Emmaline, I find your willingness to deceive me with such a trivial portrayal *tiresome*."

They stopped on the terrace, the only immediate couple present as a quadrille began inside.

Emily tried to yank her arm free from his firm grip, but proved outmatched by his strength. She glared at him balefully. "Fine, *my lord*. I am a spinster who has far too much time available to read. Books. I enjoy everything from gothic romance to the very enlightened writings of Mary Wollstonecraft. I am more and more content each day with my spinster status, and find this entire charade to be wearing. This is not the first ball you have paid particular attention to me in the past few weeks."

Lord Brougham took a step toward her, causing her to take one in retreat. Undeterred, she continued her unladylike tirade.

"And I will tell you, my lord, I learned my lesson well after Lord Wilton. I will not be made light of again. Furthermore, I am no green girl to be toyed with. I am not susceptible to being coaxed into dark gardens for illicit trysts. Nor am I one to surrender stolen kisses in dark corners."

She found herself pressed against a stone balustrade, cloaked in shadows, with the burning heat of a masculine form bearing down on her.

"On the contrary, my lady, I am no Lord Wilton. As for coaxing you into a dark garden, while possibly appealing, I have far more proper intentions where you are concerned." He stepped into her person, her skirts bunching around his ankles as he took hold of her upper arms. "Unfortunately, I find I am not beyond stealing *a kiss* in dark corners."

With a gasp, Emily found her lips captured by his. Despite the layers upon layers of clothing that separated them, she was sure she could feel the heat of his body searing through her gown and underthings. He tasted faintly of brandy as his tongue twined around hers in the most shocking encounter of her spinsterhood. Of course, she had read of such embraces, but she had long ago given up thoughts of ever experiencing such a thing.

With a soft little moan, she surrendered to the foreign sensation of his kiss and relished the way her body reacted. Her skin felt tight, as though overly stretched, and her nipples grew sensitive as they pressed against the fine linen of her chemise.

Too soon, he drew back from her and released her shoulders. Lips flat, as though he disapproved of her, he stepped backward. "Do not believe that you are safe from men like me at any age, my lady. I suggest you return to Lady Vardy immediately, and do not stray onto terraces with men you do not wish to kiss."

Shaken to her very core, she fled the darkened terrace and went in search of Lady Vardy. All the while, Emily grappled with the snarl of conflicting emotions tangled within. Her body clamored for more of the wonderful tingling sensation Lord Brougham's kiss had caused, but her head screamed for her to run away from the man. He was far too domineering and insightful. A man like that would see past her ruse and quickly discern her thieving ways—and more importantly—the reasons for her actions. He was not someone she could trust—not that she trusted anyone anymore.

Chapter Three

Two nights later, Emily skipped the Wharton ball, tired of the wallflowers and the charade. For the moment, their debtors were satisfied, though how long that would last was a question she preferred not to answer. Her brother had gone out, as usual, with his wild friends—she truly hated the group of rich, spoiled lords he traipsed about with—eschewing her offer of a cozy family night at home. It was difficult not to be angry about being cast aside so easily, particularly with all she did to keep him out of debtor's prison.

Admittedly, her brother remained ignorant of the fact she had taken to thievery to help clear their debts. But he did know she had taken over managing their accounts and ensuring the bills were paid. Considering how dire things were when she did so, how could he not wonder at the sudden dearth of collectors knocking at their door? Even if he imagined her as some kind of wizard with the finances, should he not at least be more grateful? Perhaps more resolved not to be such a spendthrift? More ashamed of the fact his sister had had to save his title and the roof over their heads? She sighed. Not Arthur. No, he had chosen to go carousing with his cronies yet again, in lieu of spending time with her.

Despite his obtuseness about their finances, he was still her brother. He was still the one who had pushed little Johnny Redmond into the mud after the boy pulled her hair—and not for the first time—when they were children. Arthur was the one who would sneak into her room when she was sick and bring her sweetmeats he'd filched from the cook. And when their parents had died ten years earlier in a house fire, thanks to her father drunkenly stumbling into a gas lamp, Arthur was the one who had made sure that she had her first season as soon as their year of mourning ended. Little good it did her in catching a husband, though.

The household had retired for the night, and she was on her way upstairs when the front door slammed open. Her brother spilled unceremoniously through the entry and onto the foyer floor, landing with his arms and legs all askew. Shocked by his disgraceful sprawl, she flew down the stairs, concerned he was injured. As she came to the bottom of the steps, she could hear him moaning. And then his head flopped to his right and toward her, revealing his split lip, black eye, and bloody nose. Pulling up short at the reek of alcohol, she looked down at the mess that was her brother. "Arthur, what on earth has happened?"

His only response was another moan.

With a sigh of resignation, she knelt next to him and tried to assess how badly he was hurt.

Behind her, Palmer, their longtime butler, scuffed into the foyer. "My lady, is everything well?"

"I fear not, Palmer. Lord Dunmere seems to have gotten himself foxed, as well as soundly trounced. Do help me get him up and into the study for now. Then we can assess his apparent injuries."

"Very good, my lady." Palmer knelt on Arthur's other side and helped shoulder his weight as they hauled him up and into the next room.

As they settled him on the leather couch, her brother roused. "Emily! What the blazes are you doing in Lucifer's?"

She wanted to moan herself upon hearing his question. It was bad enough handling the multitude of collectors and merchants knocking on their doors, but now he had taken to visiting gambling hells?

"Palmer, would you please see that Mrs. Halliwell puts a good beef stock on? I suspect we shall need it in a few hours."

"Of course, my lady." Palmer bowed and left her alone with her brother.

Arthur had dozed off again, so she set to searching his pockets. She needed to know what he'd been up to, and chances were his pockets would tell the tale. Inside one, she found a slip of paper with a long list of numbers and initials jotted down. As she continued searching his interior coat pockets, her hands shook. If the list was what she suspected—IOUs—they were in serious trouble. By the time she found the second list—bigger in both length and in denominations—fury, fear, and desolation overwhelmed her. With a rough shake of her brother's shoulder, she woke him once more. "Arthur. Arthur, you will wake up this instant and tell me what is going on!"

"Emily?" He sat up slowly, looking blindly around with his damaged left eye. "I must be batty with drink." He rubbed his face and peered right past her again. Then he flopped back on the couch and groaned. "Bloody hell. She'll kill me when she finds out about what I owe Lucifer."

"Arthur. I already know. I am standing right here." She wanted to hit her idiotic brother, but his face was already battered enough for one night.

Opening both eyes, the left one only a slit, he peered at her. "Double damn. I'd hoped you were a figment of my imagination."

"Well, I'm not. Now, time to tell me what you've done." She held up the slips of paper she'd found.

"Bollocks. You found 'em. You always were too quick for me, little Em." He slurred the last part so badly, she had to stop and think to be sure she understood what he was saying.

"Don't you dare trot that old nickname out now. It will do you no good with me. I found them all, Arthur. By my accounting, nearly a thousand pounds in IOUs." She had to work very hard not to shriek the words.

"Oh good, she didn't find the fiver." His mumbled relief punched her square in the gut.

"No, I didn't find the fiver. But now that I know, who do you owe a fiver to? And what exactly is a fiver?" Her fury was quickly rising and drowning the fear and desolation. Her brother had gone out and beggared them by losing a fortune they did not have in one single night, or so it seemed.

"Five thousand pounds." He moaned and slung an arm over his eyes, but when his limb hit his black eye, he winced in pain. "And to Lucifer himself."

Emily felt all the blood drain from her head as her stomach twisted in her belly. *How did one gamble so much money away?*

Fighting off the nausea, she pushed herself to focus on the immediate issue. "All right. Arthur, who beat you up?"

She was getting angrier and angrier, and not just with her brother, but with all men. With a society that wouldn't allow grown women to walk alone, but would stand by and watch as young men drove their families into the poorhouse with nary a twitch.

After all, lords will be lords. The notion made her want to stamp her foot and wave her fist at such inequity.

But more importantly, his behavior—not unlike her father's selfish drunkenness—felt like yet another betrayal. Another instance of a man putting his own desires before the needs of his family. The needs of the very ones who depend upon him for their survival. Fury seared through her and made her hands clench into fists as she fought the urge to slap him across the face. But further violence served no purpose. Her brother was already so battered.

"Oh, that was some of Lucifer's goons. It was a friendly reminder that the first of my debts are coming due and I have yet to make a payment. Now leave off, lil Em." He slurred even more as he rolled over toward the back of the couch. "So tired."

"Yes, I can imagine." She turned on her heel and went to the kitchen. There she found a rag and some cool water. Once she returned to the study, she placed the damp rag on her brother's eye and covered him with a blanket. There was little else she could do for him until morning, so she went to bed. Of course, she doubted she would be sleeping much, not with the realization that her brother had just put them so far in hock, she would have to rob a bank to save them. Anger had long since overridden the exhaustion that had tugged at her earlier as she had planned to retire. Perhaps a book might help clear her mind and allow her to rest.

The next afternoon, Emily slipped out of the house after her lady's companion, great-aunt Hortense, had gone upstairs for her afternoon nap. She found herself knocking on the door of Lucifer's, all the while willing her hands to cease their shaking. At this point, she wasn't sure they would ever stop trembling. As the door opened, her heart leaped into her throat at the sight of the large and terribly scarred man who appeared.

He looked her up and down. "We ain't giving to charity."

Then the door began to close.

With a harrumph of indignation, she slapped her hand on the door and jammed the rather insubstantial toe of her kid boot into the opening. "I am not here soliciting donations. I wish to speak with the proprietor."

"There ain't no such thing here." The words came out more of a rumble than proper communication.

But Emily persevered. "The owner. I would like to speak with the owner, please."

The man stopped and considered her request. "Well, why didn't you say so in the first place? He's not taking callers."

And the door resumed closing.

She held fast. "I am here about my brother's debt. I am sure he will see me about the five thousand pounds Lord Dunmere owes him."

The man paused again, opened the entry, and waved her in. Once she was inside, he closed the door, cutting off the majority of the light that had shone into the space. A few streaks slipped past heavy curtains to highlight bits of burgundy and gold in the medium-size foyer.

"Wait here," he said, and then he walked away. Lumbered, really, but she was too nervous to be amused by the awkward gait of the huge man.

Curiosity and an irrepressible need to move about had her looking inside the adjacent rooms. The two spaces appeared as mirror images of each other. The same colors and decorations, same tables and chairs. She was inspecting one of them when the shuffle of footsteps alerted her to the arrival of someone. She spun about to find another tall man looming over her as a beam of light splashed across him.

"I was told an elegant-but-persistent lady wished to see me about a rather large debt."

A dichotomous picture of a ruffian who must have employed the most talented of valets stood before Emily.

She blinked slowly. While he was burly and somewhat menacing, his finely turned cravat and impeccably groomed beard suggested the beast had been civilized. She certainly hoped that was true for her sake. "You are the owner of this establishment?"

He nodded and took a step back, almost as though shrinking away from the light, which made it hard to inspect him further in the shadows. "Frank Lucifer, at your service. And you are?"

"Lady Emmaline Winterburn. My brother is the Earl of Dunmere."

She resisted the urge both to curtsey and to follow the mysterious man out of the light. Though being illuminated so her every expression was visible felt like a distinct disadvantage at the moment.

"Ah, yes." He bowed to her. "Welcome to Lucifer's. Please, come upstairs, where we may better conduct business."

The man took her hand and placed it on his arm, as comfortable with the gesture as any gentleman of her acquaintance. They walked through the foyer and up the stairs. There, they strolled along a gallery that overlooked the main rooms she had been peeking at earlier.

"I've never seen you here before, have I?" he asked.

"Of course not. That would be inappropriate. This visit is also unsuitable, though unfortunately necessary."

"Yes, I rarely see ladies of such quality and breeding." His gaze swept her from head to toe in the much-better-lit area they walked through. They continued all the way to the end, and then he stopped before a set of double doors and opened one. "Please, join me."

Fear had her belly flipping as she stepped into what she was sure would turn out to be his bedroom, whereupon he would proceed to ravish her. Except, she walked into a well-lit office that boasted an elegant mahogany desk that would have given any lord she'd ever met a serious case of envy. The beautifully carved wood piece made a bold statement about both the man and his expectations. It also shifted her hope for how the conversation might go. Perhaps Mr. Lucifer would prove to be more of a gentleman than she had anticipated.

The man in question followed her into the room and indicated a chair on one side of the desk.

"Thank you for seeing me, Mr. Lucifer." She took the offered seat and waited as he prowled around the massive piece of furniture.

"Now, what may I do for you?" He settled back into his chair and waited.

Everything about the man was dark and forbidding. She took in his sun-bronzed skin, midnight hair, and eyes so dark as to appear black. His intense gaze left her feeling much like a butterfly pinned for inspection. Fidgeting in her seat, she tried to find the words to express what she needed. "I understand my brother owes you a rather large sum of money, and that payment is due in the next few months."

"That is correct. In fact, the first thousand pounds is due by the end of the month. Do you need the exact figure?" His dark gaze held her in her seat.

Her heartbeat sped up as her palms grew damp. "I do not. What I need is time, Mr. Lucifer."

His brow creased. "I have given your brother the standard payment schedule. He agreed to it before I loaned him the money, which he then proceeded to lose."

"Back to you, no doubt," she snapped, her nerves fraying under the stress.

The darkly handsome man grinned at her. "Indeed, I believe a fair portion of that money—if not all of it—was, in fact, lost at my tables. However, that does not alleviate the debt he owes me."

She wanted to smack the smirk right off the man's face. "It does not. However, I had hoped that you might take pity on me, if not him, and give us a bit more time to get the money together. We've had"—she hesitated, grappling for the best turn of phrase—"a bit of a challenging year. We are certainly good for the debt, but a year would be far more manageable than three months to repay you without further damaging our financial situation."

The man frowned. "And why is your situation different from that of any other bloke who comes into my establishment and requests a loan because they do not have the blunt to play?" He leaned on the desk. "Why should you have a year when the standard agreement for repayment is four months?"

Emily's heart sank. Despite his handsome features and pretty manners, the man was proving to be as unfeeling and hardened as she had originally expected. "I see. I should have expected someone who makes their fortune on the foul luck of others would not have a heart. May I make one stipulation to my brother's agreement?"

His smile long gone, Lucifer sat back in his chair. "You may make a *request*."

"I would like you to promise me that you will not make further loans to my brother, nor will you allow him to gamble in your establishment."

Emily waited, her heart constricting painfully.

"You do pay attention to details, do you not?" A grudging respect shone in his eyes as he assessed her.

"Someone must. Do you agree?" She pressed her request.

One brow rose near his hairline. "And should I refuse? What will you do?"

"Mr. Lucifer, you know very well I have little recourse should you refuse. It is unkind of you to point that out to a lady who has come to you for some assistance for her rather precarious position. I shall ensure you are paid, regardless. What I am asking for is an opportunity to ensure my brother does not continue to beggar us."

"You do realize there are infinite options for a man who has the determination to gamble away his family's fortune."

"I am no fool. But this would be one less option for me to worry over." She folded her hands together in her lap, hoping for even this small boon.

"You have caught me in a weak moment. I respect a lady who has the gumption to take a thing head-on without sniveling or batting her lashes. Despite it being generally bad for business, I shall bar your brother. But do not bandy that information about London. I do not need a string of women in here begging for the same service. I have a business to run."

"You have my word, Mr. Lucifer." She rose and turned to walk out. "You will hear from me in a few weeks to arrange payment."

She had reached the office door when he stopped her with a question. "How are you going to manage the debt?"

She froze and considered how she was going to do exactly that. Two of her favorite books came to mind, *A General History of the Pyrates* and *Rookwood: A Romance*. Sailing the high seas wasn't terribly practical, but then, neither was becoming a highwayman. Although... both had a common element. Theft on its own, however, was imminently practical when one regularly received invitations to balls in all the wealthiest homes.

She decided to be frank with Mr. Lucifer. He likely wouldn't believe her anyway. "I plan to steal the money."

As expected, he laughed loudly as she retraced her steps through the building. At the door, she found the man with the scars waiting for her. He quickly opened the door and then locked it behind her as she stepped out onto the street.

It seemed she had some planning to do.

Chapter Four

Cooper was intrigued. Lady Emmaline maintained the appearance of a veritable wallflower. She leaned toward more subtle gowns, often in subdued tones of blues, browns, and greens. Tonight, however, her gown was a dark green material contrasted by a pale green trimming about the neckline. With her golden-brown hair swept back into a sedate set of rolls that framed her face, she looked every inch the self-effacing spinster.

But with a keen eye trained on her as he approached, he did not miss the flicker of annoyance that danced within her hazel eyes upon spying him. Not for the first time, he wondered what truly lay beneath the milksop façade of Lady Emmaline. During the Harringtons' ball, he had no doubt sensed something more beneath the surface, particularly when his lips had met hers. Despite being a relatively chaste kiss when compared to others he'd experienced over the years, something about it remained with him. In fact, he had been unable to cease thinking about having Lady Emmaline in his arms once more.

He stopped before Lady Vardy, her chaperone, first. Then he turned to the woman who had unexpectedly dominated his thoughts of late and bowed, all the while enjoying the view of her breasts his courtesy provided. "Lady Emmaline, you look lovely. If I may, I should like to claim a dance or two from you this evening."

"Thank you, my lord." She studied him for a moment. Suspicion turned her gaze hard and assessing before she nodded and ever so slowly produced her dance card.

For a moment, he swore she would pull it back before he could take it. Then he selected his dances—two waltzes, of course—and handed it back to her.

She looked down at her card and frowned slightly. "You are *too* kind."

Satisfied with having achieved his immediate goal, he retreated until his first dance. Of course, he had not missed the dearth of other dances filled in on her card. There was merely one other name beyond his. It made him wonder what had occurred to cause her to be so lacking in attention. She'd mentioned the incident with Lord Wilton. Could that cad's actions have so damaged her prospects? He had vaguely remembered Lord Wilton paying her some notice a few years before, and his investigation had mentioned the occurrence as well, but since that time, she'd slipped into obscurity. Was that by happenstance, or by design?

The next two dances plodded along, particularly considering the young ladies he was forced by etiquette to partner with. Upon delivering his last debutante to her beaming mother, he was able to head off to collect Lady Emmaline. He found her just as he had left her earlier, standing by Lady Vardy.

"I believe this dance is mine." He bowed over her hand.

She curtsied. "You are correct, my lord."

He led her onto the floor, and they took their place. The music commenced, and he swept her into the close-hold rotation of a waltz. Determined to get to know her better—after all, he intended to offer for her once they were well enough acquainted—he ventured conversation. "Are you enjoying the festivities?"

Emily offered a guarded smile. "I suppose I am. And you, my lord, are you enjoying yourself?"

"I am now." He offered her a conspiratorial smile that she did not return. "At my age, I find the young chits rather overeager."

She neither smiled nor frowned at his comment. "Do you? I have come to understand a man of this set"—she lifted her hand in indication of the crowded ballroom—"enjoys such fawning attention."

Aghast at such a notion, Cooper blurted, "Good God! What would make you think such a thing?"

His companion's cheeks became dusted with a fetching light pink. It was strange to find himself growing more physically attracted to the woman he had selected for his bride. Mostly because he'd chosen her based on the fact she specifically did not fire his lust. She was a reserved, all but overlooked prospect, who, in theory, would jump at the opportunity he offered in the form of marriage. Or, at least, that had been his initial perspective. As he got to know Lady Emmaline, he was discovering that his perceptions might have been more than a little wrong.

"As I spend a great amount of time at balls watching you and your contemporaries swirling those very chits around the dance floor in lieu of older specimens such as myself, I should think it an obvious conclusion." She dared a glance up at his face, but then quickly returned to staring at his bow tie.

The woman had a valid point that he found difficult to refute, so he decided to switch topics. "I understand that supper will be served soon. It would be a great honor if I could escort you in."

To Cooper's surprise, that skeptical hardness returned to her lovely green-and-brown gaze.

"My lord, you seem to be paying *particular* attention to me. If I were a younger woman, I would think you were courting me. But as we both know I am well on the shelf, I can't imagine what might be behind such attention." She paused as her cheeks colored an even darker pink. With a careful glance about, as if to ensure their conversation was private, she asked, "Are you perchance trying to lure me astray, like some merry widow? Let me be clear: I am neither merry nor a widow."

He burst out laughing as he spun her about the floor in time to the music. Her question had both surprised and delighted him. A refreshing candor that he had only recently discovered lurked within the sedate woman he had chosen to pursue. Once he reined in his mirth, he realized the rather cagey lady in question was not at all amused. "Forgive me, it was not that you are not worthy of luring astray, but merely that you asked me outright if that were my intention."

Brow creased in doubt, she frowned at him even as she continued to follow his lead. "And is it? You have yet to answer the question, my lord. And do not pretend I do not know of your reputation."

He sobered at her pointed reference to his membership in the Lustful Lords. It seemed he might have underestimated a spinster's willingness to overlook his less socially acceptable entertainments—particularly *this* spinster. She was proving to be a mistrustful sort.

"I would never pretend to be other than what I am. I have never hidden my more prurient leanings, nor do I intend to start now. But the answer to your query is no, Lady Emmaline. I do not intend to ravish you."

Though if they continued this line of conversation, he might find the suggestion had more merit than he'd first suspected. Nevertheless, the conversation was taking a turn into territory best addressed in a more private setting than the ballroom floor.

"Whyever not?" She followed his lead easily enough in dancing, but less so in the conversation.

"I am not prone to despoiling innocents, even those set upon the shelf." He hoped she would accept his response and leave the subject alone.

"That is not what people say about you and your friends. But it's neither here nor there, since I will not allow you to *despoil* me, in any event."

Her haughty dismissal of his intentions, real or otherwise, disturbed him considering his recent warning to her about shadowed terraces and kissing. But before he could retort, she continued on.

"Well, I daresay I would not have allowed you any such liberties that would lead to ravishment."

Her innocent insistence rankled.

"I suggest you may wish to rethink such boastfulness, my lady. If you will recall the Harringtons' ball, I neatly steered you into the shadows and stole a kiss, despite your best intentions. Most young ladies do not intend to be ravished, but merely find themselves as such."

Something dangerous deep inside him had been piqued by her defiance.

And suddenly, his thoughts shifted from stolen kisses to images of a bound Lady Emmaline with her backside pink from his spankings. His cock twitched eagerly in his trousers, hinting at a soon-to-be uncomfortable situation. For the moment, all was manageable with the assistance of his partner's skirts, but it would soon be outright embarrassing if he could not regain control of himself.

Emily gasped at his pointed reminder of their kiss. But before she could muster a response, the waltz ended. As she regained her wits, Lord Brougham led her back in the direction of Lady Vardy.

"Were I you, I would not assume any such future opportunities, my lord. I am not a woman to be trifled with." They arrived back at Lady Vardy's side. "Thank you for the dance, my lord."

"My pleasure, Lady Emmaline. I look forward to escorting you in to supper later."

With a smile and a wink, Cooper left his adversary with her chaperone and repressed the urge to whistle a tune at having outmaneuvered her so neatly.

Emily remained where she was, standing mutely next to Lady Vardy. She was far more preoccupied with the wild tumble of emotions that rolled through her than with whatever platitudes her deceased mother's best friend was speaking at the moment. Indignation that Lord Brougham would manhandle her in such a fashion. And, oddly enough, frustration that he had not, in fact, attempted to kiss her again. As they had swept about the ballroom sparring verbally, she'd wanted nothing more than to feel his lips on hers. It had come as quite a shock.

Of course, despite walking a fine line with Society, he had proven to be mostly a gentleman. Although the fact he had claimed her as a supper partner without her actual agreement was awfully high-handed, but short of explaining to Lady Vardy why she had no desire to dine with the man, she had no choice but to join him for supper.

Still preoccupied with thoughts of the very distracting Lord Brougham, she tried to calm her thoughts and focus on the real reason she had attended the ball—and it definitely was *not* related to strong arms or sandalwood and leather scents. Lord Brougham and his second dance—let alone supper—could go hang. Determined to accomplish her true purpose and forget the man who messed with that kernel of hope that she kept buried deep down inside, she turned to her chaperone. "Lady Vardy, I believe I require a visit to the ladies' retiring room."

To Emily's relief—and immense good luck—Lord Vardy appeared by his wife's side. "Madam, I was wondering if you might enjoy a turn about the dance floor."

Her chaperone cast a glance at her, then looked back at her husband. "I am—"

"My lady, please do not hesitate on my behalf. I am certain I shall muddle through just fine for one dance."

Emily smiled and nodded as she slipped away from Lord and Lady Vardy.

As usual, it was easy enough to skirt the mass of bodies and make her way past the retiring rooms and up the stairs to the private living quarters. Ever cautious, she quietly crept down the hall, peeking into the various rooms until she discovered the chamber she sought. With a lamp burning low on a nearby table allowing enough light to determine it was the correct room, she let herself inside Lady Kilpatrick's chamber. Since the lady in question wore a very potent perfume, Fleurs de Bulgarie, originally created for Queen Victoria, Emily's nose offered further confirmation she had the correct room.

The heady scent of rose and bergamot hung heavy in the air as she looked about for some trinket or bauble to liberate. Finally, she found a stash of jewels in a dresser drawer. A particularly lovely choker studded with diamonds and rubies caught her eye. Determined to acquire more valuable pieces now that her brother's debt had reached outrageous proportions, she pushed away the misgivings that prodded her to put the necklace back.

Voices carried down the hallway, making her close the drawer and place the lamp back on the table it had been sitting on when she entered. Then the voices came closer, growing louder, and Emily's heart pounded. With no time to fiddle with her secret seam, she jammed the jewelry down her cleavage, making sure to tuck it deep between her breasts.

The hard stones and bulky gold setting dug into her skin, having managed to slide behind her chemise and corset. But with no time to adjust the piece, she dashed into the adjoining room and shut the door between them. Now in Lord Kilpatrick's more masculine chamber, she waited. The door to the room she had just vacated opened, and two maids entered.

"Lady Kilpatrick is insisting on having one of her new silk shawls brought down for supper," one of the maids said.

"I certainly hope she doesn't spill anything on it. She blamed me for not getting the last stain out of her favorite tea gown. As if any person might be able to remove tea from cream lace. I spent hours removing and replacing the lace trim," the other woman said.

Terrified of being discovered, Emily stood pressed against the door. Her hands trembled as she listened to the two women continue to ramble on about Lady Kilpatrick. The voice of the woman who'd had to replace the lace grew louder. "Now Lord Kilpatrick, he's as kind a soul as is possible. Perhaps I should just straighten up *his* room."

The woman was standing near the door that separated Emily from discovery. Sweat beaded on her brow, and her stomach twisted as she held her breath. *Please God, don't let her come in here.*

The knob started to twist, and Emily swore her heart would break free from her chest. A glance around the room offered no place to quickly hide. The closet and hall door were too far away in the cavernous chamber.

The other maid snorted. "Kind, my fat arse. He's as many hands as a sea monster has legs! Every time I have to clean his study, the man finds a way to be in there so he can touch me."

The knob rotated back in place with a snap.

"Polly Bodsworth, you shouldn't tell such lies!" The maid by the door sounded outraged.

"Don't you Polly Bodsworth me, Kathleen. I'm not telling lies at all. My wee brother has one of those picture books some rich person gave to charity. It has all kinds of sea monsters in it, and one of them has eight legs that wrap around a ship at sea. I'll tell you that's how I feel when Lord

Kilpatrick corners me alone. It's disgusting." Polly sniffed. "But if you don't believe me, then that's your business."

And then sharp footsteps tapped across the floor, and a door slammed closed. A moment later, Kathleen ran after her friend. "Polly, wait!"

Once both women had departed the room, Emily heaved a huge sigh of relief. Desperate to return to the ball, for she had been gone for far too long, she opened the master's chamber door and crept down the hall.

Nearly back on the main floor, she slipped through the crowd toward the ladies' retiring room. But then a firm hand grabbed her upper arm and quickly drew her into the Fitzpatrick's library.

"Where the devil have you been?" Lord Brougham's warm baritone held a note of panic as he released her arm.

Determined to brazen out the moment, she blinked as though in surprise. "Why, I have been in the ladies' retiring room."

"Last I checked, the ladies' retiring room is not on the second floor." He let both brows rise nearly to his hairline.

Concerned now that he might have some suspicion of her, she strove for her placid-spinster countenance. "It was terribly crowded in the retiring room. I needed a moment of peace, so I slipped upstairs and ducked into a guest room for a moment."

His gaze narrowed, as though he found that story highly suspicious. "You know there have been rumors floating about. It seems more than a few hostesses have discovered missing items of jewelry after their soirees."

"Have they? Why, I had not heard such rumors, my lord." She pressed a hand to her chest, causing the diamond-and-ruby necklace to dig cruelly into her flesh.

"I suggest you curtail any wanderings. As we established at the Harringtons' ball and again here earlier, it can be dangerous for a woman to be gadding about unchaperoned during a ball." He grunted a bit, as though punctuating his point.

Annoyance overriding her good sense, she rolled her eyes. "As I told you earlier, my lord, I am not a woman to be trifled with. I am quite capable of taking care of myself."

In a fit of pique, she turned and stormed toward the closed library door. But before she could attain the portal, Lord Brougham grabbed her arm once more and spun her about to face him. Trapped with one arm behind her back, her wrist held firmly in his grip and her chest pressed indelicately against his chest, she sucked in a gulp of air.

"Do not be so ridiculous, Lady Emmaline. You are a delicate woman, and no match for some villain who may be prowling about the upper stories of the *ton*'s balls."

Anger radiated off his body as he stared down at her. His nostrils flared, and then his lips captured hers in another kiss.

Despite the illicit items digging into her chest, Emily found herself instantly swept up in the moment. Her heart raced—for an entirely different reason—and the warm heat of his mouth overwhelmed her ability to think, let alone speak. All she could do was taste, and revel in the feel of him as he kissed her for the second time.

As though he, too, had lost all reason, Lord Brougham allowed his kisses to trail down her neck and over her collarbones. Tingles danced across her body, causing her core to throb. He then lowered them to the nearby couch.

"Emmaline," Lord Brougham moaned as he continued to pepper her skin with kisses.

And then he eased the front of her gown down, exposing more of her breasts. He busily followed the material down over the tops of her breasts, still kissing her wherever new flesh was exposed.

Suddenly warning bells sounded in her head: *the necklace!*

"What the bloody hell?" Lord Brougham was tugging on the item in question when it slid free from between her breasts.

Chapter Five

Cooper stared at the very expensive trinket he had found nestled in Lady Emmaline's bosom. The cockstand he'd had only a moment before wilted as the implications of what he had discovered took root.

"That is my necklace. Please return it to me, my lord." Emily sat up, pulling at her bodice.

"Why is it you have a necklace stuffed down your corset?" He held the item in question aloft as he examined what appeared to be a rather valuable item.

Panic flashed across her face for a moment, but then calmness settled over her features. "I had thought to wear the blasted piece this evening, but as we were driving, Lady Vardy convinced me it was extravagant. Lacking a safe place to keep the bauble, I stuffed it down my dress."

He stood and inspected it more closely. "Diamonds and rubies?"

He looked back at Lady Emmaline, who currently had a set of simple pearl-drop earrings dangling from her lobes. In mere moments, he put all the facts together. He'd seen her leave Lady Vardy's side, and had followed her to ensure she reached the ladies' retiring room. It was an obvious destination, so he'd been surprised when she'd sailed right past it and up the stairs to the living quarters.

Considering the rumors he'd mentioned, he'd had little desire to be caught wandering about upstairs. The *ton* already thought him barely respectable. If he added "accused thief" to his list of sins, he would be utterly objectionable. So, he'd placed himself at the bottom of the stairs, just behind them in the shadows, and waited. She had been gone nearly half an hour when worry set in. Then, just as he was about to charge up the stairs after her, she had appeared.

It had occurred to him she might be meeting someone for an illicit tryst, but there was no question she kissed like a novice. He found it hard to imagine she had taken a lover. The notion of the ball-attending thief had flitted through his thoughts, but mostly as a threat to her safety. It had never really occurred to him that *she* might be the thief.

"I tell you it is mine, my lord. Do you question my truthfulness?" She rose from the couch, anger infusing her words with just enough outrage to make him want to believe her.

But there was no possibility she was telling the truth. While no fashion expert himself—his valet would likely suggest he was a fashion imbecile—he knew well enough that women did not mix diamonds and rubies with pearls. Not to mention, she had never, in the time he'd been getting to know her, worn anything so ostentatious.

He turned to face her. "I believe I am, Lady Emmaline."

Furious, she stormed up to him and attempted to snatch the necklace from his grasp.

Holding it high above her head, he wrapped his free arm around her and pulled her against him. "Ah, ah, ah, my Lady Hellion. First you will admit the truth to me."

First? He couldn't help but wonder at himself. The woman he had intended to make his countess was, in fact, a thief. He should be hauling her out of the library and into the ballroom to have the authorities summoned. But he quickly realized he had no intention of doing any such thing.

"Very well, my lord. If I admit such a thing, will you return the necklace to me?" Her lips pressed together, emphasizing her stubborn aspect.

"That rather depends on what you have to say." He couldn't hide his smirk. Intuition told him this was going to be an interesting turn of events in his courtship of Lady Emmaline.

She growled at him a little. He found it adorable.

"Fine, my lord. I stole the necklace."

She said what he had expected, though with ill grace. Clearly, she was not as entertained by events as he.

"Why, Lady Emmaline? I have not heard of any financial woes related to your family. What could be driving you to such an action?"

His mind ticked through what he knew of her family. Her parents were both dead, killed in a tragic house fire. Her brother didn't particularly stand out in any fashion among the *ton*, but then that had seemed typical of her family until now.

In short order, the fear and anger slipped from her face like a mask tossed aside. In its place appeared the neutral expression he had originally associated with her. One that hinted that she found the whole event tiresome, but was too polite to ever say so.

"Boredom, Lord Brougham. Night after night, year after year of attending balls, only to dance once or twice, and then be forgotten once more. Eventually, a woman will find a way of entertaining herself."

Cooper blinked. Boredom? That seemed preposterous. "If ennui is your issue, perhaps I can offer you something to busy yourself with?"

"Doubtful, my lord." She dismissed his suggestion out of hand, without having even heard it.

More than a little affronted, he straightened up. "Perhaps, Lady Emmaline, you should consider my suggestion. Under the circumstances."

With her nose wrinkled, she again conceded to hear him out. "Very well, my lord. Suggest away."

"Marry me." He blurted the words out in the most unromantic fashion possible. Of course, the entire scenario was terribly unsentimental.

The blasted woman laughed. She actually guffawed as she held her stomach and bent over as far as her corset would allow.

Feeling peeved about the whole thing, Cooper stood there and waited for her mirth to subside. Finally, as she settled down, he spoke. "I fail to see the humor in this."

"You have just suggested that I, a known thief—at least by you—marry you." She chuckled again. "You do, of course, realize how ridiculous that sounds?"

He refrained from grinding his teeth—barely. "I don't see why it is so ridiculous. I need a wife, and you clearly need a husband to take you in hand and curtail such fiendish activities."

Lady Emmaline finally ceased laughing. Her features shifted from mirth to a studied seriousness, her gaze full of calculation as she rose. "You may stop right there, Lord Brougham." She held up one trembling hand. "I shall save you any further embarrassment by clearly stating my position on marriage."

She tucked her hands behind her back, placing one in the other, then turned to pace as she spoke. "You may not have realized it because men of our social standing often overlook me, but I am a spinster. *Firmly* on the shelf. And I must say that I have come to find a certain peace in my lot. I have no interest in taking on a husband, or the various responsibilities that come with marriage. I answer to no one but myself, and if I should desire to spend all my pin money on frivolous things, there is no one who can gainsay me on this. I have no need of a man telling me what to do or thinking he knows best. Nothing you can say shall sway my thinking."

She ceased moving and turned to face him, defiance radiating from her person in almost palpable waves.

"Not even a promise of financial security?"

Cooper could not understand how a woman who was apparently stealing could turn down such an offer. It made no sense, unless she was quite serious about being bored and not stealing for financial gain.

Her face hardened, the muscles around her jaw tensing. "I am not for sale, my lord."

"Lady Emmaline, I made no such suggestion. I merely pointed out the fiscal advantages of marriage to me. There are others, you know." He was miffed that she had taken his carrot and turned it rotten. "I can also offer you the social acceptance of being an earl's wife, a home that has been in my family since the Tudors reigned, and an opportunity to be a mother."

To his great surprise, none of what he metaphorically laid before her caused a softening of her features. Her chin remained tilted—mutinous, he'd daresay—and her lips firmly pressed together. Beneath the stubborn glint in her gaze, he could still see the suspicion lurking.

"None of what you propose is of interest to me, my lord. I am comfortably on the shelf."

He frowned. "What of marital relations? You have no interest in experiencing the intimacy between a man and a woman?"

The firm resolve on her face wobbled.

Seeing a chink in her armor, he pressed. "As my wife, I can show you the delights of the bedroom. I *am* one of the Lustful Lords."

Determination renewed, he saw the moment she weighed the suggestion and discarded his lure. "Whatever *prowess* you possess in the bedroom is doubtful to be worth a life of indentured servitude as Lady Brougham."

Cooper admitted to himself that the lady's words stung. As a lifelong bachelor, he had never intended to marry. Certainly he knew it was his duty, but in some strange corner of his mind, he had believed he might stave off that fate until the ripe old age of fifty, or possibly even sixty. Just the other day there had been an article in the paper telling of a man just turned seventy-five, who'd fathered twins! But here he was still in his prime, not even forty yet, and he had somehow succumbed to the pressure to secure the future of the earldom.

Then a thought occurred to him. "I see. Indentured servitude?"

"Just so." She nodded decisively.

"Please excuse my forwardness, but might I suggest that the notion of the delights of the bedroom seemed to contain some potential appeal to you?"

She eyed him warily. "I might concede to a certain curiosity about all the hullabaloo."

He mentally rubbed his hands together. His pulse picked up slightly as he cornered his quarry. "Interesting. You are certainly an unconventional woman." He stepped closer to her. "So may I offer you an unconventional proposal? An arrangement that will allow you to indulge your curiosity while not surrendering yourself to indentured servitude?"

Lady Emmaline continued to watch him, but nodded. "I'm listening."

Having had a small taste of holding her and kissing her, he needed more. Needed a way to have her in his arms so that he could show her how they might just work. "Will you be my mistress?"

Yet another chuckle from her was not the response he expected.

"I cannot take a lover."

"Why not? You have no intention of marrying, so you are not giving away what is rightfully your future husband's. Many a widow has taken a lover after discovering the pleasures of the marriage bed. Are you so willing to give up the possibility of experiencing that satisfaction?"

Consideration whirled to life in her perceptive gaze as she returned to the settee. "Perhaps. Perhaps not. What would be the terms of such an arrangement if I were to say yes? And where would this affair take place?"

Cooper grappled for a moment for what might be basic terms he would include. "We would meet at The Market. I am already a member and known visitor. You could continue to wear a mask and cloak to meet me, or I am sure Madame Celeste would arrange for a more discreet arrival around the back. As for the terms, we would need to write them all down, but Celeste has a standard contract we could use, and then tailor it to any specific requirements."

"A contract?"

"The Market requires such for all extended assignations." He shrugged one shoulder.

Lady Emmaline paused for a few moments. "And the terms of this contract?"

"Well, for example, I would require that you be available upon my request."

She hesitated a moment before responding. "I would need at least twenty-four hours' notice so I could plan to be out for the evening. Lady Vardy is no easy chaperone to escape. Also, what I do when I am not with you is my business."

"Twenty-four hours is acceptable." He drew a deep breath and reminded himself that if he did not relent in some fashion, she would say no. "And I agree not to badger you about your activities when not with me. However, I am the only lover you will have for the length of our arrangement."

"I see." Her hand fluttered to her throat in a thoughtless gesture that suggested she found the notion intriguing. "How..." She cleared her throat. "How long would this *arrangement* last?"

"We could start with three months and then reassess. If we like, we can renew it for longer, or make any necessary changes."

"That sounds fair. Will I need to become a member of The Market to visit frequently?" She bit her lip as though the notion concerned her.

"I shall address the issue with Madame Celeste." He would either cover her membership fees or arrange a guest pass. Either way, he would see to it. One last demand occurred to him, a necessity if his plan was going to work. "I also want the right to call on you—"

"Absolutely not. I shall not allow you to court me." Her spine stiffened, and her chin tilted just so. "As I have clearly stated, I have no intention of marrying."

"Not as a lover, but as a friend. One day every fortnight should be enough to establish a friendship without causing tongues to wag."

She hesitated, letting the silence linger as the strains of music from the ballroom filtered through the wood doors.

For a moment, he thought she might back out, but then she offered him a slow nod of agreement. "I don't like your last demand, but I shall agree with the stipulation that your visits will not include gifts or anything that resembles courting."

"Agreed. However, the first visit does not count since the contract will not have been signed." Pleased with his last addition, he wrapped an arm around her. "Now, to seal our preliminary bargain with a kiss."

And then he crashed his lips down on hers before she could object. Tongues tangled, he tried to drink her in, needed to take a piece of her with him just in case she changed her mind before he could get the contract settled.

Chapter Six

Emily had risen early—truly, she had simply not been able to sleep after her encounter with Lord Brougham the night before—but it was late afternoon now, and she had yet to see her brother. Arthur had hidden away in his study all day, ostensibly reviewing the ledgers with his man of affairs. It was more likely he was tending an aching head while counting up his vowels from the previous night's gambling. Tucked away in her room, she was organizing her spoils to sell when the tap-tap-tap of the front door knocker echoed throughout the house.

With an economy of motion, she wrapped up her ill-gotten gains and hid them back into the far corner of her bottom drawer, along with the few trousseau items she'd placed there once upon a time.

While she was not expecting any visitors, they were in principle at home to callers, so she smoothed her skirts and checked her hair for loose strands in case someone had come to call.

Mrs. Peppers knocked on her door a few moments later. "My lady, you have a—um, you have a gentleman caller."

"I do?" She felt as surprised as her housekeeper sounded.

"Indeed, my lady. He's downstairs with a posy and everything." The kind older woman's rosy cheeks and twinkling eyes belied her pleasure at such an event. "Why, your mama would be so excited. Bless her soul."

Yes, her mother would have been excited, except Emily very much doubted this call would have been made if her mother was still alive. There was only one man it could be.

"Please tell Lord Brougham I shall be down directly, and let Aunt Hortense know we have a visitor."

"Very good, my lady." Mrs. Peppers left with a spring in her step.

Emily, on the other hand, drew a deep breath and tried to calm her nerves. Chances were Arthur would never notice either Cooper's visits or her absences. And, in the end, she would have an opportunity to experience a part of life she had long thought lost to her. It was not as though he was going to ravish her in the front drawing room. She had nothing to be nervous about. With that reminder firmly in her head, she glided downstairs.

In the least shabby of all the public rooms, she found Cooper staring out a window, alone. It would seem her great-aunt was either napping or slow to arrive. Either option might be a boon, both considering Lord Brougham likely had the contract with him, and that great-aunt Hortense had a disconcerting tendency to say the most inappropriate things.

At the sound of her entrance, Cooper turned, a devastatingly genuine look of pleasure on his face. "Lady Emmaline, it is lovely to see you again."

"Good day, Lord Brougham." She stopped and curtsied before him. "You are looking handsome today." She hoped she sounded cordial, because frankly, he'd taken her breath away when he turned. His blond hair glinted like gold in the sunlight, and the Corbeau green of his frock coat made his brown eyes appear even richer.

"Thank you, but please, Lady Emmaline. We should dispense with such formalities. My friends call me Cooper, or you may call me Robert." He kissed her hand.

Emily sucked in her breath. *Robert?* She could never call him by his given name. It was far too intimate.

"Cooper shall do nicely, I think. Please call me Emily."

Her cheeks warmed even as she reminded herself the man was a means to an end. She needed him to stay quiet, and if she got to indulge in a bit of personal exploration as well, then all the better.

"It suits you. Now, as promised, I come bearing gifts." He held the flowers out to her.

Hands clasped together, she froze. "As I recall, we discussed that there would be no gifts," she said, teeth gritted.

"We did. But as I stated at the time, the first visit does not count as the contract has not been signed." He pressed the flowers on her, looking as pleased as a boy who'd found the cookie jar.

She shot him a speaking glare as Aunt Hortense trundled into the room. How had she not caught such a specious argument at the time? Perhaps negotiating while still under the influence of his rather heady kisses was not the best policy? With a nod to him, she accepted the flowers and made a note that there would be no further negotiations under such circumstances.

"Don't mind me. Keep on about your visit. It's not as though the girl has so many male callers. Too much longer, and the bloom will be off her fern."

Aunt Hortense propped herself up in the far corner and promptly dozed off, her ear trumpet in hand.

Emily stared at her aunt in mortification and confusion—a fairly regular occurrence with the elderly woman. She looked back at Cooper and found both his brows raised.

He cleared his throat. "I had not realized ferns lost their bloom so easily."

She stifled a laugh as she glared at her caller.

Undeterred by their interruption, he next produced a box of chocolates.

She sighed. "How many more gifts did you bring?"

Humor took his countenance from dazzling to breathtaking. "All of them."

"All of what?" Now she was quite confused.

"All the gifts I would have given you over the course of our visits. Since I was only permitted this one opportunity to lavish you with tokens, I did my best to cover everything." He walked to the drawing room door and opened it. "Come, Mrs. Peppers, I told you I would convince her to accept all the gifts."

Her housekeeper walked in, beaming from ear to ear as she led a procession of men and women carrying bouquets, chocolates, books, and even a few boxes she was certain came from a modiste.

"Cooper, this is outside of enough. I cannot possibly accept all these gifts from you." She walked over to the plain boxes with simple ribbons around them. Opening one, she held up a fetching bonnet with feathers and ribbons in the first stare of fashion. She had never owned such a luxurious head cover. "And this? This is practically a declaration of our betrothal. No other man would be permitted such leeway."

Her great-aunt snuffled and snorted in her sleep, drawing their attention for a moment, but then the frail woman settled back into a deep snooze.

"I'm sorry, but you forced my hand. If you will not accept everything, then give it away, for I shall not accept any of it back." He stared her down as the servants departed the room. Once they were alone again, he stepped closer to her. "Do I need to convince you to accept all my gifts?"

Had it grown warm in the house? She tugged at the high collar of her day dress. "I— Cooper, I simply can't—"

Closing the last bit of distance between them until her skirts wrapped around his boots, he said, "I see I must convince you." And then he kissed her.

Emily's head spun as his arms circled her and pressed her closer to his chest. The man plundered her mouth, stealing her breath and all rational thought. Her body's desires took over, urging her to take what he offered, throw caution to the wind, and simply—feel.

With a soft, breathy moan, she capitulated. Melting into his body, she stopped fighting the myriad sensations the man evoked with his touch, his spicy, woodsy scent, and the earthy taste on his lips and tongue. Had he taken a drink before coming to shore up his nerves? How intriguing to think she might cause such a confident—some would say *too* confident—man to need some sort of artificial bolstering.

As she reveled in his kiss, her body came alive. Tingles danced over her skin, a feather-light touch that made her heart race, while her nipples pebbled to hard nubs that chafed against her linens and corset. And between her thighs, she recognized a dampness that spoke far too plainly of her desire for the man holding her.

Slowly, he pulled back from the kiss, dropping nibbles along her jaw that shot little trills of pleasure over her form. Once he was looking her in the eyes, his hands at her shoulders as a steadying influence, he smiled. "Please, take the gifts as a token of my friendship and affection for you."

Oh, how she wanted to say yes, but propriety dictated she say no. Casting another glance in the direction of her still-sleeping chaperone, she bit her lip. Of course, ignoring propriety had become such a routine part of her life, she considered doing it once more. Gifts were few and far between in her life, let alone anything intended solely for her. She eyed the tip of a teal feather poking from the hat box and bit her lip in indecision. If nothing else, she could pawn the items and put the money toward her brother's debt. Decision made, she nodded at Cooper. "Very well, I shall accept your highly inappropriate gifts. But the bargain remains. No further trinkets."

"Agreed." The man beamed as though she'd granted him his fondest wish. "Now, on to other business. Please, take a seat." He ushered her over to the settee. Once she sat, he took the cushion next to hers and opened the folio sitting on the drawing room table. Lowering his voice to ensure their witness remained as she was—asleep—Cooper continued. "This is the standard contract for The Market, with a few changes per our agreed-upon terms. Please read through it carefully to be certain everything is as you remember agreeing to."

Emily perused the one-page contract, taking careful note to ensure the stipulations were in accordance with her memory. Satisfied, she nodded and nudged the folio back toward him. "It all looks in order."

"Good. Did you also notice that either one of us may break the contract with forty-eight hours' notice in writing?" He reached into his coat pocket and produced a fountain pen.

"I did notice that line. I am fine with the addition." She nodded, all business even as her pulse thrummed wildly beneath her skin. The rush of the forbidden made her jittery with excitement.

"Very good." He leaned over and signed his name with a flourish to both copies of the agreement. Next, she took the pen and followed suit. Once she was done, he handed her a copy. "For you, my lady."

"Thank you." She set the document aside and folded her hands in her lap. For an awkward moment, she wondered if he might suddenly leap upon her person, but then she reminded herself that Cooper was a gentleman, and they had *both* signed the contract.

Cooper shifted on the seat next to Emily, who seemed terribly uncomfortable now that the contract had been signed. Deciding he needed to get her past this awkwardness, he angled his body toward her and asked the one question he knew would get her past whatever reticence had settled in. "Tell me again why marriage is impossible?"

She huffed in a most unladylike manner. "I have already explained this."

He worked very hard to keep a straight face. "Have you? I don't recall having that conversation."

"You remember it very well. You had just pulled a necklace from my bosom," she hissed at him.

Determined to have a bit of fun, he drew his brows together. "Truly? I should think I would remember that."

Realization caused her mouth to pinch. "Do not provoke me. I am no simpering miss to be cowed by such behavior. I am not wifely material for the same reasons your ridiculous ploy to rile me shall fail."

He could see her struggle for composure until a calmness fell over her features.

"I am too independent to make a good wife."

Giving in, he grinned unrepentantly, "Ah, yes. I do remember you mentioning such a notion."

"It is no mere *notion*, as you put it. It is fact. No man wants a thief for a wife." Her gaze softened and grew a bit damp as she struggled with the truth as she knew it.

For a moment, he considered pulling her into his arms and comforting her. But he knew it would only reinforce her belief that he saw her as weak. The truth was he'd never met such a strong woman. She was fierce and fiery, determined to come out ahead in a way that stroked his most dominant instincts to life. He wanted to protect her, help her. Not because she was weak, but because he could make her life better. Safer, even.

Frustration and a little bitterness slipped through his determination to win her. "Chin up, Emily. I'm sure you'll find some poor fool to marry who wouldn't notice a little theft here and there."

"Do stop your irksome prattle. If you are going to stay, we should have tea and speak of civilized things." She cast a glance at the pile of gifts, and then at her great-aunt.

"Perhaps I should leave you to sort through your new things." He turned his knees so he faced her. Despite hating the need to end their visit, he dared not overstay his welcome. Gaining her trust was a key part of his grand plan to convince her to marry him.

To his surprise, she offered a genuine smile. "You should stay and see me enjoy your gifts. I'll have Mrs. Peppers bring a tea tray."

"Never say I passed an opportunity to take tea with a beautiful woman." He settled back on the sofa and waited for her to rise and approach the boxes.

She did stand, but first, she rang for her housekeeper and ordered their repast. Then she approached the gifts. "The hat is just lovely. You have excellent taste."

"I'm glad you think so. Now open the rest so I may enjoy your enthusiastic delight."

He settled back and took in the engaging sight of Emily amidst her presents. In general, she had been nothing like what he'd expected. Recalling his foolish belief that she'd be a docile spinster, he snorted to himself. Now he was looking forward to unleashing the hellion in his bed.

Chapter Seven

Cooper had thought to leave well enough alone after having made plans with Emily to meet for the first time at The Market, but once he'd found out—purely by accident—that she would be attending the theater that evening, he couldn't pass up the opportunity to see her sooner than planned. With that in mind, he'd called on each of the Lustful Lords and extended an invitation for them to join him in his box.

He arrived first, followed quickly by Lord Wolfington and Lord Lincolnshire. Neither man was accompanied by a lady, so the three chatted about their plans for later that evening.

"Is everyone planning to attend The Market later?" Wolf settled into a chair, stretching his long legs out.

Linc laughed as he followed suit. "Don't we always?"

Cooper lifted one shoulder as he scanned the boxes across the theater for the woman who had captured his interest. "I have plans."

Linc sat up. "What do you mean you have plans?"

"I'm meeting a woman at The Market, but not with you lot." Cooper continued his perusal of the other box occupants.

"Another man succumbs to the wiles of a woman." Wolf sighed and shook his head. "It's a bloody travesty, the second Lustful Lord to fall under the yoke of domestication."

"If you were to assume the woman who has enticed me is domesticated, you would be mistaken." Cooper laughed, trying to picture Emily as a demure domestic woman, which was odd considering he'd once counted her his ideal candidate for a stable, scandal-less wife.

As Linc and Wolf considered his statement, Lord and Lady Stonemere entered his box. It was the first group outing the man had attended since his marriage. His lady wife, though dressed in the first stare of fashion, also exuded a sensuality that had Linc and Wolf standing up and taking notice. Normally, Cooper would join them, particularly having sampled her wares along with her husband, but tonight his mind was focused entirely on Lady Emmaline—his hellion.

As the newcomers were welcomed by Linc and Wolf, a flash of lavender caught his eye. He turned to focus on the new arrivals across the theater—not that he'd been cataloging each empty box—and found the very object of his desire, Lady Emmaline.

His gaze stroked over the artful folds of her gown and the appealing dip of her neckline as he relished what the night held. When their gazes locked, her eyes widened in surprise at finding him so near. Then there was a movement in the back of the box she occupied, and her back was presented. As he imagined bending her over later and plunging deep within her hot core, his cock grew hard and his breath shallow. Need had him by the balls, and he wouldn't have it any other way.

"Cooper, what are you staring at that you have yet to say hello?" Stone ripped him from his deeply sensual thoughts and returned him to the moment.

"My future, but I am glad to see you and your lovely lady wife." Cooper bowed over Lady Theodora Stonemere's hand and then hugged his friend. Images of the one night spent in bed with Stone—and more particularly Theo—flickered dully in his head. A faded image that seemed to grow more and more faint after each encounter with Emily. For months after, if he were honest, he had wrestled with a terrible bout of jealousy. He found it hard to believe Society could produce two unique and engaging women, but to his great stroke of luck, it seemed it had.

Stone raised his brows and looked at Cooper curiously. Clearly, he had questions. "Dare I assume love has struck our merry band again?"

"Let's call it infatuation for the moment." Cooper tipped the corner of his mouth up ruefully. "The object of said infatuation is less than welcoming of any deeper sentiment."

Stone, Linc, and Wolf all laughed while Theo patted his arm. "If anyone can convince her of the merits of love, it's you."

He couldn't hide his surprise, even as his friends laughed harder. For far too long, he had been about the hunt, and then an entanglement-free arrangement. He'd cut Sarah, the merry widow with whom he'd had a dalliance, loose once he'd decided to do his duty. But his friends likely remembered him waxing poetic about his easy arrangement with her not all that long ago.

"While I have my doubts, she's a stubborn, freethinking woman such as yourself. But I do aim to try to sway her to my thinking." Cooper offered a roguish grin and a wink.

Theo narrowed her eyes at him for a moment before a beatific smile appeared on her face. "Then I wish you all the joy Stone had convincing me to settle down."

Cooper wanted to groan at the politest curse he'd ever been gifted. "Theo! I thought you liked me."

Everyone laughed again, since they were all well aware of the struggle Stone and Theo had gone through to make their marriage work. But it seemed they were doing well together in the end.

"I do like you, immensely." She cast an inquiring look at her husband, who nodded. "Which is why I am asking you to stand as godfather to our next child when he or she is born."

Cooper would do anything for Stone, his best friend, and possibly more for the spirited woman he'd married. "Of course, whenever that day comes, you may count on me once more."

Their box grew very quiet.

"But I am asking you now, Cooper." Theo's brows rose high up toward her hair as she waited for him to comprehend her statement.

Pregnant? Theo was pregnant? Again? Cooper was both pleased and a little worried all at once. After all, it was the logical outcome of marriage and then marital relations, but somehow, even with Theo having recently given birth to her and Stone's first child, it seemed shocking. After taking a moment to let it sink in, he felt the joy for his friends burst through the chaos of all the other emotions. "Congratulations!" He scooped Theo into a tight hug.

Once he let go and stepped back, he caught Emily staring at him from across the theater, one brow sharply raised. Her little display of jealousy pleased him as he turned to thump Stone on the back.

Then the lights flickered, so they all took their seats. Cooper was man enough to admit it was good having Stone about again, even if it was only while they were at the theater.

Emily sat in a blue room in The Market, her pulse racing as she toyed with the mask she'd worn into the establishment and waited for Cooper to join her. She assumed it was known as the blue room since every fabric covering almost every surface was some shade of blue. Despite the multitude of blues, the palette worked together, running from the palest cornflower to the deepest navy. She studied the space for a moment more before her focus shifted to her own internal thoughts, particularly the ease with which she had escaped for the evening.

It turned out slipping away once Arthur had engaged in his nocturnal carousing was far too simple. With Aunt Hortense as her sole chaperone at home, there had been no one to gainsay her when she blithely announced she was going out to the theater with Lady Gladstone—a theater lover through and through, who would likely let her slip away without much fuss—and her daughter. To her surprise, the very man she was to meet later also appeared at the theater.

Watching him greet a woman in his box whom he then publicly touched in a terribly intimate way—a mere hug, mind you, but one simply did not embrace in public—caused her to doubt his trustworthiness. Of course, sitting alone waiting for him as she stewed over what she had seen had her questioning everything she had agreed to—possibly even her sanity.

A sharp knock sounded, driving her to her feet as the door swung open and delivered Cooper into the room. "Ah, there you are. I hope I did not keep you waiting long."

He crossed over to her and pressed a kiss to her cheek in greeting. It was such a casually intimate gesture, she pressed her palm to the spot that seemed to tingle from his lips as she tried to absorb an unexpected swell of emotion. "No, of course not."

He stripped his coat off and laid it carefully over the arm of a brocade-covered wingback chair. "May I offer you something to drink?"

"Whatever you're having is fine."

Without any further comment, he poured a whisky for her and one for himself. After handing her a glass, he sat in another chair and perused her from head to toe.

Earlier that evening, she had considered her choice of dress carefully. She had opted for a green watered silk with an organza overlay and a plunging scooped neckline that was as daring as propriety would allow a spinster. But when his gaze lingered at her breasts, almost caressing them, she found herself excited despite the displeasure lingering from the theater.

"Come here." He waved her over to where he sat regally in his chair.

She harrumphed and remained seated as she sipped the whisky he'd poured her. Not anticipating the burn from the liquor, she coughed and sputtered. Once she recovered from the unexpected momentary lack of oxygen, she pinned her companion with a glare. "I believe you need to explain that woman in your box at the theater before I shall come anywhere near you."

Cooper blinked, almost as though confused for a moment. Then a smile split his kissable lips before a chuckle escaped. He laughed for what seemed an eternity, all while she sat fuming. Partly because she was jealous—there was no denying the aberrant emotion—and partly because she was terrified of all the things this dangerous man already made her feel.

Once he managed to tame his mirth, he looked at her, his eyes nearly watering. "Are you referring to Lady Stonemere? My best friend's *wife*?"

Emily gave him a cold stare. "The very one you embraced in a public spectacle this evening? If that is *she*, then yes."

He stopped and blinked. "Yes, well she shared some good tidings with me, and I believe I became overwhelmed with the news. I suppose hugging her was a bit inappropriate, but we—Stone, Theo, and I—are quite close."

His phrasing struck her as odd. She narrowed her gaze at him. "How close?"

Cooper glanced away from her and then back, but more in the vicinity of her feet as his cheeks flushed.

Her free hand fluttered to her throat and rose from her seat. "Oh, my. How *close*?"

He rose, set his glass on a nearby table, and strode over to where she stood. "I shall not disclose another's secrets. You may rest assured there is nothing between Theo and me but companionable affection. If Stone thought for one moment either of us harbored some romantic feeling, I assure you he would trounce me soundly and tie his wife to their bed after spanking her thoroughly."

"Perhaps you shared too much, at any rate? I cannot imagine any lady of the *ton* allowing her husband to spank her and tie her to the bed." She gnashed her teeth, unsure she believed another lady might welcome such treatment.

He took her drink and set it aside, then pulled her into his arms. "Ah, but then you have yet to be properly spanked while tied to *my* bed."

Rich male laughter surrounded her until he swooped in and stole a kiss, their lips melding together as they pressed closer. She whimpered and opened to him, unable to resist his sensual assault. And if the kisses she'd experienced with him were any evidence, she thought she might enjoy anything he wished to do to her. But she would *never* admit that to him.

As his scent and taste overwhelmed her senses, she felt his clever fingers working the laces of her dress loose. Her heart sped up as she realized there was no turning back from what lay ahead. She wanted to know the touch of a man, but she could not deny the agitation that made her limbs restless.

The men in her life had been less than reliable, most betraying her in one fashion or another. Her reserves of fortitude had been well used up by her brother of late, she had little left to deal with another man who might be of a similar bent. She pressed a palm to his chest. "Cooper, do not toy with me. Our agreement stated we would remain faithful for the duration of the contract."

She ignored the squeezing sensation that gripped her heart.

"And I told you, there is nothing but platonic love between Theo and me. She belongs to Stone." Then, like an expert, he worked her gown open and then over her head. Next, he started on the rest of her undergarments, each layer coming away as he pressed kisses to her shoulders, her neck, the tops of her breasts, and then even her back.

All the while, she considered his words. She believed him, and yet there was this uncontrollable doubt that assailed her. With a sigh, she set the unwanted emotion aside. After all, she had no time for such entanglements. This was about her sexual exploration, nothing more.

When she finally stood wearing naught but her stockings and garters, she bent to pluck them free, but he stopped her.

"Those can stay. I will enjoy the silky feel of your stockings as you wrap your legs around me." His wolfish grin had her thighs squeezing together as her center grew damp with need.

"Oh. Well, if you prefer them." She straightened up and stepped closer to him. She worked his tie free and then started on his shirt as he tugged at his trousers and slipped his shoes off. Within moments, he was naked, his cock springing up from a nest of blond curls. She imagined many men looked ridiculous in this state, but somehow it made Cooper look even more beautiful, more appealing.

Her previous rancor forgotten, she stood awkwardly, wanting very much to cover herself. Of their own volition, her arms crossed over her breasts, but Cooper intercepted them midpath. "You are a beautiful woman with nothing to be ashamed of."

She glanced at the bed and back to him as her cheeks heated. "Could we..."

"Shhh." He stepped into her and pulled her into his arms. "I promise I will be as gentle as I can."

Then he swooped down and captured her lips in a searing kiss that had her forgetting about their nudity. Her pulse thrummed under her skin, a steady drumbeat of desire. His tongue tangled with hers, a wet heat that was both sensual and demanding.

Between her thighs, she ached with a need that made her wish to press closer to him. To find some part of him that might relieve the pressure. Why she wanted to do such a thing or even where the notion had sprung from eluded her, considering her years of training to be a good wife had not prepared her for such desires. Of course, neither had her years of being a freethinker and, even of late, a thief.

She hated it when her mind took over and nearly paralyzed her with too many thoughts. It didn't happen often these days, but every once in a while, when she pushed up against some unforeseen boundary, her old habit popped up. And still, despite the whirlwind of thoughts spinning through her mind, she managed to lose herself in his kiss.

Finally, he broke away, gasping for the same much-needed air as her. After a breath or two, he demanded, "On the bed."

Again, her mind raced as she struggled within. She stood there frozen in indecision. Then he moved a foot or so away from her, and she wondered what he was about.

"I am going to assume that all that good breeding that makes you Lady Emmaline is interfering with your desires. Yes?"

She nodded.

"I see. Well, fortunately for you, I am an expert at getting past these issues. If you want something or want me to do something, you must state it clearly for me."

Her face grew very hot as she imagined explaining what she had wanted to do only moments earlier.

"Otherwise, I shall simply do as I wish." He waited for her to react. When she said nothing, he scooped her into his arms.

The next Emily knew, she was on the bed with Cooper coming down beside her. His bulk created a dip in the mattress, which caused her to roll into his side.

He faced her, lying on his side, and tipped her chin up to him. He kissed her again, a soft sweet press of his lips. Then he dropped kisses down her cheek, along her neck, and over her collarbones.

All the while, her nipples felt swollen and the ache between her thighs grew more intense. A soft whimper escaped her as Cooper latched on to one nipple and sucked. Her upper back arched up off the bed, pushing more of her breast into his mouth. His big, warm hands chased away the chill of the English night more effectively than the fire that crackled merrily in the fireplace across the room.

He moved lower, still using his lips to brand a trail over her skin as he kissed down her ribs and across her belly until his face was far too near the spot that ached with some need she did not understand.

And then he wedged his shoulders between her thighs and let his warm breath feather across her skin.

She jerked partway up, her weight on her elbows. "Cooper! What are you doing?"

He grinned at her over the length of her body. "I'm preparing to sample your sweet, sweet pussy."

Emily gasped at his words, shocked to hear such language. But then he flicked the very spot that ached so severely, and her body trembled with pleasure. He licked her flesh, a long slow stroke that sent sparks of heat up her limbs and had her moaning with need.

"That's it, lie back and enjoy the sensations. Let me make you feel good." His voice sounded low and rough, not at all like his usual smooth baritone.

When he pushed his tongue into her, all coherent thought fled. He licked and suckled at her swollen flesh, increasing the pressure that felt like steam trapped in a kettle. When he slid something long and hard inside her, she bucked against him and cried out. "Please, Cooper!"

Without a reply, he focused on that sensitive bundle of nerves, licking and lapping at it while he pumped his finger in and out. When he added a second finger and amped up the suction on her nub, her world exploded. She cried out an incoherent string of words as lights danced behind her eyes and her body seemed to shatter into thousands of pieces.

Chapter Eight

Cooper rose up from between her thighs and laid next to a still slightly dazed Emily. As she returned to herself, he stroked her body. Long gentle touches to both bring her back to him and to keep her now sensitized body still humming. What came next would not be as enjoyable for her, but it was a necessary step.

While he'd not bedded a virgin before, he was aware enough about the mechanics to realize that a swift approach would get them past the painful part. His cock ached with the desire to be inside his little hellion, but he refused to rush her. And so, counter to his usual style, he lay there continuing to stroke her skin until her lashes fluttered, and then her beautiful hazel eyes appeared.

"That was…" Her cheeks were still flushed from her orgasm.

He resisted the urge to command her to tell him what she was thinking. But he reminded himself this was how married men treated their wives. In fact, he'd already broken protocol by stripping her naked and loving her with his mouth. But there were only so many concessions a man could make.

"There is more to come if you're ready." He pressed a kiss to her shoulder, finding the urge to lick and taste every inch of her all but impossible to resist.

Her nipples tightened into peaks either from his words or his touch, he didn't particularly care which once she nodded her head.

He hesitated. Normally, he would require verbal consent. There was far more pleasure in a shared experience. Perhaps some things shouldn't be changed?

"Say yes. I want to be sure you are ready for this. No regrets come morning."

"We are far past the point where regrets could be avoided if I were to have them." She paused and snared his gaze with her own. "Please, take me."

Cooper groaned, her words making him desperate with desire. He wanted to thrust into her and fuck until his top blew off. But his sweet Emily was not ready for such vigorous activity. Instead, he levered himself over her and knelt between her spread thighs. There, he donned a French letter he'd kept handy for the evening and pressed his tip against her still-soaked pussy. Leaning over her, braced on his arms, he warned her, "This will hurt the first time, and there is little I can do to mitigate it for you."

"Go ahead, I'm ready." She looked up at him, a wariness in her gaze that gave him pause.

Still determined to try to make her first time as pleasurable as possible, he rubbed the tip of his cock along her slit until she writhed against him once more. Then, he paused at her opening, took a moment to appreciate her gift to him, and pushed into her. He sank about halfway on one firm thrust and then seated himself to the root with a second.

Emily cried out, her hazel eyes wide in surprise as the green flecks glowed in the gaslight.

He placed a gentle kiss on her forehead as she trembled beneath him. "The pain will pass in a moment or two."

She nodded as her white teeth nibbled on her lower lip, already plump from his kisses.

Still bearing his weight on his arms, he hovered over her until she squirmed beneath him a bit. "Are you well?"

"Oh my," she said. "I feel so full. I never imagined it would be like this."

He groaned, lost in the tight clasp of her pussy, the way she looked up at him with wonder and a tiny flicker of desire. Needing to move, he shifted his hips and drew back from her body until just his tip remained. Resisting the urge to thrust deeply, he pushed back inside her on a slow easy glide. With each plunge inside her, he picked up his speed but maintained the smoothness of motion. His arms quivered with his restraint as sweat slicked down his back. All the while he worked in and out of her.

Once her breath changed to panting and she gripped him more securely, both with her core and her hands, he balanced on one elbow and reached between them with his free hand. A few soft strokes over her clit and she came for him. Not as intense as her first orgasm, but under the circumstances, he was pleased she was even able to find a second release.

With his own need driving him, he rose up on his knees for better leverage and grabbed her lushly round arse as he shuttled in and out of her snug heat. Once. Twice. And then he came. His body seized up until his hips jerked haphazardly, as every inch of his skin tingled with pleasure.

And as he withdrew from her sweet clasp, he knew he had to have her again. Once would never be enough, because he greatly suspected the next time would far outstrip the first.

Cooper walked into the Kilpatricks' ball accompanied by Stone and Theo; however, he only had one woman on his mind. He deftly surveyed the crowd in search of Lady Emmaline. Her golden-brown hair offered her a certain anonymity in a sea of such similar hair colors, and it was the gleam in her hazel eyes that made her stand out. Finally, he caught a glimpse of her as she walked behind Lady Vardy, her usual chaperone. They appeared to be heading toward the refreshments.

"Stone, may I fetch anything from the refreshments for you and your lady wife?" He did not bother to look at his friend as he tossed the question over his shoulder.

Stone chuckled behind him. "Considering we've only just arrived, I can't imagine either of us being in need of nourishment so soon. But do go about your business. Do not delay on our accounts."

Ignoring his friends' laughter, Cooper took off in the direction of his quarry. Perhaps he was being a bit fanciful, but it seemed to him that it had been too long since he last saw

Lady Emmaline. Was it only the previous night that he had held her in his arms for the first time? He could not help but admire the straight column of her back as he approached her and her companion.

"Lady Vardy." He bowed and kissed the woman's hand. "Lady Emmaline." He bowed again, repeating the gesture, but this time, he lingered as long as was polite while he stroked the underside of her hand in as intimate a gesture as he could muster under the circumstances.

"Lord Brougham." Emily turned a fetching shade of pink as she curtsied.

He released her hand and offered a dashing smile—or at least he hoped she found it so. "I have come to claim a dance or two with you."

"Have you? I don't recall—" She stopped midthought and glanced at an all-too-interested Lady Vardy.

"What don't you recall, Lady Emmaline?" Lady Vardy was too earnest in her query for anyone's comfort.

Emily glanced at him, and he could see the wheels turning as she tried to muster up some plausible answer.

"I'm afraid I've caught the lady off guard." Cooper pressed a hand to his chest as though he were responsible for the confusion. "When last I saw Lady Emmaline, having called on her earlier this week for a friendly visit, I had told her I would not be attending the Kilpatricks' soiree. But as it turned out, I was able to make it. It seems my unexpected arrival has flustered her."

Cooper couldn't resist the urge to tease Emily just a little more. He leaned closer to Lady Vardy and put his hand up as though shielding his next words. "My lady, I believe she may harbor a tendre for me."

As he had hopped, the matronly woman tittered and smacked his arm with her fan. Emily's gaze shifted from calculation to shock to outrage. She sputtered for a moment and then snapped her mouth shut, as she must have realized she could neither acknowledge nor deny his claim. If she refused to respond, then Lady Vardy would rightly assume he was being playful.

"May I, Lady Emmaline?" Cooper pointed to her dance card and waited for her to relinquish the small paper with far too many blanks on it.

She did so with relatively good grace, and he promptly picked the two waltzes for his dances. It might have been pushing the socially acceptable boundaries, but he was a Lustful Lord. Appearances had to be maintained where they could.

"Lady Vardy, would you mind if I escorted Lady Emmaline over to meet Lord and Lady Stonemere? They are two of my dearest friends."

"Of course, you may. I shall be right here when you are finished saying hello." Lady Vardy indicated a spot out of the way

"Thank you, my lady." He scooped up Emily's hand, tucking it in the crook of his arm, and escorted her over to where his friends stood. After the formal introductions, Cooper turned to Emily. "Lord and Lady Stonemere were only just wed."

Emmaline smiled. "Felicitations, Lord and Lady Stonemere."

"Thank you, my lady." Theo beamed at her husband, and for a moment, jealousy pierced Cooper's heart. He wanted what his friends had, and strangely, he very much wanted it with the woman standing next to him.

"Lady Stonemere, I believe you and Lady Emmaline share some of the same notions on the independence of women."

Cooper heard Emily snort softly.

"I wouldn't wish to bore anyone with such conversation, my lord," Emily demurred as she glared at him.

Theo leaned in excitedly. "Lady Emmaline, please tell me you have read Wollstonecraft."

Nonplussed, Emily swung her gaze from Theo to Cooper and then back. "I have, my lady."

The ladies launched into a discussion of the merits of *A Vindication of the Rights of Woman,* leaving Stone free to ask questions.

"Rather unusual of you to introduce someone to us."

Cooper could feel his face heating, but did his best to ignore the sensation. "I suspected your wife would find her engaging."

He refused to say so aloud, but he hoped Theo might be a softening influence on Emily. Show her that married life might not be so repugnant.

Stone's eyebrows rose in disbelief. "May I suggest you not leave her alone with my wife if you wish her to be less independent? While Theo has settled into marriage, that is not indicative of her willfulness having been curbed." Stone leaned closer to Cooper and lowered his voice. "She still provides plenty of reasons for me to spank her."

Cooper chuckled and shook his head.

"Gentlemen, please excuse us for a short while." Theo hooked her arm in Emily's, and together, the women sailed off toward the ladies' retiring room.

Cooper caught the ladies making plans for a visit soon. Despite being content with that arrangement, he couldn't help but worry that Emily had maneuvered Theo into separating them for a reason.

"Stone, I had best follow after them. Lady Emmaline has a knack for getting into trouble."

"Trouble?" his friend asked, only slightly surprised.

"Just so. Excuse me." Cooper nodded and went to hover outside the ladies' retiring room, using a nearby alcove as an excellent vantage point.

Just as he had suspected, a short time passed before Emily slipped from the room on the heels of a small group of ladies, and she was without Theo. As his little hellion slipped past, he reached out from the alcove and dragged her into the curtained shadows. "And where do you think you are going, my lady?"

"What the devil are you doing?" Emily hissed. "If we were caught in here, I would be ruined!"

"Do cease your nonsense, Emily. You were sneaking off to steal again." Anger swept through Cooper in an unexpected wave. The woman had no care for herself. Not a one. Someone needed to, and it seemed to be falling to him. "Do not think to lie to me."

"I do not owe you any explanations, my lord." Her brows lowered over her sparkling hazel eyes as her mouth flattened to a stern line.

So, she reverted to formality to create distance, did she? He refused to allow her to employ such tactics.

"My lord?"

He took a half step closer to her, closing the little distance he had allowed.

Her gaze darted sharply toward the curtained entrance of the alcove.

"I think not, my little hellion. You appear to have an affinity for living dangerously. I find myself intrigued by such a notion." He shifted his grip from her forearm to her waist, where he wrapped her up and hauled her against his chest.

Her breath hitched as her gaze drifted down to his lips, which pleased him immensely. No man wished to think he was the sole half affected so strongly by the other.

"I find myself intrigued by you," he said. And then he captured her lips with his.

She stiffened for a moment, her hands pressed to his chest. But as he slipped his tongue deeper into her mouth to savor her exquisite taste, she melted into him with a soft moan. His cock hardened at the small sound of surrender, and more still as her arms twined around his neck.

Frustrated that she responded so sweetly to his touch but would not trust him with her secrets, he exerted the little dominance he could. Turning slightly, he walked her backward until his hand hit the wall and he could press her up against the support. As they kissed, tongues dueling, hands roaming, he needed more, *wanted* more.

Determined to show her how thrilling they could be together, he broke their kiss and sank to his knees. "Place your foot on the bench."

"Cooper?"

Hearing his name spoken as a breathy whisper from her lips sent shivers down his spine. The depth of his need for this woman after only one night shook him to his very core, yet he could not relent, *would not* relent. "Do as you're told, Emily."

He lifted her skirts to help her move her foot as directed, and then he slipped under her skirts and parted her pantalets. Her quim was already wet as he leaned in and licked her. A muffled whimper from above had him worrying, so he retreated for a moment. "You must keep your voice down."

He saw her nod in the shadows of the alcove and returned to his task. With single-minded focus, he delved past her nether lips and stroked his tongue over the little sensitive nub, then back down to her soaked opening. Another low moan vibrated through her, but not as loud as before. Determined to make her climax, he swirled his tongue over her clit with a relentless rhythm. Then he added two fingers to fill her, and she gasped as her hips bucked.

All the while, her sweet-tart taste teased his tongue and lips, making him desperate for more of her. He continued lapping at her center until a tightly drawn breath forewarned him of her coming orgasm. Her body tensed, and then she came. Her release coated his tongue and fingers as she came apart above him. He pinned her hips to the wall as best he could as she shook. The one leg she stood on started to give out. Steadying her as he backed out from under her skirts, he rose up to face her as she gathered her composure.

Before he could warn her off, she shoved off the wall and into his arms. Pressing her lips to his, she kissed him deeply, her body mashed against his throbbing erection. Then she paused and pulled back slightly. "Is that what..."

"Yes, that is you on my lips. I intended to wipe my mouth before kissing you, but you rather got ahead of me." He chuckled a little.

She hesitated. "I like the way I taste on your lips. Knowing you brought me such pleasure that way, I find it...arousing."

And then she swept in and kissed him once more. Suddenly, Cooper realized that if they continued as they were, he was going to impale her on his cock right there in the alcove of the Kilpatricks' home. He'd already far exceeded his initial intentions—merely to steal a kiss and hopefully stop her from thievery. Pulling away, he said, "You should return to Lady Vardy. She will be worried about you by now."

It was a bit like pouring a bucket of water on a drunk. The fog of desire cleared, and she stepped back from him, her arms dropping to her sides. "Oh my. How long have I been gone from the ballroom?"

"Not so long it cannot be explained away. But you must return soon." He glanced down at his own rather obvious issue. "I believe I shall stay here a bit longer, which should help avoid any suspicion."

Righting her dress and pressing her hands to her heated cheeks, Emily nodded. "Right, then. I suppose I shall see you soon."

"Without a doubt." He nodded.

As she opened the curtain and let more light into the space, Cooper caught a glimpse of Emily's kiss-swollen lips and pink cheeks. Groaning to himself, he swore they were doomed.

Chapter Nine

The late afternoon sun shined down on Emily as she walked smartly along Brewer Street. For the occasion, she had donned her most worn and repaired gown and shoes. Borrowing one of the maid's straw bonnets, she had slipped from the house with a basket for marketing. As she drew closer to her destination, her heart raced and her palms grew sweaty.

It reminded her of how she had felt during her first encounter with Cooper—her first time with any man. To her great surprise, he had first brought her to orgasm with his mouth, and then impaled her with his rather fine cock. Certainly, it had hurt with his first intrusion, but he had quickly showed her how much pleasure there was to be had with each other. And every time she'd interacted with him since then, he had surprised her with some new arousing experience.

However, today her nervousness had nothing to do with Cooper and everything to do with the jewels she carried in her reticule. Despite knowing the shop owner cared little about the origins of her goods, wariness—or perhaps guilt—had her questioning the intelligence of conducting her own business. But, of course, she had no one else who could handle such a transaction on her behalf. With a fortitude born of desperation, she turned the corner onto Bridle Lane and sought out the shop with owners of somewhat questionable ethics.

The street—really more of an alley—was quite narrow and practically empty. Head up as she took in her surroundings, she found the discreet entrance to Fletcher & Sons. Beneath the bold lettering was written: *Pawn brokers for all your needs.*

With a deep breath, she opened the door and approached the counter along the back portion of the shop. The counter was divided into small cubbyholes to protect the client's dignity, for which Emily was grateful.

"Good afternoon, ma'am. How may I assist you?" A man, Mr. Fletcher, she assumed, appeared before her booth, bearing a smile that failed to reach his eyes.

"I have some items I must pawn." She reached into her basket and pulled out her stash of stolen jewelry. Along with the necklace Cooper had once pulled free of her breasts, there was a bracelet, a number of pairs of earbobs, and more rings than she could fit on her ten fingers.

The broker's eyes suddenly lit up as he assessed her wares. He picked up one of the rings and produced a small magnification lens to inspect the item closer. With a grunt, he set the ring down and picked up another. This continued as he looked at each piece on the counter. All the while, she resisted the urge to fist her hands in her skirts.

Once he had examined each piece, he looked back at her, eyeing her dress and the obviously repaired spots. "How much are you seeking for the baubles?"

Emily's gaze narrowed. "Baubles? Each piece is valuable in its own right. Do not think to undercut their worth, Mr. Fletcher."

The man grunted again. "How much do you need?"

"Three thousand pounds." She tried to breathe after speaking such a sum. Still only part of what her brother owed, but a start if she could get as much.

The man snorted. "Two thousand."

"That will not do, Mr. Fletcher." She stood straighter and assumed the look and tone she used with recalcitrant servants. "Twenty-eight hundred."

"Twenty-five hundred and not a bit more." He growled the words more than spoke them.

Disappointed she could not get more but unwilling to bicker further, she accepted his offer. "Agreed. And you will hold the items for a year?"

He shoved a handwritten ticket across the counter and pointed to the terms of pawn posted on the wall behind him. "That's the policy. I'll just be a moment."

And then he disappeared into the back room for a few moments. When he returned, he handed her the stack of notes and glanced around the front of his shop. "Do you not have a man to escort you home?"

Panic flared as she grappled for a plausible answer. "The drunken lout wouldn't do me a bit of good if he were here."

"'Tis a sad state of affairs when a woman cannot count on her menfolk. I shall have one of my boys walk you home," Mr. Fletcher offered.

"Not at all. I'll just be on my way. But thank you."

And then she quickly walked out of the shop and down the lane until she could slip back into the busier foot traffic on Brewer. Once she was safely lost among the crowds, she headed back toward home.

~

Dress changed after her foray to the pawnbroker, she felt much more herself as she settled in the front salon. Despite a few setbacks as a jewel thief, she had managed to collect over half of what Arthur owed in gambling debts. But she couldn't deny she was quickly running out of time. Perhaps paying Mr. Lucifer a visit and offering a substantial payment might convince him to give her more time? It was certainly worth the effort to try.

"Lady Emmaline, Lord Brougham to see you," Mrs. Peppers announced with so much pomp and circumstance, Emily wanted to chuckle.

Cooper strode into the room, hands tucked behind his back, and stopped in the middle of the sitting area. Her housekeeper quickly departed, leaving the two of them alone—ostensibly to go in search of Aunt Hortense, though Emily knew she'd only just laid down for her nap.

As soon as her footsteps faded into the depths of the house, Cooper started moving slowly toward where she sat on a settee. "You have been a rather busy woman today."

Curious, a statement more than a question.

"I believe all ladies are taught to stay busy. Idle hands and all that."

"Yes, but I am not sure when they came up with that they anticipated a woman such as yourself." He stopped just in front of where she sat. "In fact, I would guess they never imagined a lady thief at all when that was first conceived."

"Perhaps not." She firmed her chin and waited. It was obvious what this conversation was to be about. "Might I remind you, Cooper, we have an agreement in place."

He held up the newspaper he had clutched and spread it out so the headline was readable. PRINCE VISITS UNITED STATES!

"Oh, that's lovely. I hope he was well received." Emily smiled intently, knowing full well that was not the part that had drawn his concern.

"Not the bloody headline. Look at the lower right corner." His face had turned a rather alarming shade of red, and a very large vein appeared to pulse on the side of his head.

She leaned forward and blinked a few times as she perused the small bit just above the fold of the paper. The story described a bold fellow who had taken to robbing the homes of London's elite during their fêtes. That—much smaller—headline read: THE WALTZING THIEF STRIKES AGAIN!

She leaned back and folded her hands in her lap. "I am well aware the Waltzing Thief was recently in action."

He leaned down and practically hissed at her. "When will you cease these ridiculously risky activities?"

Feeling mulish, she pressed her lips together and took a deep breath. "I never agreed to stop. In fact, I stipulated that what I did outside of our arrangement was my business."

Cooper stared at her for a few heartbeats and then cursed as he stepped back. "Why do you insist on doing this? You are going to get yourself killed!"

"I shall do no such thing."

As though she was so inept as to get caught. Besides, she had to do it, and she couldn't get caught. If she either quit or was caught before she had the money to pay off Lucifer, her brother was as good as dead.

Cooper's face stilled as he stood across the room from her. Thunderclouds seemed to roll into the room as his jaw grew rigid and his brown eyes turned nearly black. "I know you won't, because I forbid you to continue. You will cease this insanity at once."

Fury pushed Emily from her seat. "Forbid?" she asked softly as she crossed the room. "You forbid me to steal?"

Doubt flashed through his gaze. "Indeed. Someone must, as it seems your brother is incapable of acting as your guardian."

Too angry to snort at the notion of Arthur acting as her guardian, she focused on her next breath. *Utter nonsense.* "Cooper, I suggest you leave this instant, while I still consider our arrangement intact—despite your very obvious impingement of the terms we both agreed to. I shall not be treated like some green chit barely out of the schoolroom. I am a grown woman who knows her own mind. And at this moment, I am quite keen on the notion of planting you a facer."

The man whom she normally found so attractive it was all she could do to control her urges around him had driven her to a rather indecorous threat of violence. Not at all a ladylike notion, yet a very appropriate one for the moment.

He narrowed his gaze at her before he had the gall to toss the paper on a nearby table. Then he stepped into her person, hauled her into his arms, and captured her lips with his.

She wanted to be furious at him, and still was if she were honest, but apparently, that did nothing to abate her body's response to his touch. Arms clamped tightly around her, he left her no place to retreat, and she was quick to acknowledge that she did not wish for one.

As their tongues dueled, slipping and sliding against each other, she allowed her anger to be tempered by the headiness of his kiss. Her body throbbed with the need to feel him, to take him within and lead the way to a pleasure she had not known before his presence in her life.

Setting her away from him as abruptly as he had swooped in to kiss her, he dragged a ragged breath into his lungs and stared at her with wild eyes. For a moment, she was unsure what he would do, but then without a further word, he spun around leaving her standing there alone, lips tingling from such a passionate embrace.

Cooper sat in White's and stared at the fire crackling merrily as he nursed a whisky.

"I've found him." Linc's boisterous voice broke through Cooper's line of thought as his friends pulled up chairs around him. The rain had started just after he'd stepped into the all-male enclave, and it had not let up since. As a result, his damp friends crowded around the fireplace.

Flint, Linc, and Wolf each eyed him in turn. He could see the question in their gazes as they warmed themselves. Once their hands had dried, he poured them each a glass of whisky from the bottle at his left. The service at White's was impeccable, so there had been no need to request the glasses required.

After a few moments of companionable silence, during which Cooper considered what he was going to ask of his friends, he broke the peace. "I need your help with...a situation."

Flint responded first. "Ask away. Whatever it is, consider it done."

Linc and Wolf both nodded in agreement.

"I shall require your discretion in this matter." He paused. Was he going too far? His heart lurched at the notion of Emily being caught in the process of robbing someone. "I have taken a marked interest in Lady Emmaline Winterburn, sister of the Earl of Dunmere."

The other three groaned, Linc the loudest. "Not you as well, Cooper? I thought you were sure to remain a bachelor forever."

He smiled ruefully. "I'm afraid I have met the absolute antithesis of what I believed my ideal wife to be, but something about her compels me. The trouble is, she refuses to consider marriage at all, and she seems to have taken up stealing while attending the *ton's* entertainments." He let his words slip past their whisky-soaked awareness.

Wolf put it together first. "Damn your eyes!" He leaned forward and lowered his voice, "Are you saying the Waltzing Thief is a woman?"

"Why yes, I am. I thought I had her attention redirected toward more carnal pursuits, but then I saw this morning's edition of the *Times*." Cooper sighed and pinched the bridge of his nose.

"Why not walk away?" Linc asked the very question Cooper had been asking himself since that morning.

But then the heated kiss he'd stolen before he'd last left her replayed in his mind, a reminder that something about the woman had wrapped itself around his soul and wouldn't surrender. "I'm afraid it isn't so simple now. I find myself quite enamored with the hellion."

His friends all looked aghast at his declaration, but he had spent the morning accepting the truth of his dilemma.

"Since I cannot leave her without trying to save her, I need your help. Lady Emmaline is no bored Society miss out for a lark. I thought perhaps it was the excitement of the activity, but when I spoke to her today and demanded she cease, I saw a desperation in her gaze that I had not noticed before. Something is driving her to rob people, and if I don't discover what it is, quickly, I may be too late to save her."

Flint looked at Linc and Wolf, then back to Cooper. "We are at your service. How may we assist you?"

He laid out his plan to track Emily with their help. They all agreed, and after a bit more discussion, they rose to part ways. Flint was taking the first watch and headed off to his post for the rest of the rainy afternoon.

Alone again, Cooper sat brooding. How could he have been so stupid as to get involved with Lady Emmaline? He should have stayed the course with his plan to find a sweet, submissive chit with no scandal to be found in her family. Instead, he'd snatched up a little hellion who stole jewels during balls for thrills.

Or perhaps he was missing a key piece of the story. The Earl of Dunmere did not appear to be down on his luck, or no more so than many lords in these modern times. Certainly, he owed creditors and was always good for a wager at a party, but nothing had struck Cooper as being irregular.

But now? With Emily refusing to shift her thrill seeking to the bedroom with him—as he had hoped she would once he made the offer—he had to suspect Dunmere and his sister were in poor financial shape. The problem was, if she wouldn't trust him with the truth, he would have to discover it on his own. But once he knew for certain, what would he do about it?

Chapter Ten

Emily woke up and immediately dressed. She had a full morning ahead of her, despite spending a late night at The Market in Cooper's arms. It still amazed her how unexpected he proved to be in bed. Of course, her only knowledge outside her experiences with him suggested that one was to lie very still and think of other things until the man was finished. Fortunately for her, she had been quickly disabused of that notion, and Cooper had done so in the most delightful way. On the other hand, she wasn't having married sex, so perhaps that was the difference?

An hour later, she found herself standing once more on the doorstep of Lucifer's gambling hell. Her belly flip-flopped as she thought back to her previous visit. The man had been fierce and a little frightening, but she had come with a purpose then. And her purpose remained unchanged. Lifting her arm, she rapped firmly on the door. She waited a few moments and then knocked once more. Standing on the doorstep, she resisted the urge to tap her foot as she waited. Raising her arm another time to knock, she was startled when the wood surface swung open.

Emily once more faced the very large man with the ugly, jagged scar running from his temple near his hairline down to the corner of his mouth. He frowned. "You again."

"Yes, me again. I need to speak with Mr. Lucifer." She stuck her chin up, letting her stubborn nature take over and carry her beyond the pounding of her heart.

"Come inside." He opened the door, letting her into the dimly lit foyer. Nothing had changed since her last visit, not that she had expected that to occur. "Sit." He pointed at the same seat she had occupied previously.

With the exception of knowing what Lucifer looked like and more or less how he would behave, she felt every ounce of the same trepidation she had previously. Sweaty hands, a light tremble in her limbs, and the throb of her pulse had her sitting on edge. When the scarred giant returned, she stood, prepared to be escorted upstairs as she was last time.

"Lucifer cannot see you. You'll have to come back during business hours." The large man lumbered toward the entrance.

Determined to conduct her business now, before the hell's more unsavory clientele arrived, she turned on her heel and took off up the stairs. Fleeter of foot than the doorkeeper—despite her skirts—she was halfway to the second floor before he'd even turned.

At the top, she turned right and walked the length of the gallery to the same double doors she had previously passed through. Inside, she found Lucifer's office empty. Disappointed, she turned to leave when a door she'd not noticed during her first visit opened.

"I should have known a woman like you would not take no for an answer." A deep voice resonated into the open space.

She turned only to find herself confronted with the man's bare chest. Having only seen Cooper's before that moment, in lieu of blushing and running from the room, she stopped and considered his physique. Where Cooper was leaner and roped with muscles, Lucifer was built like a man who had labored all his life. His torso and arms were packed with muscle and dusted with dark hair. Suspenders hung from the waist of his trousers, which were still partially open and offering a peek at more.

He chuckled. "My, my. It seems much has changed since your last visit."

Her gaze snapped up to his face. "I can't imagine what you are suggesting."

"The shy blushing girl has become a brazen woman. Tell me, Lady Emmaline." He stalked across the room to where she stood. "Who has had the pleasure of introducing you to the carnal arts?"

Pulling herself together, she ignored his teasing. "Mr. Lucifer, I am here to conduct business. Shirtless or no, I believe you are still interested in money?"

His brows rose, but he couldn't hide his grin. "You are correct, my lady. Shirtless or no, I am indeed still interested in money. The question is, how much?"

"Fifteen hundred pounds." She reached into her reticule and pulled the bills out. "I need more time to gather the rest."

He wrapped his fingers around the wad of paper. "I told you, no more time. You had ninety days. Now you have sixty."

Panic swamped Emily. There were two house parties left in the hunting season. After that, she'd have to begin pawning their things, and she was certain there would not be enough to cover the remaining balance.

Lucifer stepped closer to her, reached out with his free hand, and stroked her cheek with a fingertip. "I told you, Lady Emmaline. I am not an unreasonable man. I would be amenable to working out Arthur's debt in trade."

She smacked his hand away. "And I told you, Mr. Lucifer, I am *not* that kind of woman. I shall get you the rest of the money."

Somehow. She spun in a whirl of fabric and stormed from the room.

"Gordie!" Lucifer bellowed from the door of his office. "Ensure Lady Emmaline knows the way out, and no more bloody visitors!"

Emily was met on the stairs by the scarred giant, Gordie, she assumed, and was shown to the door. Not that she couldn't find it as easily as she had found Lucifer's office again. As she was all but pushed out into the glare of the midmorning sun, she stumbled.

A handsome gentleman with black hair and deep blue eyes caught her arm and righted her. "Are you well, miss?"

Embarrassment heated her cheeks as she took in the man's finely cut suit and aristocratic air. His classically Greek nose was long and straight, which only seemed to highlight his questioning gaze at finding a woman dressed as she was stumbling from a gambling hell.

"I am fine, thank you, sir." And then she darted off down the street where she'd left the carriage waiting as fast as her legs would carry her.

She needed to complete her shopping, and then it would be time for afternoon calls. It had become imperative that she pinpoint the wealthiest of the guests who would be traveling to the Marquis of Holden's house party. She had to come up with another twenty-five hundred pounds before mid-November.

Sitting on a settee in Lady Stonemere's—or Theo's, as she was bid to call her—drawing room was proving to be an unusual experience. After all, it was not every day she visited with a marchioness and a former madame at the same time.

"And how were your errands this morning, Emily?" Theo asked.

"Mostly uneventful." Emily dearly wished she knew Theo and her other new friends better. She could certainly use some advice. But how did one broach such a vulgar topic as money? No, better she keep her own counsel.

Lizzy, Theo's sister, who had dark blonde hair, soft gray eyes, and had married the Marquess of Carlisle, smiled. "I do hate running errands. They are most tedious."

Marie, the former madame now married to Baron Heartfield, offered a wicked grin. "One simply needs to know how to enliven the process."

Theo and Lizzy chuckled while Emily sat a little confused by the exchange.

"Do share more of your sage advice, Marie. I fear Stone is getting a bit complacent again what with my pregnancy. He could use a reminder of whom he is married to," Theo encouraged her friend.

"Well, the other day, Heart surprised me by joining me for my errands." Marie glanced about the group and then lowered her voice a bit. "While amorous activities in the carriage are not a new idea, typically we had restrained ourselves to long carriage rides. At first, he merely teased me between stops so that I was forced to conduct business in a rather flushed state. Eventually, Heart succumbed to his baser instincts. Our poor driver ended up circling London aimlessly as we repeatedly ordered him to keep driving."

Emily laughed a little, along with everyone else, despite her astonishment at such an intimate tale being shared, and that married people behaved in such a manner.

Marie noticed her discomfiture. "Oh, dear." She shushed Lizzy and Theo. "I fear I've shocked Emily with my story."

"Only a little." Emily couldn't control the heat rising in her cheeks.

Theo smiled gently. "Well, I daresay if Cooper is as taken with you as I believe, you may find out firsthand how husbands sometimes behave."

"Oh, heavens no, Theo. I have no intention of ever marrying...anyone." Emily ignored the first inkling of doubt she'd had in a long while as she said the words that were once an incontrovertible truth.

"Surely, you jest. Cooper is a bit wild, I will admit, but he is a good man with a rather soft heart. I don't see how you could do better in selecting a husband, since Stone is quite taken." Theo looked at her, all expectation and a bit of worry.

Emily hesitated but plunged ahead. "I have never seen a *ton* marriage that inspired anything but dread. When I was a girl, I held girlish dreams about marriage and love. But as I've gotten older and wiser, I realize spinsterhood is the better choice, since one cannot become a widow without having been married."

"And I take it you have relayed to Cooper your unwillingness to wed." Theo's brows drew together.

"Indeed. I have made it eminently clear I have no intention of marrying," Emily assured her new—though possibly short-lived—friend.

Theo sighed. "Well then, I suppose Cooper knows well enough what he is about. But if we might offer another view of married life?"

Emily glanced at the three women, and for the first time, she realized that not one of them had that pinched look that most of their female peers seemed to carry. These women looked serene. Content, even. "Please do."

Theo settled back. "Lizzy here married for love. She and Carlisle fell madly in love in the usual fashion over waltzes in the ballroom and warm punch. Then once they were wed, the man did a full retreat from her. With Marie's help, Lizzy was able to tempt her husband back into the marriage. It turned out that as large as he is, he feared hurting poor little Lizzy. She had to take the bull by the horn, so to speak, to show him she was no wilting lily."

Lizzy smiled and nodded. "Sometimes men take to a notion, and it requires a great deal of effort to break them of it."

"Marie, on the other hand, was the madame of The Market when her long-lost sweetheart reappeared in her life trying to rescue her. Of course, she neither required rescuing nor wanted it."

Emily couldn't help but identify with such a sentiment. "And how did you show him the truth?"

"Ah, my dear. That's the crux of the thing. While I was content in my life and quite self-sufficient, I had missed the truth. I was lonely. For quite a while, I made every attempt to dissuade Heart from his notion of saving me through marriage. I did shocking things with him in the bedroom to prove that I neither required saving nor was adequate marriage material."

Marie laughed. Her golden-blonde hair glinted in the sunshine as her blue eyes danced with merriment. She was a beautiful woman with lush curves that made Emily wonder if she even needed to tightly lace her corset.

"And how did you convince him?" Emily was eager for a solution to her problem.

"I convinced him that I was no longer the girl he remembered. He convinced me it was the woman he was after. Now I am both self-sufficient and happy." The older woman's genuine smile was hard to discredit.

"And then there is Stone and me. He inherited me along with his title, and he wanted none of it. As for me, I was so busy managing everything, I nearly missed the truth about my husband. While he can be a high-handed sort at times, he loves me. I keep him from being stodgy, and he keeps me from being reckless." Theo glanced around conspiratorially. "Sometimes that results in him spanking me when I've been particularly reckless."

Emily gasped. "It's true?"

Theo winked and grinned naughtily. "I wouldn't dare equivocate."

Her mind spinning with the confirmation of what Cooper had once told her, she tried to reconcile her old perception of marriage with all the new information she had so recently received. And while Cooper had been amorous at every turn, she still could not picture such behavior continuing after they were wed. Doubt about her long-held view crept in until she added in the fact that upon her marriage, she would legally cease to exist as a person, becoming her husband's chattel. She still could not stomach such an arrangement.

After all, she currently had the best of both worlds, didn't she? A so far satisfying intimate arrangement and all the freedom she could eke out as a spinster. Could marriage to Cooper be worth giving that up? What if she could have it all, like her newfound friends seemed to?

Emily arrived home to find her brother sitting in his study. He was looking at the daily newspaper, and for a moment, her heart lurched. Would he discover her secret? Was there something new about the Waltzing Thief? Fear grabbed hold of her, all but choking off her ability to breathe. To think.

But then a rush of fury swept in. He should bloody well know what she had been doing. Perhaps then he might reconsider how he spent his evenings. Anger spiked her pulse and had her fisting her hands as she stalked into the room, spoiling for a fight.

"Arthur." She strode across the space. "Have you reviewed the invitations I left for you?"

He looked up from his paper in surprise. "I did not see any invitations."

Emily spied the stack she'd left in the middle of his desk now neatly perched on the right corner. "Didn't you? They seem to have migrated from where I left them." She lifted one eyebrow.

Her brother's cheeks took on a faint pink tinge. "I did not realize you wished me to look at them." He cleared his throat. "I will, of course, take care of that at once."

She sighed. "Very well. Supper will be served at seven."

She turned to leave him before her tart tongue took hold once more.

"Oh, did I not tell you?" Arthur's words halted her progress and had her turning around. "I'm dining at White's this evening." He grabbed the pile of invitations

She knew what would come next. He would be out with his cronies racking up even more debt. Every muscle in her body grew so rigid, and she had to force the words past her clenched teeth. "And then?"

He looked up from the invitation he was reading. "And then I shall be out for the evening."

"Doing what?" She drew a deep breath, trying to stem the tide of her fury.

Nonplussed, Arthur stared at her. "I haven't been in leading strings in a very long time. As I recall, I do not owe you an accounting of my whereabouts as you are neither my mother nor my wife."

Emily growled at her brother. "You unmitigated ass. I am the woman who ensures that your house is cleaned and your meals are on the table. I may not have given birth to you, and I certainly did not marry you, but I am your de facto hostess."

Not to mention your acting man-of-affairs.

"And I value all that you do, Em. But I do not owe you an explanation. I apologize if I failed to mention my supper plans, but do not think you have some say over my comings and goings." Arthur tried to look stern as he pressed his lips together.

And just like that, her temper snapped. "So, I shall sit here alone—again—while you traipse off across London racking up chits and vowels we cannot afford! Arthur, for once in your life, think about me. Think about how your fun affects not only me, but Aunt Hortense and our staff."

He snorted and tossed the invitations on the desk. "Em, I sit in parliament all day, listening to droning speeches and pointless debates. How can you begrudge me a bit of relaxation?"

The fact that he was honestly bewildered, or appeared to be, at any rate, crushed the fight in Emily. She'd always known he was oblivious. She'd just told herself that it was his way of coping. She never truly believed he could be so idiotic, so utterly obtuse as to not understand their situation.

"You are a bloody fool!" Seething mad, she spun around and fled to her room for fear she might do or—more aptly—say something she shouldn't. Because as angry as Arthur made her, she was not going to make her aunt and the staff suffer any more than necessary.

Her brother, on the other hand, could go hang.

Chapter Eleven

July 1861

Cooper sat in his study, not so patiently waiting to hear word from Flint. He was the one currently tailing Emily, since she wouldn't recognize him. Restlessness pushed him from his seat and had him pacing the length of the study. The room was long and narrow, giving him plenty of distance to travel before he was required to turn around and head in the other direction. He'd considered, and discarded, the notion of having a drink multiple times over the course of the morning, primarily because he needed his wits about him once he did have information he could act on.

The concern of the moment was that while he was certain there was some underlying issue driving Emily to rob unsuspecting hostesses, until he knew what it was, he could do nothing. And that was something he'd failed at his entire life. He'd always been action oriented, even as a child. Adulthood had proven no different. He was not a man of leisure as a general rule. He rode daily, attended to estate business, and managed a few discreet philanthropic endeavors.

A knock on the door interrupted his pacing and produced Flint, much to Cooper's surprise. "Why the devil are *you* here?"

"I had Linc pick up the watch at her home after she ran her morning errands because I knew you would wish to hear where she'd been."

Flint strode in and made himself comfortable in a chair.

"What news?" Cooper's heart skipped a beat. *Could there be another man?* He knew it to be a foolish thought, but doubt assailed him for the briefest of moments as he waited for his friend to speak.

Flint hesitated a moment. "Her first stop this morning was Lucifer's."

Cooper blinked. "The gambling hell?"

"The very same." Flint shrugged. "She was there perhaps half an hour."

Fury spun through Cooper as all the possibilities whirled through his mind. "And you did not see fit to send for me? She could have been ravished or killed in that den!"

"Cooper, it's Lucifer's. It's not as if she strolled into Mad Molly's. Lucifer is mostly a gentleman." Flint's tone admonished Cooper as much as his words. "He rarely kills anyone, since he far prefers to be paid the money owed him."

"What the blazes was she doing there?"

Cooper's mind flitted toward another man but once more dismissed it as quickly. Then he considered that she might have a gambling issue. But his little hellion had far too much self-discipline for such dissipation. Perhaps the man was a buyer of her stolen goods? That made infinitely more sense than any other possibility he had identified.

"I do not know, though she was sound of body and appeared unmolested when she departed. I had considered knocking on the door to see if I could ascertain why she was inside for so long, but then she tumbled right out of the building and practically into my arms. Once she was steady on her feet, she pulled away from me and set off briskly down the street."

"Did you speak?" Worry gnawed at Cooper, making him fidget worse than before.

Flint nodded. "Briefly. I asked if she was well. She said she was and then took off. I followed her as she did some shopping, picking up a few items here and there, and then she went home. That was when I sent for Linc, so he could take over and I could come here."

Cooper pinched the bridge of his nose and considered his options. He could confront Emily and demand she tell him where she had been and why, which would likely cause her to break their arrangement since his inquiry violated one of the terms. *Or* he could visit Lucifer and see why Emily had been there. He *still* couldn't imagine her as a gambler, let alone someone who gambled at a hell. But clearly, she had some business with the man or she wouldn't have visited such a place.

"I had my man do a passing check to ensure no scandal was associated with the family, and that all seemed as expected with their finances, but now I wonder if there might be something else there of import. I know Lucifer also provides high-interest loans, so perhaps the family needed some blunt to float things through the season?"

Flint shrugged. "They wouldn't be the first of the *ton* to find themselves in such straits."

"I believe it is time I pay Mr. Lucifer a visit and get the truth of the matter," Cooper said as he rose from his desk.

Flint nodded in agreement as they went in search of the man with the answers.

Cooper and Flint finally walked into Lucifer's just after the gambling hell opened its doors for the night. Their efforts to see the owner of the club earlier that day had proven futile, ending with them retiring to their club for a while. They had then agreed to meet when the establishment opened. At eight o'clock, it was just humming to life with staff bustling about making last-minute preparations. A behemoth of a man greeted them and bid them to wait while he went in search of his boss.

At first glance in the dimly lit main gambling rooms, the club offered the appearance of extravagant opulence. There was blue velvet draped everywhere, with gold fringe dangling around its edges. The floors were black-and-white tile, which Cooper imagined held up well to the nightly crowds that gathered around the blue-felt-covered gambling tables. He counted a dozen card tables on each side of the hell.

Upon closer inspection, the truth of Lucifer's shone through. Many of the floor tiles were cracked. The drapes were a thin velvet material—not the thick lush velvet found in White's—with burn holes tucked into the folds, and the fringe was tattered and fraying in places. The tables appeared to be in decent shape, as they were a vital part of the hell's success.

Having just returned to the foyer from their circuit of the gambling rooms, the oversized brute returned. "Mr. Lucifer will see you now."

With a nod, they followed the man up the stairs and along an upper gallery. They entered a large, spacious office through double doors and found Lucifer sitting behind an imposing desk with a stack of papers to his left and a glass of whisky on his right.

The dark-haired man wore a close-cropped beard that added to his sinister look. But it was his dark eyes that seemed to penetrate a man, seeing deep within to his innermost secrets and weaknesses. Perhaps they were merely fanciful thoughts, but Cooper much preferred to conduct his business and be gone.

The darker man stood up. "Good evening, Lord Brougham, Lord Flintshire. How may I be of service to you?"

Cooper stepped closer to the desk and shook hands with the self-made man—by all accounts, Lucifer had grown up in the gutters of Seven Dials and built the empire he now ran. "I've come to speak with you about Lady Emmaline Winterburn."

"Please, sit." Lucifer waved them over to the chairs across from his desk. "May I offer you something to drink?"

Cooper and Flint both declined and waited silently for their host to get down to business.

Settling back into his chair, Lucifer offered a wry twist of his lips. "I'm afraid I am unable to discuss my clientele. You see, they expect a certain level of confidentiality."

Cooper sighed. "Mr. Lucifer, I am aware that Lady Emmaline has been here to visit you. In light of this knowledge, I am concerned that she may be under some financial obligation to you. If that were the case, I would be interested in settling her debt on her behalf."

"Intriguing." Lucifer reached for his glass and took a drink. "However, Lady Emmaline herself is in no debt to me."

Confused, Cooper sat forward. "I do not understand. If she has no business with you, then why would she frequent your establishment?"

Lucifer smiled, a sly, knowing grin. "I said she had no *debt*. I did not say she did not have business. She has taken an interest in her brother's activities of late, and the rather unfortunate—for him—outcome."

Cooper and Flint looked at each other. Of course. Dunmere was running with a rather wild set these days, and it seemed his pockets were not so deep as his cronies'.

"And Lady Emmaline's interest, I assume, is in squaring the debt with you?"

"Indeed. Though I do believe she is in danger of coming up short, my lord."

Bloody hell.

"I believe we can see to it that that is not the case."

Cooper reached inside his coat to retrieve his cheque-book.

Lucifer hesitated, despite the opportunity to be paid.

"While I would gladly settle the debt here and now, I do fear the lady in question might take exception to such intervention on her behalf."

"And why would you care about whether Lady Emmaline might take exception or not?"

Lucifer grinned. "Well, she is a feisty thing. Would you believe me if I suggested I feared for my well-being?"

"Mr. Lucifer. I believe you are a man who is in business to make money. While I do not engage in trade, I am no fool. Now, I would like to settle the debt and be on about my evening." Cooper couldn't tamp down his impatience.

"And normally, you would be right. But I find myself interested in possibly helping Lady Emmaline when she fails to satisfy the debt."

The lascivious gleam in Lucifer's eyes was more than Cooper was willing to tolerate.

"Lady Emmaline is *mine*. In any event, she would never succumb to your unscrupulous offer. I suggest you name the amount owed you and train your sights on another desperate woman," Cooper snarled, his anger far outstripping his well-ingrained manners.

Lucifer's brows rose high above his dark eyes. "I see. I suppose I should have known that if you were here tracking her movements, she had some tie to you." The man sighed. "Well, that is damned disappointing."

Lucifer opened a ledger sitting in the middle of his desk and flipped through a few pages. Finally, he looked up from his notations. "Dunmere owed me five thousand pounds. Lady Emmaline recently made a payment of fifteen hundred pounds, so that leaves…"

"Thirty-five hundred pounds." Cooper cut the man off as he wrote out the cheque. "And shall I make this payable directly to you?"

"That will suffice, my lord." Lucifer watched carefully as Cooper handed him the cheque. "Though, as you seem to be so generously absolving Lord Dunmere's debt, you may wish to know I am not his only debt holder."

Flint, who had remained silent throughout their exchange, sat up. "Who else might hold his vowels?"

"Mind you, it is merely rumor. But I have heard that he owes Lord Worthington a small—though not inconsiderable—amount." Lucifer rose from his desk after tucking the cheque in his ledger. "Now, if you gentlemen wouldn't mind, I do have a business to run."

Cooper and Flint stood to go, but Cooper hesitated. "I would appreciate your discretion with regard to our business here. Particularly where Lady Emmaline is concerned."

Lucifer did not miss a step as he strode to the double doors of his office and opened them. "You may rest assured that, if at all possible, I plan to avoid Lady Emmaline, considering the nature of our business." He hesitated. "Of course, should you tire of her quickly, I could certainly be persuaded to take her off your hands."

Cooper glared at the unscrupulous gambling hell owner and growled. "The hell you will. She's *mine*."

Chapter Twelve

Two days later, with all of Lord Dunmere's vowels in hand, Cooper paid him a visit during a time when he knew Emily would be out. A bleary-eyed, more masculine version of Emily peered at him from across a walnut desk that seemed to be the only quality piece of furniture in the study.

"To what do I owe the honor of another visit from the esteemed Lord Brougham?"

Cooper wanted to smack the fool. Instead, he opted for a little shock value. He held up the pile of chits he now possessed. "I should think you would be a bit more cordial to the man who currently holds all seventy-eight hundred pounds of your debt in his hand."

Dunmere sat up, his already pale face now ashen. "All of my debt? What do you want?"

"Besides payment?" Cooper let his annoyance shine through.

"I assume there is something more at play here than a man looking to turn a profit. I doubt debt collection is the most profitable of investments."

Apparently, her brother, when cornered, showed small flashes of the steel found deep within his sister.

Perhaps the man was salvageable? He decided to get straight to the point. "You are correct, Dunmere. I am here because I want your sister."

The once-pale man turned flush—with laughter. He literally bent over himself guffawing.

Cooper sat and waited for the man's humor to subside. It took longer than he liked.

Finally, Dunmere straightened in his chair and leaned back, once more the insouciant lord, with the exception of the occasional chuckle that still burst free. "I'm afraid you may have misspent your money if you think you can buy my influence over my sister. She'd be far more inclined to sell herself in a direct transaction than to bend to my will."

Bloody hell! Cooper wanted to throttle the foolish man. "I do not need your *influence* so much as I need you to cease being a burden on your sister."

The last vestiges of the man's good humor dissipated in the blink of an eye. "Here now, I shall not have a man, one whose reputation for debauchery far outstrips any vice I may have, sit in my home and question my manhood."

"Good God, man! You have no idea what your hellion sister has been up to, have you?" Cooper was incredulous. He'd assumed the man simply had turned a blind eye to serve his own purposes. He had not expected him to be so deep in his own world that he was oblivious.

Dunmere sat forward. "What do you mean by calling Emily a hellion? She is a wonderful woman who does her very best to care for me and manage this household under rather difficult circumstances." He snorted. "The woman practically blends into the woodwork at balls!"

Cooper made a tsking sound as he shook his head. "Lord Dunmere, your sister is a master at getting people to see what she wants. Or, more correctly, presenting the appearance of what they wish to see."

"Do not be ridiculous." The man waved his hand in punctuation.

"Are you aware that your sister knows of your gambling debts?" Cold determination filled Cooper as he started down the path of truth with Emily's brother.

The man looked down at his hands. Cooper assumed he was hiding his shame.

"I am. You may have noticed she has stripped this house bare to try to raise the funds for me."

"Are you also aware that she has visited Mr. Lucifer multiple times in relation to your debt?" Cooper waited as he gauged the man's response.

Her brother's face first drained of all color then. After a moment of sheer terror, he turned purple with fury. "You dare suggest such vile things about my sister?"

"I speak only the truth. A rather unsavory one, though not of the nature you are thinking." Cooper paused to draw a breath. "Arthur... Do you mind if I call you Arthur? I believe we shall be brothers-in-law soon enough. The point of fact is, she visited the man to assess your debt and try to get it lowered. Failing in that, she has since set out on her own to clear your marker. At least the large one she knows about."

Confusion clouded strangely familiar blue eyes. "If you aren't suggesting something salacious, then how is she paying off my debts? The house is barely standing, she has stripped it so clean, and I know it barely covers our month-to-month expenses, let alone pays back what I now owe you."

"Precisely. How do you think your sister has managed to pay off fifteen hundred pounds of your debt?" Cooper let one brow rise.

"I don't know, and I am not sure I wish to." Arthur blanched, a shadow of fear flitting across his haggard features.

Cooper wasn't sure how the man was still upright with all the wild swings in temperament on top of the headache and dyspepsia he was clearly suffering. He'd have cast up his own accounts if he hadn't been sober as a judge at the moment. "No, you don't, but I shall tell you anyhow. Your sweet wallflower sister is a thief."

"The hell, you say!" Arthur snarled as he shot forward across the desk to grab for Cooper.

Seated more than far enough back to avoid being touched, he pressed on. "In fact, your sister is the Waltzing Thief the papers have been writing about of late."

"You lie." Arthur slumped over his desk and slithered back into his chair. "Please tell me you are lying."

But there was no doubt in Cooper's mind her brother knew he was not lying, even as he still tried to deny the truth. "I wish I could. As it stands, I cannot. Returning to your earlier question of what I want besides the money you owe me. Through circumstances that I shall not delve into, I have become quite enamored of Lady Emmaline. I daresay I love her."

Arthur looked up after yet another shock, though this one appeared to be far less disturbing. "And what of her? Does she love you?"

"Ah, you see, that is the quandary. Your sister, being of a stubborn bent, would not likely admit she did, even should it be the truth. I am slowly working her toward being comfortable with the notion. However, that will take time. Time I do not have if she continues to steal from hostesses during the balls she attends. What I need is for you to cease your childish behavior. Stop the gambling. Cut ties with those bad seeds you call friends, and take your estate in hand."

"You call my friends bad seeds? What of your lot?" Arthur glared, clearly not pleased with Cooper's demand.

"My friends are all bricks to a man. They have been and will continue to be reliable sorts who come when called, and sometimes even when I have not asked. They may enjoy the fleshly pleasures, but they do not allow such endeavors to interfere with their obligations to their titles and their families. You would do well to ape them."

Arthur sighed. "And if I refuse?"

"If you refuse, I shall begin proceedings to take what remains of your holdings to satisfy your debts. I shall tell your sister the full scope of the debt you owe, and then I shall give her all your holdings and the monies I seize. You, my lord, will then be beholden to your younger sister for every scrap you eat, every piece of clothing on your back, and every farthing you spend."

Cooper waited and hoped the man would see reason.

Silence stretched out between the two, almost a battle of wills. Which was ridiculous, because clearly, Cooper was the stronger of the two. Finally, Arthur caved and groaned in defeat as he let his head plop into his hands.

"You're right. I have been a wastrel of man. When my father died, the estate was so deep in debt, it wiped everything out to bring us back into the black. At first, the gambling went well. I was winning, able to fund my sister's first season. But then my luck turned." He shook his head. "It was a slow slide into the gutters, but it was inexorable. One day, I looked up, and things were so bad, I had no idea where to start to fix them."

Cooper let his disdain for Arthur slip away. The man seemed to want to do better if given the chance. "Consider your debt absolved. As long as you head down the right path and stay true, your debt is forgiven. Should you slip, I shall do as promised and take everything and give it to your sister."

"You realize she'd never marry you then." Arthur's point was one Cooper had considered.

"But she would be happy, and that is all I care about." Cooper rose. "I suggest you join me at White's tomorrow for lunch. I shall introduce you to my friends, and I promise you, things will begin to turn around. You may also have your man of affairs call on mine."

Arthur also stood. "I'm afraid I had to let my man go a few months prior." He turned a bit pink as he admitted yet another failing.

"Very well, then. I shall have my man send one of his junior associates over to begin getting your situation sorted. I am sure he has a young enterprising man amongst his staff who might be just what you need to turn things around." Cooper nodded and turned to go, but stopped. "One last thing. Not a word of any of this to Emily. She is not to know I am the one who bought your debt out. She will see it as manipulation, not assistance. Also, you should escort your sister to the Landstones' ball and stay out of the card rooms. Perhaps with you there and paying attention, she will be less...reckless."

"Of course, Lord Brougham." Arthur nodded solemnly.

"Cooper will do in private. As I said, I aim for us to be in-laws. No point in standing on ceremony."

And then he departed, leaving behind the man he had torn down humbled. He hoped rebuilding him into the man he should have been would prove to be easier.

Chapter Thirteen

Emily wore her second-best gown for the Landstones' ball. The dress bore up well under the weight of the added lace, mostly intended to hide the more worn spots of the gown. With her hair curled nicely to hang by her face and a pair of comfortable slippers on her feet, she felt certain tonight would be an excellent evening. She needed a good haul if she was going to make up the ground she had lost due to Cooper's relentless interruptions.

It seemed every time she was about to slip off to acquire a few new items at a ball, the dratted man popped up and hustled her off into some deserted alcove or empty library. Granted, she thoroughly enjoyed their activities once they were there, but nonetheless, they were a distraction. Once more, she divested herself of Lady Vardy—and, to her great surprise, her brother—and moved toward the ladies' retiring room.

Typically, when Arthur deigned to attend a ball with her, he disappeared into the card room upon their arrival. Tonight, after depositing Aunt Hortense with the other matrons, he had opted to remain with her and Lady Vardy—in the ballroom! He'd even gone so far as to commit to a number of dances. Emily wondered if he might be making a foray into the marriage market.

Happily, she had yet to see Cooper at the ball, so she took the opportunity to slip upstairs and take care of what had become rather pressing business. As usual, she made her way down the darkened hall, opening each door in turn until she found what appeared to be Lady Landstone's bedroom.

With a sigh of relief, she slipped inside the room and closed the door behind her. In the chamber, moonlight filtered in through the window, providing the only source of light. Unlike the owners of many of the other bedchambers she had stolen into over the previous months, Lady Landstone appeared to be fastidious. Emily commenced searching the drawers for any valuables. Finding none, she moved to the closet.

As she was opening a drawer, the soft click of the bedroom door closing alerted her that someone had come in. Instantly, her heart skipped a beat. If she were caught digging through Lady Landstone's closet, there was no question she would be in a great deal of trouble. Leaving off where she was, she crept to the closet door and peeked into the chamber.

To her horror, it was no maid in the room.

She gasped, drawing the notice of the man—he had a short but broad build—who spun around with a curse.

Emily dashed toward the bedroom door, determined to flee certain disaster. Despite her cumbersome skirts, she was nearly to the point of her escape when a meaty fist snagged the back of her dress. The man yanked on the material to halt her advance, much to the detriment of the lace embellishment. She heard the shredding sound of her middling stitchwork giving way as all momentum stopped.

"What 'ave we here?" The man's rough speech indicated to Emily that he was certainly not one of her peers.

It was something of a relief as it made it highly unlikely she would be identified and humiliated in a public fashion by a fellow thief. But it did not mean the man was not a threat to her person. He spun her about and grabbed her wrist, his hand as strong as any manacle.

He dragged her closer to the window so he could get a look at her. "My, my. A real lady, I'd warrant."

Emily mustered her best outraged-lady tone. "Unhand me this instant."

The man laughed. "I think not. I came for the pretty baubles, but I seem to have found a whole different set."

Terrified, she placed her hands against his chest and attempted to push him away to no avail. Far stronger than she, he leered at her breasts and then reached up to fist the front of her gown and yank. Fabric rended, but not so much as to grant him access.

Out of the corner of her eye, Emily spotted a hefty candle-holder. Shifting one hand from holding him off, she reached for the heavy artifact. The man managed to lean in, grabbing her breast through her clothes. His shift in weight brought her that much closer to the candleholder and allowed her to wrap her hand around it.

Removing her other hand, she let him come closer still as she raised the metal ornament with both hands and crashed it down on the back of his head. With a muffled *umph*, he collapsed on the floor, letting her go. Tears welling in her eyes, she dropped the household weapon and fled the chamber.

Her feet skimmed the hallway as quickly as her skirts would allow. Heaving for air, whether from the fear pulsing through her body, the constriction of her corset, her uncontrollable sobbing, or the simple act of running when she had not moved so quickly since she was a girl, she didn't know. Nor did she particularly care at the moment. Regardless of the cause, it was making breathing difficult.

Once she reached the top of the stairs that led back to the public areas of the Landstones' home, she paused for a moment and tried to calm herself. Cheeks wet with tears and face warm from her exertions, she was certain she looked a fright. A stop in the ladies' retiring room was most certainly in order, and then, if possible, a speedy departure. If she could alert the Landstones to the prowler, she would. But she had no way to explain her presence upstairs. Pushing the guilt aside, she headed for the relative safety of the retiring room, when all she wanted was to retreat to her bedroom, sip a cup of hot chocolate, and curl up under the covers.

As it turned out, her wishes were not to be.

Emily hovered just outside the busy room for the female attendees, crossing her arms to hide her damaged bodice while a gaggle of young girls tittered and walked by. More than one looked at her queerly as they passed. Finally able to pass, she took a single step forward when a masculine hand on her arm waylaid her. Shocked by such a familiar gesture, she did not need to look to gather who the owner of the hand was. But despite her desperate desire to flee into the retiring room, Cooper turned her about.

"Lady Emmaline—" A sharp indrawn breath cut off whatever he'd been about to say. "What the devil happened to you?"

"Lord Brougham, please. I'd like to make use of the retiring room. I'm sure whatever you needed can wait a few moments." She struggled not to plead and hoped he didn't detect the waver in her voice.

Without a further word of acknowledgment, he turned unceremoniously and dragged her behind him into a nearby drawing room. With the door closed and the two of them alone, he pulled her into his arms. "What has happened?"

His simple question, but more so the obvious concern that laced his words, caused her tears to return in full force. The next thing she knew, she had soaked Cooper's waistcoat and shirtfront as her fear rolled through her body like a squall hitting the shore. Time slipped away as she let her heart-wrenching fear escape along with her tears. As she calmed, Cooper rubbed her back and crooned soft, meaningless words to her until all that remained were the soft hiccups of the emotionally spent.

"Now—" He set her back from him slightly, and for the first time, she was sure, took in her total appearance. His gaze touched on the torn front of her bodice, her tearstained face, and her disheveled hair. A low, fearsome growl escaped him. "Whoever did this to you...I shall kill him."

Emily blinked, surprised by the ferocious anger that rolled off him in waves. "Cooper, I—" She tried to form the words to explain. But all her thoughts rushed through her mind at once, tripping and tumbling over each other. Strangely, she could sit back and understand the occurrence for what it was. Clearly, she had had a shock.

"Did someone attack you?" He barked the question at her, his impatience for an answer as plain as the soaked necktie drooping around his throat.

"Yes, but—" Dread shot through her. He would be furious when she told him what had happened. But mostly—she was afraid—furious with *her*.

He growled again. "Bloody hell, woman! Tell me who did this to you so I may avenge your honor!"

Her own fury rising at his belligerent demand, she snarled at him. "It is none of your concern."

"The hell it's not. Tell me this instant, or I shall go find your brother and bring him back here."

The glint in his eye warned her the threat to retrieve her brother was not made idly.

Damn the man to perdition. "Fine. I was upstairs making a new acquisition when I ran into an unexpected prowler. We tussled a bit, but I escaped and came directly downstairs."

Cooper looked as if he wanted to kill someone, and, as she had worried, she wasn't sure if it was her or the other thief.

Once more his gaze touched on her disarray, but with each spot on her person he shifted to, something in his eyes grew wilder, darker. And Emily could admit to herself that his darkness, the profound commanding anger that flared to life deep in the chocolate depths of his eyes, roused something in her, soothing the panic and fear in a most unexpected way.

And then he hauled her into his arms and snared her mouth with his. She melted against him, a strangely safe harbor in the momentary storm. Tongues twined as their bodies fused as closely as fashion allowed. If they had been at The Market, she would have happily stripped bare so that she could absorb his heat and the succor he offered. For the moment, his arms and lips would have to suffice.

The steely embrace pressed her closer to him, so she slid her arms up around his neck. Hanging on for dear life as he took possession of her mouth and perhaps a small part of her soul, she reveled in the taste of fine whisky, a hint of tobacco, and some indefinable spice that was all Cooper. He moaned into the kiss, even as his growing erection became more prominent.

What had started as an angry exchange had ignited into white-hot passion that was quickly flaring out of control. And in that moment, Emily was happy to burn.

A loud gasp that had clearly not come from either her or Cooper ended their kiss as they broke apart and turned to face her brother, Lord and Lady Landstone, as well as another man Emily did not recognize.

The unknown party raised a finger and pointed at them. "There is your thief."

Emily blanched, all the blood draining from her face. Did he mean her? Was he the man she had encountered upstairs? Everything had happened so quickly, and with the shadows of the room, she would hardly recognize her attacker were he standing two feet from her in a ballroom.

Lady Landstone took in the vignette before her and bellowed loud enough half the ballroom could hear. "Lord Brougham, Lady Emmaline, what is the meaning of this?"

Emily suddenly noticed the cooler air caressing her bosom and remembered her damaged bodice. "Oh!" She gathered the sagging fabric to her chest and stared Lady Landstone down. "I don't know what you mean."

The stranger once again inserted himself into the moment. "She must be the thief."

Cooper grew agitated with the man's more specific pronouncement. "I do not know who you are, sir. But I suggest you cease your baseless conjecture and"—he eyed the man's rougher clothing—"stay out of dealings that do not concern you."

Lord Landstone stepped forward. "Here now, Lord Brougham. This man is here at my behest. Afraid of being robbed during the ball, we hired Mr. Paget as some insurance against the possibility. As we had feared, he caught a man red-handed."

A gusty sigh escaped Cooper. "My lord, if you say he caught a man, why would he stand there and claim Lady Emmaline is a thief?"

Mr. Paget harrumphed loudly. "The man I apprehended stated that he had a run-in with a lady thief, which was why he was so easily detained. The lady in question had knocked him out with a candleholder during a struggle."

Cooper cast a wary glance at her, and Emily swallowed, trying to regain her composure in light of the situation. She was trying to step in as the discussion continued to flow around her as though she were not the accused.

"And since when did the word of a thief become worthy of levying such accusations against a lady?" Cooper demanded.

"Since we opened the door of our drawing room only to discover Lady Emmaline's dress has been damaged as though she were part of a struggle." Lady Landstone answered, daring to point out the glaringly obvious disarray of Emily's garments.

The room fell silent as a low murmur swept from the Landstones backward across the ballroom.

Emily suddenly lurched into the hushed chasm. "I am no thief. Such accusations are ridiculous."

Lady Landstone's gaze grew sharp and probing. "Then please, explain how your dress came to be in such a state."

Emily looked down and hesitated. One heartbeat. Two. "I'm terribly clumsy. I was attempting to slip in here for a small reprieve from the festivities, and my bodice caught on the door latch, tearing a bit as I came in."

Mr. Paget snorted in clear disbelief. Lord Landstone eyed the height of the door handle and then Emily's bodice. She could see the moment he rejected her version of events.

"Lady Emmaline, it pains me to point out that the hardware on the door is not of sufficient height to cause such damage." Lord Landstone's slightly jowly face had something of a hangdog expression.

Cooper straightened up and tugged on the front lapels of his frock coat. "Lady Emmaline is attempting to protect me, I am afraid."

"You are the thief?" Lady Landstone sounded as confused as Emily felt.

"No, my lady. But I am guilty of ravishing her here in your drawing room. Which is how her dress became damaged. I was a bit carried away by the *intimate* moment."

Everyone froze as his words landed like loose pearls on a parquet floor. Explosive little pings pierced the quiet, followed by the soft rolling hum of news flying through the ballroom. Emily stood there in shock as her reputation disintegrated before her very eyes. She looked at Cooper, horror and sadness overwhelming her surprise. "Please, my lord. Do *not* do this."

He shook his head. "I merely speak the truth, my lady. I refuse to see you stand accused a thief."

Fury rushed through her at his interference, but there was little she could do. The damage was done. She was ruined.

Chapter Fourteen

Lord Landstone promptly closed the still gaping doors of the drawing room, shutting out the rest of the ballgoers. Emily sat down on the nearby settee, cold and still as a statue. As the brute of a man had labeled her a thief, Cooper's voice had rung out and ended her life as she knew it. He'd ruined her with a few words. It wouldn't have mattered if they had not been in the slightest true. The mere fact that he had linked their names in such an intimate manner in such a public forum relegated her to the status of ruined.

Desperation surged through her trembling frame, scattering her thoughts.

Mr. Paget—completely indifferent to her discomfort and the tattered state of her life—had moved to hover over her as though she might try to run. Certainly, she would have, if given the chance, but it still annoyed her that he had assumed. With Cooper and Arthur to her right, Aunt Hortense seated off to the side, and the Landstones and Mr. Paget to her left—at least Lady Vardy was still in the ballroom—it almost didn't matter what the outcome of the next few moments was. Her life was irrevocably changing, and it was all utterly beyond her control.

Mr. Landstone's deep bass was a rumble that suddenly caused Emily's stomach to roil. "Now, I believe our friend here is claiming that Lady Emmaline is a thief, and Lord Brougham has countered that claim by saying she has been amorously engaged with him. My lady, could you perhaps help us out and clarify which man is correct?"

She resisted the urge to roll her eyes. "My lord, you give me so many cheery options. Could it not be that neither man is correct? Perhaps I am both not a thief *and* not amorously engaged, as you so politely put it."

Cooper sighed. Arthur glared. But she tilted her chin and fell silent.

"That may be true, my lady. However, if you cannot prove that you were not with Lord Brougham, then I shall have to leave the resolution of the other claim to the authorities. Which I might remind you would mean jail, for at least the short term, a public trial, and potentially *transportation*." The man ended on the most ominous note possible, letting his tone drop low and deep to great effect.

She felt the blood leach from her head as it all plummeted somewhere south of her clacking knees. Stubborn to a fault, she pressed on with her argument. "But my lord, either choice is imprisonment. One a cage of steel, the other gilded in gold, perhaps, but a cage nonetheless."

Cooper growled beside her.

Lord Landstone pinched the bridge of his nose. "My lady, both men cannot be wrong."

Of course not. Men in general were thought never to be wrong. Oddly enough, both men were correct. But what could she say that was not incriminating in one capacity or another?

Emily wanted to be sick. Very, very sick—all over Cooper's shoes, preferably.

After she sat mutely for a few moments, her brother finally spoke. "Do not be foolish. What's done is done. Do not make this any worse than it is. Admit"—he looked furious as he slashed a glance at Cooper—"what has happened, and then we can go home to sort out this disaster."

She remained in her seat as a dizzy spell swept over her. Acknowledge her ruin? In public? Never. Besides, if the two meddling men had left well enough alone, she would not be in this situation. The ridiculous detective—or whatever he was—could search her person, and he would find nothing to indicate she was the villain. Not that it mattered any longer. The damage to her reputation was done.

Cooper huffed. "Lady Landstone, Lady Emmaline has a small dark birthmark on her upper right thigh on the inside of her leg. If you might validate that what I say is true, we could dispense with this charade."

Lady Landstone blushed to the roots of her hair, but she nodded. "Of course, I will do so in the name of justice."

But then Aunt Hortense spoke up from her perch in the corner. "No need to embarrass the girl further. I can assure you she has a mark such as Lord Brougham describes."

Emily watched the private inquiry agent's face turn red as he gaped after Aunt Hortense concurred with Cooper and he realized his culprit had just been exonerated.

"There, now that we've established that Lady Emmaline is innocent, I believe Lord Dunmere and I have matters to discuss. Lady Landstone, is there a more private room we can make use of?" Cooper asked as a matter of manners.

"We'll leave you to your discussions here, my lord." And then she and her husband exited the room with the reluctant detective in their wake.

As they left, Emily felt as if her future had walked out with them.

Once the door closed, silence reigned until they were certain they were alone. Cooper turned to face her, but she refused to look at him as fury surged forward to replace her disbelief.

He sighed. "You cannot ignore me and expect me to go away."

"If you please, my lord. Do not address me so informally." Emily's lips felt stiff as she seethed beneath her calm exterior.

Arthur sat next to her as he tried to take her hand in his. "Emily, please. I believe Lord Brougham saved your life. That brute would have strung you up from the nearest tree."

She turned to him. "And you. How does it feel to be complicit in the charade that has ruined your sister's reputation and made Aunt Hortense complicit in your deception, as well as an incompetent chaperone?"

Her brother snorted, slanting a glance at the now sleeping woman in the corner of the room. "Nobody in their right mind would believe Aunt Hortense to be a competent chaperone—one can only imagine what our parents were thinking when they named her such. And what the busybodies won't know is that we saved you from being hanged for a thief."

Molten anger burned through the last of her reserves. "By whose estimation? How can you be sure they would have had any evidence to call the magistrate, much less find me guilty? If you two fools had simply followed my lead, this conversation would not be happening. Unlike you two, I was well prepared for the potential consequences of my activities." She stopped and stared at Arthur. "Wait just one minute. Why are you assuming I would be found guilty? It's as if you know what has been happening while you've been out getting soused and throwing all our money away."

Her brother shut his mouth and darted a glance at Cooper. "I assumed they would have manufactured whatever evidence they needed. Though I am not"—he cleared his throat—"sure why they focused on you."

Emily rolled her eyes. "Arthur, you're a terrible liar."

She rose and faced Cooper. "What did you tell my brother?"

"That I suspected you were taking some rather terrible risks, and I suggested he should put a stop to such behavior." He made a face of exasperation. "Clearly, I was too late."

"You, sir, are a bastard, and I regret ever making your acquaintance." She drew a deep breath. "Now, if you two are finished, I am ready to depart. I suggest you come along if you plan to ride with Aunt Hortense and me." She started across the room. "I suspect Lady Vardy will be seeking out other transportation home."

"Emily." She stopped as Cooper called out. "You shall marry me so we can end this farce and move past it. And you shall cease your risky activity."

She whipped around. "I shall do no such thing. I told you long ago marriage was out of the question. *Nothing* has changed."

She wheeled around and sailed out of the room as her brother sputtered to life behind her. "But you can't be serious! You're ruined!"

Both the men in her life could go to hell. She would not be forced into marriage to appease Society.

Cooper turned to Arthur as the door slammed shut, and sighed. "She will realize very soon she has no other choice but to marry me."

"That may be true, but she will not like it any more then than she does now." He shook his head. "I fear she is a stubborn woman who may never soften under the circumstances."

Cooper considered the fury he had seen burning in her eyes. There was no doubt in his mind that where there was passion—even angry passion—he could turn the tide his way. But first, he needed her to agree to the wedding.

"Tell me, Arthur, have you never put your foot down with her?" Cooper was curious.

Her brother offered him a sheepish look of apology. "More often than not, it was her putting her foot down with me." He gave a soft sigh of resignation. "I'm afraid I was a coddled sort. Emily was the one who kept me from turning spoiled as we grew up. She frequently reined me in when I grew too wild or too demanding. Our parents never denied either of us anything. But unlike my levelheaded sister, I often took advantage of their generosity. It seemed there was always more to come. Of course, everything changed when they died. I learned the truth of our lifestyle and then did my own damage to boot."

His gaze bore a hole in the floor of the drawing room.

Cooper nodded. "Well, the issue here is that you must intervene with your sister."

Arthur looked up from the floor in surprise. "Me?"

"Absolutely. For the first time, you, Arthur, are going to put your foot down with that little hellion you call sister." Cooper grinned and slapped him on the back.

"Indeed, it's high time you reined that girl in. She's like a runaway donkey." Aunt Hortense seemed to come awake with no warning, but obviously she had heard enough to understand what was going on.

Arthur sputtered. "B-but—"

"Enough." The elderly woman rose from her seat. "If you can't make her do as she should, then you need to find some leverage to use against her. Family is the way to sway the girl. For once your tendency toward selfishness may actually serve another." With that declaration, she hobbled from the room, leaving two rather shocked men in her wake.

Cooper shook his head at the wily old bird. "She's right, it must be done. Emily is out of her depth. After all these years of her helping you out, and with you taking the reins as the head of the family, it falls to you to help her. Besides, it will be excellent practice for when you marry." Cooper slung an arm about him and led him over to the decanters on the sideboard.

Arthur chuckled. "I have no intention of marrying. And if I do, I shall marry a biddable woman. One who is sweet and kind. I would never be so foolish as to fall in love with a woman such as my sister." He preened at his pronouncement. And then realized what he'd implied. "Oh, not to say…"

Cooper huffed. "Never mind that. I like your sister just fine as she is. But I shall warn you, better men than me have sworn the same thing, and none of us have accomplished the task. We have all married handfuls, and I suspect you will be no less fortunate." He poured two fingers of whisky and tossed it back.

Arthur considered his words and then shook his head. "No, I shall stick to my plan. A biddable woman if I must."

Cooper simply smiled and nodded at his future brother-in-law.

Arthur stopped. "By the by, should we not tell Emily that the debts are paid? Seems as though it would have stopped this foolishness sooner." Concern creased his brow.

"With our nuptials looming, I see little opportunity for her to get into further trouble."

Cooper sidestepped the issue. And it was an issue, but for entirely different reasons than Arthur realized. If Emily was to be his wife, he needed to know she trusted him as he trusted her. He wanted to give her more time to do just that on her own. Perhaps that made him imprudent, or perhaps that made him a romantic at heart. In either case, he didn't wish to think on it too much.

Chapter Fifteen

T he ride home had been quiet, tense. Aunt Hortense had dozed most of the thankfully short distance. Her brother, while never a very talkative sort, had proven especially silent and brooding. And nothing had changed upon their arrival. It wasn't until the next morning that her new reality began to intrude. The morning papers arrived, and within the gossip columns an all-too-familiar tale played out.

A certain Lady E— was accused of being the Waltzing Thief, but it was proven she could not be because she had been having a romp with Lord B—!

Emily sighed. She had hoped by slipping away from the Landstones' ball, the gossip would dissipate. Apparently not true. Nevertheless, she would brazen the chattering of bored ladies and lords if it meant retaining her autonomy. Soon enough, she would come of an age where she would no longer matter in Society. She was even willing to consider moving to the country if she could retain her independence. She sighed. Then another piece of gossip caught her eye...

Lord D—, who has been a frequenter of gambling hells all over London of late, seems to have disappeared from the landscape. Could this be a sign of reformation?

A small shred of hope wiggled in her heart. Could Arthur be making the shift from inveterate gambler to upstanding lord of the realm? Hopeful, though not convinced, she set the rag aside and took a sip of her morning coffee. She found the bitter brew to be fortifying, especially when facing what promised to be a trying day.

No sooner had she set her cup down than her brother strode into the morning room. "We need to discuss this matter of you and Brougham."

Her spine stiffened, and her lips pressed together. Taking a deep breath and releasing it, she looked at Arthur. "There is nothing to discuss. I refuse to marry him."

His deep brown eyes with flecks of gold held pain as his brow furrowed. For a moment, she wanted to take the words back, if only to ease that pain. Clearly, he was worried about her—and about time, too!

"Please, Emily. Be reasonable, I ask so little of you—"

Anger surged through her. "Ask so little? Perhaps you do not form the words, but you no doubt leave all responsibility for this house and the bloody earldom for me to deal with! For once, I am asking you to do something for *me*."

"Do not force me to do something neither of us wishes. You have been ruined, and that must be rectified. Lord Brougham has done the right thing. He's offered for your hand."

"No, Arthur. It is a no today, it will be a no tomorrow, and it will be a no the day after. I shall not marry that man. He ruined me in order to force my hand. I'll not be treated as though I am some prize to be claimed."

"The story is already in the gossip rags. There will be no more invitations, no more soirees, and no more salons. You will be a pariah. Is that what you wish?" Arthur's face grew red as he became louder with each word.

"It is my consequence to bear. Dear Lord Brougham will be welcomed back into Society with open arms, I daresay. Men never pay the toll for these affairs." She sniffed and looked away from her brother.

"Your consequence? What of the earldom? How will I ever find a wife? If you remain a pariah, do you believe I shall be welcome in Society? That the hovering mamas of the *ton* will allow me two seconds—let alone a dance—with their innocent daughters?" Frustration seethed through every syllable he uttered. "This is not a *faux pas* you can simply weather. This is the rest of your life," he bellowed, his anger filling the room.

Emily blanched. All she had ever wanted was for her brother to settle down and find a wife. It was why she had struggled to erase his debts and keep the family afloat. But she had no idea that he held any real desire to wed. It was the first he had ever mentioned a word on the subject.

Could she deny him the respectability he needed to move about Society and secure the future of the earldom, as well as his own happiness? Was her pride worth so much?

She looked back at her brother, whose face wore a mask of surprise. Had he not known he felt that way?

"I was unaware of your desire to find a wife."

The shock melted into manly disgruntlement, as though having been forced to talk about his feelings was arduous. "I can't say it is something I have thought about until recently, and even then, it still feels a far-off notion. Certainly, one day I'll need to marry."

And so, his backpedaling began.

Renewed fury sent Emily to her feet. "Damn you. How could you use my soft heart against me in such an odious fashion? That is unfair of you."

"Of course, I shall need to marry one day, but if you have been ruined, that will become far more difficult." He held his hands up, palms facing toward her in a placating manner. "I only want what is best for you."

She crossed her arms under her breasts to keep from throwing the creamer at his head. "If I agree to marry Lord Brougham, then you will agree to begin the search for a wife immediately."

Her brother paled as she waited for his response. If he wanted to use emotional blackmail, then she would do the same. It was all she could do to control her rage over his interference and the utter loss of control of her life, again.

He swallowed once. Twice. "I... I—"

"You'll need to do better than that. Otherwise, I shall be off about my business." Emily gave him the steely-eyed look of determination she had perfected as a child when Arthur had turned mulish about doing something.

He huffed out a gust of air and jammed his fingers through his slightly shaggy hair. "Fine. I shall commence looking for a wife if you agree to wed Lord Brougham."

She took a deep breath. Dear God, what had she done? There was no escape from this.

"Very well. You may tell Lord Brougham that I agree to wed."

And with that, she strode from the breakfast room before the pit in her stomach bloomed into full nausea.

Two mornings later, Emily was doing her best to remain calm as she considered what she had agreed to do. Somehow, sneaking around the homes of the *ton* to steal jewels during a crowded ball seemed less risky, less fraught with danger, than marriage to Cooper. She knew her temper was to blame for this mess. If she could have been more like the ideal Victorian woman, biddable and subservient, perhaps she would not be in this tangle. Of course, then she and her brother would likely have been living in some hovel in Cheapside or worse—on the streets—but at least she would not be facing a lifetime in a gilded cage.

Regardless, she was now faced with not only the prospect of marriage, but marriage to a man who, while desirable physically, clearly did not understand her in the least. With a sigh, she finished her morning toilet and went downstairs to try to eat breakfast.

When she entered the morning room, instead of her brother—who, strangely, had been up and about early in recent days—she was rather surprised to find her fiancé partaking of the morning repast. She supposed his appearance should have been expected at some point. After all, nearly three days had passed since she had agreed to marry the lout.

He looked up and offered a congenial smile. "Good morning. Do come in."

Feathers ruffled instantly by his proprietary behavior—as though this were *his* home and not her brother's—she halted and stared. "Cooper. You are certainly visiting betimes."

"Is it ever too early to visit one's betrothed?" He studiously slathered half a pint of preserves on a slice of toast.

Emily realized with a start that she had never taken a meal with him. For all she knew, he could have the manners of a hog at the trough. His plate was laden with food, so clearly there was no chance he would be leaving anytime soon. Of course, she would be partaking in many more meals with him in the future. What was one more?

"Don't be obtuse. You are well aware this visit is exceptionally early. However, I suppose we are engaged, so I'll cease my quibbling."

She crossed the room and took up a plate to fill with her own breakfast choices. Thankfully, he managed to keep quiet as she made her selections and sat down to eat. She was nearly halfway through a pleasantly quiet breakfast when he pushed his empty plate away and sat back.

"In light of things, I think we should be married tomorrow morning."

She nearly spat her coffee across the table as his words shattered her false sense of serenity. "We have not even posted the banns."

"No need. I obtained a special license. We could be wed as soon as today if we like." He lifted one shoulder in a half shrug and then sipped his tea.

"I see." Though she really didn't. When she had agreed to marry him, she'd assumed she'd have time to adjust to the notion—weeks, possibly even months to prepare. Clearly that was not to be the case. "I haven't had time to buy a trousseau, or even a dress."

"Do you not have something suitable in your closet?" He seemed truly flummoxed by her statement.

"You're quite right. I shall make do with what I have. After all, this is no love match."

She took another sip of her coffee and tamped down her unruly and unwelcome disappointment. It may not be a union born of love, but if she was to be forced into marriage, she had at least thought she would get to enjoy some of the usual customs.

Cooper sat still for a few moments, shifted in his chair, and then released a long, slow breath. "Is marriage to me such an awful prospect?"

She didn't bother to resist the urge to snort. "Marriage, as I said a few days ago, is a gilded cage. With the utterance of a few words and the stroke of a pen, I become chattel. Barely more important than the chair you currently occupy, in the eyes of the law."

"But have I ever treated you in such a way in the entire time of our acquaintance, or during our more intimate relationship?" There was a distinct strain in his voice, something that indicated that this was important to him.

She considered their history. "Other than occasionally being prone to hauling me about like a sack of grain, no. You have generally been respectful, if a bit high-handed. But that does not change the facts in the eyes of the law."

"So you'll punish me for our country's legal failings?" His voice was a bit hard, edging toward bitter.

"Men just like you—all privileged—fill parliament. They decide things like women not being able to own property or vote. Perhaps you are not solely to blame, but your kind are. Who else should I hold responsible?"

He growled a little and rose, tossing his napkin beside his plate.

She bit her lip, almost regretting being honest with him. "If it helps at all, it's not just you. I'd feel the same about marriage to any man."

"It does not help in the slightest." He strode toward the door but stopped without looking back at her. "We shall wed in four days. See a seamstress about a dress and send the bill to my address. Whatever it costs, just have the damned thing by then so we can marry."

And then he stormed from the house, the front door slamming shut with a resounding thud heard throughout the house.

Emily flinched but refused to cry. Whatever small connection she'd had with Cooper seemed to have been severed. And, if she were honest, it was mostly of her doing.

The question was, what—if anything—was she going to do about it?

Emily walked into Madame Le Fleur's with Aunt Hortense in tow and smiled at the shop girl who was straightening the design portfolios and dusting.

She immediately stopped and curtsied. "Good morning, my lady."

"Good morning. Is Madame Le Fleur in today?" She ignored the slow roll her stomach took. The proprietor of the shop was one of the most exclusive—and expensive—modistes in London.

"I shall see if she is available." The girl scurried into the back of the shop.

A few moments later, the ostentatious shop owner and another more circumspect woman greeted her. "I am Madame Le Fleur." The woman with yellow-blonde hair and bright green eyes smiled as she spoke in a heavy and very fake French accent. Then she indicated the woman by her side. "And this is my assistant, Mrs. Keeling."

"A pleasure. I am Lady Emmaline Winterburn, and this is my Aunt Hortense. My brother is Lord Dunmere." She nodded regally.

"How may we assist you, my lady?" The modiste wasted no time.

Emily's lips tilted up on the right side in a wry half smile. "It seems I am to be married—in four days."

The modiste gasped as though this was an unusual announcement. Emily was quite certain this was all to bolster the price she—or, more correctly, Cooper—would pay for Madame Le Fleur's services.

"Non! This is impossible!" She pressed one beringed hand to her breast.

Emily resisted the urge to roll her eyes at the woman's dramatics. "I am afraid it is true. My fiancé proves impatient. Regardless, I require a new gown for the occasion. I've been told you are the best, and my future husband can afford just that."

The woman preened for a moment at the compliment and then looked at Emily. She stepped up to her and cupped her breasts, then ran her hands down her waist, spanning the distance across, and then she stepped back and looked up and down one last time. "Did you intend to follow the Queen's example and wear white?"

"That is unnecessary." And likely inappropriate, if she were asked. "Something in a pale blue or green would be just as good as white."

The modiste leaned over to Mrs. Keeling, and the two whispered furiously for a moment, completely ignoring Emily and her aunt. After a few exchanged comments, Madam Le Fleur looked back at Emily. "I may have a few dresses that you could select from. But I shall have to inconvenience another customer, so it will not come cheaply."

"You may send the bill to the Earl of Brougham. He will be happy to pay whatever the cost is to have me suitably attired in time for our wedding."

Savage satisfaction filled her as she followed the now-eager modiste into her back room. Cooper would learn that while her hand could be forced, her will was not to be trifled with.

Chapter Sixteen

August 1861

Emily stood still as Madame Le Fleur's assistant, Mrs. Keeling, poked and prodded her for the final touches on the gown. Her *wedding* gown. Her hair was coiffed, her cheeks pink with a becoming blush—as she was assured all brides should look—and butterflies danced in her belly. A knock on the door sounded, sending said butterflies into a frenzy. She took a deep breath as Mrs. Peppers cracked the door open and then swung it wide to reveal her brother standing on the other side.

"You look lovely, Em." Arthur beamed at her.

She couldn't help but smile at him, especially when he called her Em. Things had been so tense between them since their parents' death, when their world had begun to crumble. Things had only grown worse of late with his reckless gambling and outrageous debts. But regardless of all the strife, he was still her brother, and with Aunt Hortense, her only family. She blinked back tears, certain they would destroy the effect of her hair and the bit of makeup she had allowed. "Thank you."

He held out a hand to her. "Are you about ready? Everyone is waiting downstairs."

She nodded as the butterflies suddenly clumped together and turned to lead. Downstairs, her gilded cage awaited.

Mrs. Keeling rose from where she'd been kneeling. "I'm finished, my lady. You do look lovely in that gown."

"Thank you, for everything." Emily pressed a kiss to the older woman's cheek. She had been a steadying influence the past few days as she worked diligently on the pale green Alençon lace gown.

The assistant smiled, handed her a small posy, and patted her hand before stepping away.

Emily crossed to where her brother waited, and then took his hand. They started down the hallway and he tucked her hand under his arm. "I know things have been strained lately, but I love you. You're my sister and all the family I have in the world. You know I wouldn't have pushed for you to marry if I didn't believe it was the best thing for you."

She let his words sink in as they descended the stairs. "Yes, I know you believe this is for the best." She just wished she could believe it, too. "And I know you love me, come what may, because I love you, too, and I shall always be there for you."

She squeezed his arm and smiled as she once more held back her tears. She wasn't sure if they were joyous or those of worry and fear. She'd never been much of a crier.

Crossing the foyer of Arthur's house—it was no longer hers as well—they entered the front salon. It was the room with the wide windows that allowed the rare London sunshine to pour in. There, standing in the brilliant glow, was Cooper. His golden locks shone like a halo in the sunlight as he and the parson waited for her. Aunt Hortense hovered nearby, standing as witness for Emily, and Arthur would serve as witness for Cooper. A few of Cooper's friends also sat waiting to see the happy event. She recognized Wolf and Lord and Lady Stonemere, but not the other two men standing with them. Although one of them looked vaguely familiar.

She and Arthur walked into the room and crossed to where her fiancé waited. The clergyman droned through the ceremony as Emily struggled to keep her feet firmly planted where they were. Doubts of all kind swirled through her. Would he be the same man she had met at The Market? Would he change, turning into a typical *ton* husband who ignored his wife and dallied on the side at will?

She glanced at his only friend who was married. Lord and Lady Stonemere looked happy together. Theo leaned in closely to her broad-shouldered husband, smiled up at his dark countenance, and Emily even noticed her slipping her small hand into his. When he squeezed the hand gently and lifted it for a kiss, Emily let a small glimmer of hope into her heart. Perhaps if Cooper's friend behaved in such a manner with his wife, Cooper would not be so different?

The clergyman finally got to the important part of the vows. "Will you, Lady Emmaline Dorcas Winterburn, take this man to be your lawfully wedded husband, until death do you part?"

"I shall." She answered without allowing herself to think further on the matter. What was done was done. Whether she wished for it or not, she had reaped what she'd sown.

"And will you, Lord Robert Bernard Cooper, Earl of Brougham, take this woman as your lawfully wedded wife, until death do you part?"

"I shall." Cooper sounded almost relieved as he answered the pastor.

Emily wondered if he thought she might try to dash before the ceremony was over. Obviously, she had considered it, had even had to fight her body's instinct to flee, but honor dictated she see her commitment through. She had agreed to marry him, if for her own reasons, and so she would do as promised. Had done so, in fact.

"You may kiss the bride." The pastor grinned—a touch more salaciously than Emily would have liked.

Cooper placed a hand on each shoulder and pulled her closer. Then he merely placed his lips against hers and held there for a moment. When he released her, Emily's doubts returned in full force. Was he already through with her? What was the saying about cows and milk? Was he no longer enamored of her? She blinked back tears once more, this time tears of fear that her marriage was over long before it had even started.

She turned with him to face their small party of guests while she fought hard to push a tremulous smile onto her lips. Her husband, on the other hand, grinned like a proud peacock.

After Cooper and Lord Stonemere embraced, which consisted of a manly back-slapping motion, the beaming couple turned to her and offered her their felicitations.

Emily kept her smile pasted on. "It is lovely that you both were able to come on such short notice."

"Welcome to the family!" Theo blasted Emily with a smile and pulled her in with a hug. As the two embraced, she whispered, "If you can wait a few more moments, I shall steal you away for a moment alone so you can recover."

Why she was surprised at Theo's astuteness was a mystery. Her newest friend had proven to be full of wit and wisdom during their short acquaintance. Emily merely nodded as they pulled apart.

"Lady Brougham, please excuse my excitable wife. Her typically high spirits only grow stronger on such happy occasions." Stonemere took Emily's hand and bowed formally over it. "May you find as much happiness with Cooper as I have with my Theo."

"Thank you, my lord," Emily murmured.

Cooper drew her attention and gestured at the rest of his friends. "And you have met Wolf, of course, but this is Lord Lincolnshire and Lord Flintshire."

Each in turn stepped up to greet her and wish her well. As soon as the last man had stepped away Theo followed through on her promise. "Excuse us, gentlemen, the ladies need a moment alone."

Theo towed Emily behind her as she darted into the foyer, leaving a group of stupefied men in their wake.

"The study is across the hall," Emily offered as Theo hesitated, clearly unsure of where to turn.

"Excellent!" Her friend tugged her over to the closed doors. They were tucked away from the men in a jiffy, but by the time the doors were firmly closed, Emily found herself laughing at Theo's antics.

"Much better to see you laughing rather than on the verge of tears!" Theo grinned, obviously pleased.

"Well, you are a force to be reckoned with. How could I fail to laugh with you?" Emily smiled as she sat down to catch her breath.

Theo plopped down next to her in a heap of skirts. "Now, tell me at once why you were so sad today."

Emily bit her lip, afraid to disparage Cooper to the wife of his friend.

"You must be truthful with me. You know I'll not blindly side with Cooper. I haven't yet, have I?"

Emily's head spun. "No, of course not."

"I remember the strain of my wedding day. It was quite strange, what with Stone walking about, looking like he wished nothing more than to beat me before the first day of marriage was done. It was a good thing it turns out I like a good spanking." Theo winked and chuckled.

Emily couldn't help but grin at the other woman's tale.

"Now, tell me what has you so worried on your wedding day." Theo smiled encouragingly.

Emily hesitated a moment longer, but decided she liked this forthright woman. "Well, I suppose you have heard the rumors of how our marriage came to be. I had little choice in the matter. I was ruined by Cooper—and by extension, was required to marry him." She left off the less savory description—marriage or prison.

Impossibly, Theo's grin widened. "Stone told me it was a choice of marriage or prison. I, for one, am glad you chose marriage."

Emily sat nonplussed for a moment, but then the door of the study cracked open and Arthur stuck his head in. "Will you be returning soon? The guests are hungry, and we cannot start breakfast without you."

"Oh! Yes, Arthur. Just one moment more and Lady Stonemere and I shall rejoin everyone." Emily smiled at her brother, and, for the first time that day, it felt genuine.

He closed the door, and she turned to the slightly taller woman. "I think we had best return before the men gobble up all the food without us."

Theo sighed. "Very well, but you must come back for another visit. Marie and my sister have both asked after you since the gossip first made the rounds."

Emily liked her immensely. "You can count on a visit from me. I have not had many friends in Society, and you have absolutely been a breath of fresh air."

The two were still chuckling as they rejoined the wedding party, and suddenly, Emily didn't feel so caged in. In fact, she was beginning to think perhaps life as Cooper's wife wouldn't be all bad.

Cooper paused a moment as his wife and Theo chatted happily during breakfast. In truth, it pleased him that they were getting along so well. The former would be an excellent influence on his little hellion. Theo could help Emily adjust to married life within Society, and perhaps smooth the way for their reconciliation.

The fear of losing her before he'd ever truly had her in his life plagued him. Especially when he knew there were shadows lurking all around them: his past sexual preferences, her secrets. Pitfalls lay in every direction.

Stone leaned toward him from his other side. "Have no fear of Theo saying anything untoward. She is pleased as punch to see you so happy. She would never say anything to ruin that for you."

"I am pleased to see them getting along, but I can't help but worry about that one night becoming a topic of discussion. Emily is aware that something occurred, but not the particulars." Cooper admitted his concern even as he continued to try to dismiss it from his mind.

"The hardest lesson Theo and I had to learn was that keeping secrets from each other only made things harder. Heed my hard-learned lesson and be forthcoming with your new wife. She may just surprise you." Stone returned to his breakfast without further comment.

Cooper was considering the advice given when the clinking of crystal commenced. Obeying the demands of their guests, he turned to his wife. "Is this tradition acceptable?"

Emily nodded. "I'm surprised they did not resort to such games sooner."

He shrugged and then leaned in to kiss his wife. He'd only intended to brush his lips against hers, but she placed her hands on his shoulders and pressed closer until her heat invaded his skin and reminded him of how she felt in his arms. His hands slid to her lower back, and his tongue pushed past her closed lips until he swept into her mouth and tasted the sweetness of the champagne they'd been drinking.

The hoots and hollers of his friends reminded him they were not alone, and he withdrew from their kiss. As he pulled back, he saw the sleepy look of desire in Emily's eyes. He couldn't help the sense of satisfaction that came with the knowledge that though she may be angry with him, she still wanted him physically. And that was something he could work with.

Perhaps all was not lost in their marriage just yet.

Chapter Seventeen

Cooper found himself eager for the wedding night as he changed his clothes and made himself ready for his bride. Stone's suggestion returned to him—haunted him, really. But he couldn't see giving Emily more reason to be angry with him at the moment. She had sufficient ammunition, and a rather sharp tongue as it was. If their wedding day had softened her to him in any capacity, he felt compelled to take advantage of that and see if they could find some common ground.

Even if only between the sheets.

He thought of running his hands up her muscular legs, spreading her thighs, and tasting her sweet pussy. Lapping at her until she squirmed beneath his mouth and begged him to give her release. His cock hardened at the fantasy and pressed against the flap of his trousers. Ignoring the discomfort, he tied off his dressing gown and stuck his feet into his slippers.

He knocked twice on the door separating his chamber from Emily's and then pushed it open. She stood across the room before the fire, wearing a simple white cotton nightgown. No sheer negligee, no corset and stockings, and no bare skin exposed. She was covered from her neck to her toes, as prim as any English virgin on her wedding night.

Her golden-brown hair hung loose, glowing in the firelight like a beacon in the dark chamber. Cooper found the moment more erotic than if she had waited for him stark naked and spread out upon the bed. The stillness hung heavy between them, a weighted silence broken only by the snapping of the fire and the slight hitch of her breathing as she stared at him.

Fearing any movement might break the spell, he remained rooted where he was, watching the play of emotion over her face as desire warred with anger. His hellion remained within the woman, even if she had capitulated to the marriage. With fists balled at her sides, he could see the hellion wanted blood. But if her flushed skin and choppy breaths were any indication, she also wanted to know his touch once more. Was she remembering the feel of his hands on her body and the pleasure he had given her? He certainly was.

Once more, he marveled that he had thought such an expressive, fiery woman would have made a meek, biddable wife. What a self-important, obtuse fool he'd been.

Finally, she huffed out a breath and looked away from him. "Do you plan to stand there all night?" She raised the poker and jabbed at the log uselessly. "I should think that would make consummation of this marriage rather difficult."

Freed from the spell, he walked toward her. "Always the practical one."

"Not practical, just realistic. Or I try to be." She set the hot poker back on the fireplace tool rack.

Cooper sat in the wing chair near where she still stood. "And what does your realism tell you about tonight?"

"There's no avoiding it, and why should I?" She glanced over her shoulder at him. "I'm here because I enjoyed the pleasure we found together. Why should I now cut myself off from it?"

"I see." He paused, considering his next question. "And what of your anger at me?"

She shrugged one shoulder. "What difference does that make? What difference has that ever made in the history of marriage? Men have always taken what they wanted from a woman, regardless of her choices. At least if I let you take my body, I shall still find the physical pleasure of it."

Cooper blinked. Did she think him such a barbarian that he would take her against her will? "Emily, I have never taken anything from you without your consent."

She snorted. "Of course you have. You took my choice when it was all I had left. You ruined me when I would have chosen to stand against the charges."

"That is not what I meant." Anger tinged with enough guilt to take the edge off welled within him, and made his stomach knot up.

She turned to face him. "Yes, well, men typically only see it from their perspective. Have you ever forced me to lie with you? No, of course not. Not even the first time. But this marriage is all your doing. You took my choice from me, you and my meddling brother. So I shall take what little I can from this arrangement, and I shall do it on my terms."

He felt the situation slipping from his control as quickly as every other critical moment with his hellion. "And what are those terms?"

"I expect pleasure. I shall give as good as I receive, but come the dawn, you will be gone from my chamber, not to be seen again until night falls. Outside of this chamber, we shall be civil should we meet, but do not expect my attendance at social events or other such trials."

Her hazel eyes sparkled green as she trembled with her anger.

"And if I do not agree to your terms?"

Could he make love to her at night but remain separate during the day? He had imagined laughing and arguing and chatting with his little hellion once they were married. Not living like virtual strangers.

Her gaze narrowed at him. "If you choose not to agree, then we shall see how chastity suits one such as you, *my lord.*"

He warred with the desire to rise to her challenge, seize her, and tie her to his bed so he could pleasure her until she screamed. Hands gripping the arms of the chair until he worried the wood might crack, he tried to find a way around her ultimatum without proving himself to be exactly what she claimed. At a loss, he forcibly relaxed his grip and took a deep breath. If he still had her in bed at night, he could at least work on winning her heart once more. If he was barred from her entirely, he would be without recourse.

"Very well. Pleasure by night it is." He clenched his teeth and tamped down his frustration. Why did nothing ever go as planned with her?

Emily nodded and strolled over to the bed. By the time she had reached the brocade-draped monstrosity from another era, her gown was gaping at the neckline. In a swift and unexpected motion, she whipped the gown up and over her head, exposing her naked body beneath. "Come along, Cooper. The night is slipping away from you as we speak."

Feeling like a prize stud, he stalked over to the bed and stood over her. She may have won this skirmish, but he was determined to win the war. Because, damn the woman to perdition, he loved her.

She lay on the bed, naked as the day she was born, and tried to hide the tremors snaking through her limbs. Despite all her bravado, her heart galloped in her chest as though it might break free at any moment. Had she truly just been so brazen as to give Cooper an ultimatum? To demand his husbandly services while she remained free to do as she pleased by day?

Of course, she hadn't intended to do any such thing. In fact, she'd been thinking of relenting in her anger and trying to find some common ground. But when he'd come into the room baring a sliver of his chest from the vee of his robe and looking every inch the conqueror come to claim his spoils, she'd lost control of her temper. Again. Somehow, he provoked her more than any other man she had ever met.

Her husband made her mad with desire and fierce with anger, all in the space of a few heartbeats. How was she supposed to stay calm and practical in the face of such emotional swings? How was she supposed to be the wife of someone she wanted so desperately but feared losing, as she had lost everyone else she ever cared about?

First her parents—a monumental betrayal by her father, who killed her mother by his own drunken recklessness—then her brother, betraying her with his gambling. And now Cooper. If she allowed herself to love him, she was certain she would lose him, as well. He would surely lose interest and walk away from her, or worse, stay and merely drift past her on occasion.

No, better she kept her heart safe and her independence in place. If she did not need anyone else, she could not be hurt or disappointed.

His shaft rose long and thick from his groin, seemingly undeterred by their previous conversation. One large hand reached down and wrapped around the base before he stroked the length once, twice.

She couldn't have torn her eyes from his blatantly sexual display had she wanted to. So she didn't. Instead, she watched avidly until he let go and then joined her on the bed.

"Tell me. Is there anything off-limits in our marital bed? Anything I am not permitted to taste or touch?" He lifted his brow in question even as he let his gaze roam over her naked form.

A little shiver of want slithered through her. "Nothing. If it brings us pleasure, it is allowed."

"Excellent." He offered her a feral grin and then crept between her thighs.

The heat of his hands warmed her ankles and then her calves as he slid them higher and higher up her legs until he reached her inner thighs. Then he pressed her legs open, spread her wide until there was no hiding the wetness between her legs that had started the moment he'd walked into the room. He looked his fill, almost as though he was memorizing what she looked like spread out before him.

Then he leaned over and dragged his tongue from her entrance up and over her clit. The bold stroke shot frissons of pleasure through her body, immediately putting her resolve to only seek physical pleasure at odds with the reality of just how good the man made her feel. And now all those physical feelings were tangling with her emotions in the most unwanted fashion.

He licked over her hot center once more, and a low moan escaped her. He chuckled lightly, sending a tingle through her nerves.

He pulled back from her spread thighs. "Don't hold back, sweetheart. I want to hear you call my name." And then his mouth sank down on her, seemed to swallow her whole as she cried out at the intense pleasure he wrought with his tongue and teeth.

As her hips bucked of their own free will, she focused on breathing and feeling. And there was so very much to feel. He lapped at her entrance as though savoring the sweetest nectar. Then he swirled his tongue over her sensitive little nub. As her hips wiggled and begged for more, she sank her fingers into his hair and held his head where she wanted it to ensure the peak she was hurtling toward would be reached.

Then he growled against her swollen flesh and nipped her clit, sending her over the edge of orgasm to plummet into oblivion. She cried out his name over and over as he lapped at her pussy, sending her into one paroxysm after another. Lost to everything but the feel of him between her legs, she floated slowly back to reality as he eased her return with lighter and lighter strokes of his tongue.

Once she was merely shivering with the remnants of pleasure, he crawled up her body and swept his tongue into her mouth. The sweet-tart taste of her own release coated his lips and stirred her desires anew. Ignoring the tug at her heart, she pushed Cooper off and rolled him onto his back as she landed astride his thighs.

He looked up at her, desire in his hooded gaze as he waited to see what she would do next. And truth be told, Emily wasn't sure what she wanted. For a moment, she considered taking him in her mouth and returning the attention he had just bestowed upon her, but then the selfish desire for her own pleasure won out.

Taking his cock in hand, she stroked him just as she had seen him do earlier. He closed his eyes and pumped into her hand once, twice—but then she released him and shimmied up his body so her entrance was poised over his hard shaft. "Tell me, husband." She reached down and swirled the tip of his cock around the wetness of her pussy. "Do you prefer a sedate trot, or are you more of a bruising rider?"

His eyes flew open and dropped to the spot where she was rubbing him over her heated flesh. He licked his lips as though savoring her taste. "I favor a long, hard ride. One that reminds me later why I enjoy it so much."

Emily followed her wicked impulse and formed a small pout with her lips. "Too bad. I like a nice. Slow. Controlled. Gait."

He closed his eyes and groaned as she pushed the tip of his erection inside her. Then she slowly lowered herself, inch by agonizing inch, down his length. Her leg muscles quivered with the leisurely slide of her body down onto his.

Cooper gripped the bedspread in his fists as he fought for the control he needed, but she refused to move faster. Never before had he allowed her to take any real control, so she chose to savor her moment as she sank lower on his shaft.

And when his balls finally pressed against her arse as he swelled and seemed to fill her tighter than ever, she reveled in the power she so obviously held. His labored breathing told her he was struggling to maintain his control, so she milked it for all she could get, because she knew he would soon break and take over.

Rising up only slightly faster than she'd settled down on him, she relished the thickness of him, and the hardness. She could not imagine another man filling her so perfectly, and yet she feared to trust this one with her heart. How could her body be so receptive and her brain so determined to push him away? And why did that leave her heart stuck in the middle?

After a few more slow slides up and down, she finally picked up her pace. With his hands resting on her hips, he watched her intently as she raised herself up and lowered herself down on his cock. The increasing friction both inside and against her clit pushed her to speed up with each stroke. She wanted more, needed more. Her breasts bounced and jiggled in the most obscene fashion as she tried to find a faster pace.

Finally, with a roar, Cooper lifted her off his cock, flipped her over onto her hands and knees, and plunged deep inside her from behind. Emily cried out with the force of his thrust, delighting in her power to push him past his control.

He pressed her head down to the mattress and thrust into her hard and fast. Then he slowed a bit as he leaned over her back. The wet slide of his tongue along her spine sent unexpected shocks of desire sparking through her body. Her pussy clenched his cock tight, causing them both to groan. Then he paused all movement with his hips plastered to her bottom, lodging his erection deep inside her. "Tell me what you want."

Need gripped her hard, and made it difficult to think anymore. "Please."

A soft whimper was all she could manage.

The gravelly sound of his voice refuted her simple plea. "Tell me. Tell me what you want. Say the words."

Frustrated, she tried to pull off him and shove back, but he held her hips in a firm grip. Then he reached down and wrapped one arm around her chest. He pulled her up so his chest pressed against her back while his cock remained inside her. "Tell me, my little hellion." And then he pinched her nipple, making her moan with need.

"Make me come. Please, Cooper. I need to come all over your cock."

And with the last word, he released her, pushing her back toward the mattress as he pounded into her body.

Words far beyond her ability, she made mewling noises as she thrust backward to meet him stroke for stroke. With each thrust, she climbed higher and higher.

"So tight and wet. And all for me." He yelled out and thrust with harder, shorter strokes as he reached down to rub her clit.

When his fingers stroked over her nub, she shattered in an explosive climax. He continued to pump into her as she came around him, yelling his name. "Cooper, yes!"

And then, all she could do was scream.

He continued to piston in and out of her until she faintly heard his own cry of release before he collapsed over her back.

Chapter Eighteen

He'd been married a week, and Cooper realized that he faced two rather substantial problems. First, his wife vacillated between resembling a living flame in the bedroom and a cup of tepid tea the remainder of the time. She had at least ceased the verbal attacks, but she barely acknowledged his existence otherwise. Her sulky demeanor stirred every one of his more dominant instincts to life. But that was his second issue. He had married believing he could control his sexual preferences, but now reality was setting in.

Fear pulsed thickly through his veins as he considered what to do about his wife. What if she was appalled by the notion of his dominance? Emily was so clearly an independent woman, one who supported much of Wollstonecraft's ideas, and who had so articulately expressed her dissatisfaction with the yoke of marriage, and the obviously dominant role that men held in general. How could someone who so fully believed in such notions accept his sexual need to dominate? His desire to spank her and tie her to his bed? And what peer did such things to his wife?

His logical side raised Stone as a prime example of a peer who shared his preferences. But beyond him, Cooper was unaware of any other couples who behaved in such a fashion. Unsure of what to do, and how to mitigate both his concerns, he had turned up on Stone's doorstep in the early afternoon.

His friend had looked surprised by Cooper's admission. "We have shared the same proclivities since our school days. How did you plan to deal with this once you married?"

"At some point, I anticipated a typical *ton* marriage, where my...uh...fidelity would not be an issue, allowing me to indulge my sexual needs away from the marriage bed." Cooper shifted uncomfortably in his chair. "But when I realized I wanted to marry Emily, I determined to remain respectful of her position as my wife. I had hoped more ordinary intimacy would suffice."

Stone sighed. "As I told you on your wedding day, you must not keep secrets from your wife. It will lead to no good. However, I do not think Lady Emily would take well to an unexpected immersion into your sexual desires. You will need to expose her to your needs slowly. Explore your desires together at a pace both of you can manage."

Cooper understood, but then he had to find a way to get past her demeanor. "But how can I broach such a delicate topic when she barely speaks to me outside of the bedchamber? As soon as I touch her, she sizzles with desire and need. But anywhere else, she becomes aloof and so reserved, I find it nearly impossible to speak with her."

Stone sat quietly for long, painful moments. "Start with the intimacy. The rest should work itself out as you build trust. And whatever you do, no more secrets."

Cooper was eager to begin his wife's introduction to sex as he enjoyed it. And while he adored being inside her, feeling her wrapped around him, the experience always felt as though something were missing. There was no mystery as to what the missing element was, and now he would be bringing it back into his world. Excitement surged below the hum of anticipation as he waited for Emily's maid to leave.

He finally heard the door close in the room next to his. A niggling of doubt slipped through all his musings, and for the first time since talking to Stone that afternoon, he wavered. Would his wife balk at what he had planned?

Images flashed though his mind of her in various states of passion. She often responded to his demands, happily complied with his wishes, and melted under his firm touch. Tonight would be no different, simply more.

With that reminder fresh in his mind, and his shaft already growing hard behind the flap of his trousers and hidden under his robe, he opened the door between their chambers, where Emily stood near the fire, brushing out her hair.

"Cooper. I wasn't expecting you so soon." She continued stroking the bristles over the long, gleaming strands of her golden-brown mane.

"I saw no reason to sit alone in my chamber." He walked over and sat in one of the chairs near the fire.

She bit her lip but turned back toward the fire, then added a few more strokes to her regimen. He watched her strong arms complete each long pull through her locks with a firm, steady hand. Then she set the brush aside and turned to face him. "Shall we retire to the bed?"

"Not quite yet." He took a deep breath and prepared to move forward with his plan. He held out his hand. "Would you join me here?"

She did not move a muscle. "There? On the chair?"

He patted his knee with his other hand. "I wish to speak with you, and I enjoy having you close to me."

She eyed him warily. "Why?"

He sighed. "We are married. I cannot undo what I did that night, and I am not sure that I would, since it meant protecting you."

"I could easily have managed the situation. I had no jewelry on me that was not my own, and no magistrate would have taken the word of a known criminal over that of a lady." She crossed her arms, stubborn as ever.

"Be that as it may, I miss my lady hellion—in and out of the bedroom." He hoped his plea might work. If not, he was toying with the notion of spanking her and teaching her that her refusal to engage in their marriage was unacceptable.

"Perhaps you should have thought of that before you ruined her?" She let one brow rise arrogantly.

Cooper squashed the growl that threatened to rumble from his chest. "Perhaps, but what's done is done. Will you punish me forever?"

Emily released a long, slow breath. "I do not wish to. But I do not know how to let go of this anger. How to forgive you and move on."

"Perhaps I can help you with that?" He edged forward in his chair. "Come here, wife."

This time, she moved toward him, one slow step at a time, until she stood within arm's reach. "What are you plotting, husband?"

He reached out and planted one big hand on the curve of her hip, drawing her between his legs. "Merely attempting to stay one step ahead of my hellion." He offered her a grin.

As she stood before him, her cotton nightgown draping over her curves and the fire kissing them with heat and light, Cooper bent his head until his forehead rested against her stomach. He wrapped his arms about her hips, placing his hands on the upper swells of her bottom. "I know I have hurt you beyond measure with my actions. And while I abhor the notion of having done so, please know I did so out of a desire to protect you. To care for you."

A small gasp escaped her as she laid her hands on the top of his head.

"As your husband, I will always see to your welfare—even at the detriment of my own. And I hope that we may find equal footing in this marriage as partners and lovers." He placed a kiss on her cotton-covered stomach and then tilted his head back up to look at her. "Can you find it in your tender heart to forgive me?"

She looked down at him, her eyes welling with unshed tears. "I believe I can."

He reached up and bent her over until their lips met in a tender kiss. Upon separating, he leaned back in his chair. "Now, my sweet hellion. Take off that nightgown."

She stood there a moment and blinked at him.

"Come now, you enjoy how I touch you. How I make you feel in our bed. Why the hesitation?" Curiosity pushed him as his desire for her grew with the tenseness of the moment.

"I cannot explain it." Her cheeks colored in the low firelight.

He inclined his head. "Very well, then. I shall make it an order. Do as I say, or there will be repercussions."

"What kind of repercussions?" she asked softly.

Cooper couldn't hide his smile. "Do as I ask, or I shall paddle your bottom until it is warm and pink."

She inhaled sharply, but then eyed him once more. "You would enjoy spanking me?"

He nodded. "Very much so, though only if you also enjoyed it."

"I see." Emily stood there unmoving.

He watched her, nervously waiting to see what she would do...or not do. This could be the moment that determined his future. Would he continue in marital purgatory, never to indulge his desire to own the woman in his bed mind, body, and soul? Or would his wife follow him into the sexual heaven he believed they could discover together?

A gleam of defiance lit her hazel eyes, making the green seem to grow more intense. "I suppose we shall find out soon if I enjoy it or not."

Confused for a moment, he hesitated, but then demanded again, "The nightgown, Emily."

"I think not, husband." Her little chin tilted up slightly, as though she had firmed her resolve to head down this path.

Curious to see if she was truly choosing to explore this with him, he grunted. "Go to the bed and bend over the mattress."

When his wife did as he bid her, his jaw nearly unhinged even as his cock rose to full attention. His apology had been unplanned, a spewing of his sorrow at having hurt her. But it seemed to have been the very salve she needed to allow them to move past her fury. Of course, he knew all was not perfect, but perhaps they could move forward.

He stood, divested himself of his robe, and went to the bed where his wife lay half on the mattress and half off. Bending over, he grabbed the hem of the nightgown and pulled it up until her bare arse was exposed. He reached down and caressed the left globe of her backside with a gentle touch and relished the sharp inhale of surprise that sounded from where she lay.

He placed one hand on her lower back. "My lady hellion, if we are to get on, you will need to learn to do as I say—"

She jerked up as if to stand. "Cooper—"

"—in the bedroom." He left his hand on her lower back, refusing to allow her to move.

Smoothing his hand over the other side of her bottom, he pulled back and landed the first swat. Careful not to smack her too hard, he repeated the motion on her left cheek. Then he kept going, letting each successive slap land a bit heavier until he heard her breath hitch. He paused and gently rubbed over her warming backside.

Emily moaned and pushed against his touch.

His cock ached as he let his fingers stroke lower until he found the lips of her pussy. Stroking over them, he marveled at how wet his wife had become while he'd spanked her. Drawing his hand back and ignoring another groan from her, he smacked her bottom two more times. This time, he allowed his hand to land heavily, causing her skin to glow pink in the dimness of the room.

Overwhelmed with the need to reward his hellion with all the pleasure he could give her, but equally desperate to push deep inside her, he nudged her thighs a bit wider and spread her soaked center open. After dropping his trousers and freeing his cock, he followed that desperate need and drove into her before he pulled back out. He shoved his length in again before withdrawing and allowing the delicious friction to push him to the edge. Already so close, he reached around and used his thumb to caress her little nub, which had grown swollen and distended.

Emily whimpered and pushed back into his next stroke. "Oh, God."

Yes. She was close. So close to giving him all that he wanted. "Come for me, Emily. Come for me and scream my name," he demanded, even as he drove his shaft inside her, coaxing her to explode.

And then she did as he asked. With another swipe of her clit and push of his cock, she moaned loudly. Her body convulsed with spasms, gripping his length as her orgasm slammed into her. "Cooper! Yes!"

Satisfaction pulsed through him as she ground against him, shaking with the ferocity of her release. He continued stroking into her body, shuttling in and out in a steady rhythm that quickly launched him into his own shuddering climax. With his balls drawing tight and his toes curling, he rode the wave of intense pleasure even as Emily's pussy continued to grip and release him.

Both breathing heavily, with her slumped beneath him, he withdrew and then kissed her backside. Pushing her nightgown farther up her back, he followed behind with nibbling kisses.

After pressing one last kiss between her shoulder blades, he helped her pull the bundle of material over her head. Then he helped her crawl fully onto the bed, where he tucked in beside her, letting his body snuggle next to hers.

As she returned to the present, he leaned over and kissed her fully. Their tongues twined as he savored this unguarded moment between them. He drew away from her after a few heartbeats. "Are you well, wife?"

"Yes." She sighed her response more than spoke it, but he understood.

He reached up and traced the outer edge of her areola with a fingertip, watching as her nipple tightened in reaction to the further stimulation. "There is more pleasure to come. Are you prepared for that?"

She shivered, yet looked up at him with eyes that glowed. "Please. Make me feel good."

And he did until the wee hours of the morning crept in and threatened to pull back the cover of darkness. Satisfaction that he had said what needed to be said with his body, if not words, settled in his chest. That spark of hope had him looking forward to how their marriage might shift, not to mention relishing the upcoming opportunities to show his wife the many ways one could derive pleasure.

Chapter Nineteen

Emily awoke early, after a rather unexpected night spent in her husband's arms, to discover that she was still not alone in her bed. Why was he still there? With her emotions in chaos, she was unsure of everything: herself, her husband, what they had shared, and how to look him in the eye after letting him do...what he had done to her.

Desperate to avoid the awkwardness, she had fled the house without even having had breakfast. After she'd told the driver to simply go, she had sat in the carriage and tried to push aside the images and sensations from the previous night.

As she struggled to find something other than her husband's hand on her arse to focus on, it dawned on her that she had been so wrapped up in her new marriage that she had utterly forgotten about her brother's predicament. Worse, there had been few opportunities for her to acquire the jewels she needed to raise funds, and she was due to make another payment to Mr. Lucifer.

She tried to imagine what the gambling hell owner might say when she explained her lack of funds, and suddenly, it was quite easy to imagine a man like him turning a woman over his knee, much as her husband had done to her.

A shiver chased down her spine as she remembered the delicious heat in her bottom and the wondrous sensations of Cooper's mouth on her core. But as she considered such things, doubts crept in once more. What kind of independent, modern woman allowed a man to do such things to her? To order her about? To *spank* her?

It occurred to her that Theo might be able to offer some advice—after all, she had admitted to being spanked by her husband, as well. And she certainly knew Cooper better than Emily. With that in mind, she headed to Curzon Street.

A short while later, Emily stood on the Stonemere's doorstep, grateful to see the knocker on the door. A man dressed in impeccable black livery with brown hair graying strongly at the temples opened the door. "Good morning, my lady."

Emily presented her card and waited as the distinguished servant disappeared. A moment later, the door opened again, and he ushered her into the house and into the front salon. There, Theo sat with two familiar women. "Emily! I am so glad you have come to visit!"

Theo hugged her as though they were fast friends already.

Emily smiled, a little disappointed that they were in company. She couldn't possibly share her marital issues with all of them. "I hope I am not intruding."

Theo ushered her to a seat next to her, looking utterly delighted. "Of course not! You'll remember my sister, Lady Carlisle, and our dear friend, Lady Heartfield. Lizzy was regaling us with her latest marital trials." Theo grinned. "Her poor husband can't seem to keep his hands to himself."

The three ladies laughed. Emily tried to join them, but she felt anything but merry.

Lizzy went on to finish her story. "Carlisle chased me down the hall after my outburst, dragged me back to our chamber, and paddled my bottom until we were both terribly excited."

Theo gave a little sigh of happiness and smiled. Lady Heartfield merely nodded sagely and offered a pleasantly approving look, rather like a proud parent.

Emily struggled for a moment to take in the fact that Lady Carlisle also received *and* enjoyed spankings by her husband. Perhaps she could share her concerns with these ladies after all?

"Yes, well, once Stone and I were settled and he calmed down about my being pregnant that first time, things became much more harmonious. For a short while after I told him about the first baby, I was certain I would have to resort to violence to get him to listen." Theo wrinkled her nose. "But, Marie, your advice, as usual, proved invaluable. Once I showed him we wouldn't hurt the baby with sex, he was much less grumpy. And, of course, this time around, it has not been an issue at all."

Marie nodded. "Men can be rather silly creatures at times, particularly when it comes to the women they love. I still manage to surprise Heart in the bedroom every now and then. The poor man, you'd think knowing I was once the owner of The Market, he'd be less shocked."

Theo turned to Emily. "And how is married life treating you?"

All the blood drained from her face as she imagined trying to explain the muddle she'd already made of her marriage. "Fine." She managed to choke the single word past her constricting throat.

Her new friend frowned. "Fine? No. No, no, no, no. No. What has Cooper done? I just knew he'd make a big a mess of things, not unlike Stone did when we were first married."

Emily immediately wished a giant hole would open beneath her and swallow her whole. Theo had a very determined glint in her sapphire-blue eyes, and Emily was clever enough to fear what that might mean. "Oh no! Cooper hasn't done anything..."

Hadn't he, though? Or had she been too quick to call protectiveness betrayal?

"You must spill it all now. I promise you are amongst friends, and frankly, if our sage Marie cannot solve the problem, well then, it must be impossible to do so."

Theo sounded so confident, certain that Marie could help.

Perhaps the older woman could give her some useful advice. She had to learn to trust people. Could she start with these women? Take the first step toward allowing people into her life? Determined to try, she forged ahead. She looked at the three women and then leaped. "I have a very difficult time trusting people."

There, she'd said it. Aloud, even.

Everyone remained silent and waited for her to go on.

Emily's face heated. "I was rather angry with Cooper on our wedding night after the embarrassing nature of our engagement and subsequent wedding. I told him I refused to give up the pleasure he provided in the bedroom despite being furious with him."

Theo fell back on the settee and laughed hysterically. Emily wasn't sure what she found so funny, but she waited patiently for her friend to recover.

Theo finally sat up and wiped the tears from her eyes. "I must apologize, but I find the fact that Cooper—who forever used women purely as a source of pleasure—has found himself being used in such a manner just deserts, I must say!"

Emily bit her lower lip worriedly. "The problem is, I was still furious—until last night. And now, frankly, I don't know what to do." Tears threatened as her hurt and confusion swelled from within.

Theo and Lizzy both leaned in and wrapped their arms around her to offer comfort.

"We've all been there." Lizzy squeezed her tighter and then let go.

"Indeed. Not a one of us has found love without some trials attached." Theo sat back as well. "But what else is wrong? I feel like there is more you are not sharing."

Emily hesitated a moment more, but then decided to confide in them. After all, she needed some guidance. "Last night, after a heartfelt apology for how our association was exposed, my husband revealed some tendencies in the bedroom that seem rather similar to your husbands', and I am afraid I am at a loss as to what to do."

Looking around the room for censure or judgment, she instead met three shining pairs of eyes that all seemed alight with interest.

"I cannot say I am surprised, since my husband and Cooper are such close friends." Theo declared. "Go on."

Emily offered a small smile. "Last night, he...spanked me. And I am feeling terribly confused by it."

All three women grinned, but it was Marie who asked the important question. "What is it that confuses you?"

"I enjoyed it, but I am certain I should be outraged over such a thing. That as an independent woman, I should be furious and demanding a divorce or that he never touch me again."

Emily couldn't deny feeling a bit sentimental for the not-so-long-ago time when her relationship with Cooper was much simpler.

The ladies all smiled encouragingly. Marie nodded. "It can be difficult to accept something so new and unfamiliar. Such intimacy between a man and a woman is unique and quite special. It takes a very strong man or woman to allow themselves to be made so vulnerable, to put themselves into the care of another. Did Lord Brougham do anything you did not enjoy?"

Emily dug deep and considered Marie's question. "No. Everything he did was pleasurable. Deeply, intensely pleasurable. For a short while, I might even have allowed him to do whatever he liked to my body without question. That is a bit unnerving to realize."

Theo nodded and smiled, offering encouragement. "Understandable. I remember when I first allowed Stone to take control in the bedroom, I was petrified. But I have found that with each encounter, we have grown closer. Our understanding of each other increases, which offers us greater intimacy in all aspects of our marriage. I know I can turn to him, and without question, he will be there."

Emily sighed again. If only she could share such intimacy with Cooper. It might make marriage not only bearable, but pleasurable.

She needed ideas, not merely hugs and platitudes. "What do I do?"

"I'd say you've taken the first step." Marie smiled kindly from across the tea service. "You have trusted us with your problems."

A small kernel of hope bloomed deep inside Emily's heart. Marie was right. It *was* the first step, and if she were honest, it felt good to share her burden with the others.

"Now, it sounds as though sex is not the issue here, but that doesn't mean it can't help mend your fences. If you are most comfortable with him in an intimate moment, then you must use that to begin to build trust between you two. What you do in the bedroom with your husband is nobody's concern but your own. If you enjoy the things you do together, then you should relish the joy of finding someone to share those activities with. It is a rare thing in our oh-so-civilized society for two people to find such common ground."

Theo and Lizzy both nodded in agreement.

"And if I do not wish to do something he requests—or demands?" Emily was quite sure she knew the answer, but desired the reassurance all the same.

Theo's gaze turned resolute. "Then you tell him no. You state that you are not comfortable with whatever it might be, and you do not relent. A special word might be of use. Something you would not normally say in the course of such amorous activities."

Emily thought perhaps a weight had been lifted by sharing her burden with her friends, and there was no question in her mind now. They were, in fact, friends. Yet, she still could not share her deepest, darkest secret. The one only Cooper knew. Why was it that his knowledge of that secret did not bother her in the least?

Chapter Twenty

Earlier that morning, Cooper had requested they stay home for dinner. Despite her misgivings, she had agreed. Now they sat, *just the two of them,* in the small parlor at the rear of the house.

He held the newspaper up, appearing to read some article or another. She sat with a book open on her lap. Considering she had not turned a page in nearly a quarter of an hour, she wondered what her husband thought. Certainly he knew she was no dimwit. But the problem was, with all the guidance she had received from Theo, Marie, and Lizzy, her head was spinning, trying to decide what to do, if anything.

"Book not to your liking, wife?" Cooper had lowered his paper to his lap.

Surprised she had not heard the rustling, she looked up. "Oh…no, I suppose not."

She closed the book and set it aside.

He folded his paper back up. "Well, I can't say that today's news is all that interesting. Tell me, what did you do today after distributing the new livery to the servants?"

One brow rose as a spark of humor lit his deep brown eyes.

"About that…" Emily gathered her wits and took a slow breath to calm her racing heart. "I'm afraid I ordered the new livery right after the wedding while I was still…"

"I am not concerned over the livery. While an expense, it is not one I cannot afford." He set the paper aside. "I am more interested in what you did with the rest of your day. You were gone for quite a while, and it makes me curious about what adventures you managed to find."

"Oh." She blinked at her husband. "Well, I visited with Lady Stonemere and a couple of others of her circle. I'm afraid it was not a terribly exciting adventure. Just tea with the ladies."

Cooper's eyes held more than a few questions, and a touch of concern. "That cannot be all?"

Surely he did not wish details of their conversation? She bit her lip in consternation. She certainly could not tell him that they had discussed the challenges of dealing with such dominant men, how to manage them both in and out of the bedroom, and how to learn to enjoy the specific pleasures they brought to the bedroom.

"Just tea, and hats. We discussed the latest trend in hats from Paris. Some of them are quite outrageous."

"Hats?" He looked confused, possibly even disappointed.

"Perhaps I should go check on supper." She rose to leave, but Cooper reached out and placed a hand on her wrist. Her heart skipped a beat as her skin tingled beneath the warmth of his hand.

"Please wait, I wanted to speak to you..." He released her wrist and motioned toward the seat she'd just risen from. He cleared his throat. "I wanted to discuss last night."

Her entire body flashed from cold to hot and back again as she wavered between arousal and pure embarrassment. "O-of course."

Were his cheeks turning pink? She stood there frozen by the random thoughts that continued to pop into her head, as well as her own uncertainty about all that had happened. She tried to focus on Marie's advice. If she enjoyed what they did together, it was nobody's business.

"Here." He grabbed her wrist again and tugged her toward him. "This might be easier for both of us if you sat in my lap."

Before she could object for all the obvious reasons—what if a maid walked in?—she found herself perched atop his strong thighs.

"I—" He licked his lips as though he might be nervous. "I wanted to be sure that I did not...well. That I didn't scare you last night."

"Scare me?" Confusion sliced through the jumble of her thoughts.

He swung her legs up over the arm of his chair. "Yes, scare you. We didn't precisely discuss things before we started. Typically, the kinds of things we did are agreed to beforehand to ensure everyone wants the same thing. I got rather carried away with things and failed to speak with you before the spanking."

A tremor ran through her frame as his voice grew deeper, huskier. Clearly, he found their activities as stimulating as she did. "And so now you wish to discuss this with me?"

"Well, yes." He looked unsure.

Her breath caught in her chest. "You did not scare me."

"I am glad to hear that. And if we were to possibly explore such things again, would you be opposed?" He still looked nervous.

"I rather enjoyed what we did last night, so no. I would not be opposed." She smiled even as her heartbeat continued to race.

"And if I were to demand a kiss from you now?" he asked, though there was a thread of steel to the question.

Her core grew warmer at his words, her thighs clenching together. "I would do as you wished."

Strong hands reached up to cup her face and draw her down to meet his lips. But instead of mashing their mouths together, he slid his tongue out and traced the seam of hers. "Open to me."

So she did. And he slipped inside to sip from her all too briefly. Her eyes flicked open when he retreated, only to find him studying her. Then he closed his own eyes and claimed her mouth in a fierce kiss that utterly melted her bones and muscles into a puddle of goo. All the while, his tongue tangled with hers as they slipped and twined around each other. One of his hands slipped from her jaw to slide around her back and pull her closer into his hard chest.

Beneath her, his shaft grew hard, creating a noticeable ridge against her bottom despite all her petticoats. Her own hands wrapped around his shoulders so that they were inseparable as he continued to kiss her as though his next breath depended upon it.

But then he drew back, breaking the kiss slowly with licks and nibbles. "We should stop this before it is too late."

Emily found herself summarily scooted off his lap. "Too late?"

"Um, yes. Too late to stop."

She looked down at his apparent problem. "It would seem it already has reached that point, if I may note the obvious."

"While accurate, your observation is not helpful." Cooper's mouth slanted down at one corner.

"My assistance was not requested. But if it were desired, I might be convinced to offer it."

Emily couldn't help but look down at his hardening cock and consider what it might be like to take him in her mouth. She had considered it on their wedding night but had opted for her own gratification, as she was also looking to make a point. The previous night, not unlike their other interludes, his focus had been on her pleasure.

Cooper stood as he inhaled deeply. "Woman, you test my measure."

Feeling curious about what might happen, she turned and walked over to the door of the salon. There she turned the lock before returning to where her husband stood as stiffly as his cock had become. "Perhaps a little testing is good for a man?"

He reached out and snagged the back of her neck. Then he hauled her in for another desire-soaked kiss. Though it was a short-lived kiss, he let her know without any doubt that she had succeeded in rousing his carnal instincts. As he pulled back from her, a wicked glint in his eye was all the warning she received. "On your knees, wife."

With her lower lip caught between her teeth, she did as she was told. Then he unfastened his trousers and revealed his steely shaft. Her heart lurched with her own excitement over the way their night in was unfolding.

"Take it in your mouth, hellion." There was no question the words were a demand; however, his voice was so low and gravelly, she could barely hear him.

As she shifted her weight forward to better accommodate him, her pebbled nipples scraped against the stiffness of her corset, and even with the fine linen, a shiver coursed through her. Taking the root of his length in her hand, she placed the tip of his cock against her lips. Going on instinct and curiosity, she swiped her tongue over the wet tip and discovered he bore a taste that was earthy, yet distinctly salty.

Then she took the tip in her mouth and pushed forward a bit.

Above her, he groaned. "Bloody hell."

Taking that as a good sign, she pulled back and repeated the whole series of movements, only this time, she took more of him. With each successive insertion of his cock in her mouth, she managed more of his length until she had swallowed almost all of him. With a moan and the bucking of his hips, he pumped into her mouth a few times and then drew back again. "Yes, don't stop."

His encouragement got her moving again, and she set a pace that seemed to feel good to him as she worked up and down his length. "God. That's it. Suck my cock."

His dirty words had her pussy melting with need as her lips grew swollen and a bit numb from sliding up and down his erection. Still fully clothed, she could do little for herself, so focused on ensuring he reached his orgasm.

And as she continued to work his cock in and out of her mouth, occasionally swirling over the tip with her tongue, she felt his body shudder.

"Release me before I come." He half groaned the warning.

But she refused to stop before he climaxed. So she continued to suck him until his hips took over, pumping into her mouth. Once. Twice. And then one last time, as he sank as deep as he could, his hot load erupting over her tongue. "I'm coming! Oh, God! Yes!"

The salty musk from before was back in full force, and she swallowed it all as he shook and moaned above her.

Satisfied with her performance, she released him as he drew away from her and collapsed in the nearby chair. "Thank you, wife. That was..." He blinked a few times and wiped his face. "That was quite helpful."

She stood up, smoothing out any wrinkles in her gown. Her own cheeks were warm with exertion and desire as she stood there, unsure what to do next. What did one say to their husband after sucking his cock? "Perhaps I should—"

"Do not be so quick to run, wife." Cooper reached out and snagged her wrist again. "Are you not affected by what you just did?"

Heat suffused her cheeks. "Affected?"

"Yes. Affected. Did sucking my cock make your pussy wet?" He reeled her in closer to where he sat with his trousers still open. "If I reached under your skirts and touched you, would you be hot and wet?"

Her pulse soared as desire turned to thick lava in her veins. Of course she was wet. "Y-yes."

"Good. Let me see." His demand came out in husky tones once more.

"Cooper. Supper will be ready soon. And if you keep this up, you will be back in the same predicament as before."

She strove for an imperious tone, but it all spilled out in a panicked whisper.

Her husband had a determined glint in his eye. "Lift your skirts and show me."

Reaching down with trembling hands, Emily grabbed a fistful of material and drew her skirts up. With her other fist, she reached lower down and drew up more fabric until her thighs and undergarments were exposed.

"Mmmm..." He reached between her thighs and through the slit in her pantalets to find her hot, wet center. "Indeed, you are quite wet." He drew his fingers through her dampness and then brought them to his lips. After licking them clean, he smiled at her. "A fitting appetizer." A huge but very naughty smile appeared on his lips. "And I believe I've worked up quite an appetite."

Need quivered through her while she lowered her skirts and stepped back from her husband. When her thighs rubbed together, she groaned, drawing his notice.

A look she'd never seen before came into his fathomless brown eyes. "Do not think to slip away and relieve yourself, wife. I promise after dinner, I will show you the power of anticipation when I make you scream as you come on my cock."

Chapter Twenty-One

September 1861

By the time she escaped another fitting at Madam Le Fleur's, it was early afternoon. All the while, she had stood in front of the mirror being poked and prodded, her mind had turned over her problem. She had ten days, no way to secure more money to settle Arthur's debt, and she did not have the full thirty-five hundred pounds that was outstanding. Her final foray as a jewel thief had been less than successful. Having scrounged through her own meager jewelry collection as well as a few household items she'd hoped to avoid pawning due to sentimental attachment, she'd managed to scrape together a few hundred pounds.

With the meager wad of bills in her reticule, she settled into the coach and headed toward Lucifer's. After all the ruckus of her being ruined, her rather rushed wedding, and her marital struggles, she had damn near forgotten about the debt her brother owed. Stopping up the street near a little shop, she bid her driver to stay nearby while she got out.

Once more before the door of the notorious gambling hell she knocked. This time, when the big brute who manned the door saw her, he grunted and then opened it to admit her to the foyer. He simply pointed at the chair she had sat in previously and then plodded up the stairs. He was a large man and proved remarkably cumbersome, even for someone his size.

After a few minutes, he returned. "Mr. Lucifer will see you."

She crossed the long gallery above the hall and entered through the double doors of Frank Lucifer's office. And like every other time, she was worried about the outcome. This time, things seemed even more dire than during her other visits.

She strode into his office and found the man sitting behind his oversized desk. "Lady Emmaline, to what do I owe the pleasure of a visit so soon on the heels of your previous one?"

"Mr. Lucifer, I am afraid I have had a turn of bad luck, to put it in terms you might be familiar with." Emily's gut hardened into stone. If the man didn't see fit to give her more time—and he hadn't been willing to in the past—she had no hope of satisfying Arthur's debt. God only knew what he would do to her brother.

He looked genuinely surprised by her sally. "Please, do not tell me you have fallen victim to the same malady as your brother."

The man always seemed to stir her desire to throttle someone, namely him. "Mr. Lucifer, did you fall from your bed and knock your head this morning?"

Bemused, the man rubbed his hair. "Not that I recall, my lady."

"Then why do you insist on saying such ridiculous things? No, I have not taken to gambling. But I have unfortunately seen an end come to my ability to raise the funds required to settle Arthur's debt. I have a mere three hundred pounds in my possession and no hope of expanding that further." She pulled the wad of money from her purse and set it on his desk. "I am afraid I can make no further payments on what is owed you."

The man had the nerve to grin at her. It was as though he enjoyed toying with her. Could it be that he so rarely had ladies of her caliber in his presence? Did she fascinate him? She pushed that silly notion aside. No, he was a dangerous man. He simply liked playing with those he deemed weaker than himself, and she clearly fell into that category.

"Rumor has it that you were recently married." He looked at her in expectation, both his brows rising toward his hairline.

Stunned, Emily hesitated. "I-I..." She fumbled for a moment more. "Why yes, it seems I was. How in the world did you hear such information?"

Lucifer rose from his desk and walked around to where she stood. "Ah, you see, information can be as valuable as money. I trade in both when appropriate."

"Oh." She wasn't sure she understood, and frankly wondered if this wasn't him still toying with her. "Well, I suppose I could find something of interest for you if you'd take information in lieu of money."

He laughed. "My dear, it would need to be more than the latest *on-dit* gathered from the *ton*'s ballrooms. The knowledge of your hasty nuptials was merely something I heard in passing recently. But it did make me think that perhaps you should speak to your new husband about the money."

The rock in her gut plummeted to her toes. There was no way she could explain her brother's failings to her husband. It would shame Arthur, and likely infuriate Cooper. No, that would never work. "I'm afraid that is not possible."

He reached up and traced a fingertip over her shoulder and down her arm. "I did offer another solution."

The silence hung thick and full between them as her body stiffened. She let her lashes lower to hide the anger simmering within at his proposition.

"I'd say it still stands, but something tells me you aren't the kind of woman to cuckold her husband."

She drew in a breath and raised her gaze to meet his, the full measure of her ire on display. "I am most certainly not that kind of woman, and for you to suggest otherwise is insulting. If this were a different era and you were actually a gentleman, I'd call you out for such disparagement of my honor."

The man had the audacity to grin at her. "Lucky for us this is not the right era—I will, of course, overlook the small matter of you being a woman in this supposed scenario—and I am no gentleman. If I were, I would not so easily give in to the urge to rile you up just to see your cheeks grow pink and your eyes flash."

Dear God, did the man find her attractive? She wasn't sure if she was flattered or appalled. Perhaps both, if she were honest.

"Mr. Lucifer, I shall do my best to acquire the remaining debt, but I feel certain I shall come up short based on the given timeline. If I fail, what will happen to my brother?" Fear quickly pushed aside all the other confusing emotions Frank Lucifer seemed to enjoy stirring up.

"I would not be able to let nonpayment pass." He paused, for dramatic effect, she supposed. "But, Lady Emmaline, I urge you to speak with your husband on this matter. You might find him amenable to resolving things with you."

Lucifer's low bass rumbled over her. If she were not so enamored of Cooper—even as she was still furious with him—she realized she could find Frank Lucifer very attractive in a rough sort of way. She took a clear step back, putting space between them. "And as I have told you, that is not possible. I shall find another way. You will hear from me when I have sorted things out."

She turned and strode toward the door of his office. As she neared it, his voice snared her for one last moment.

"Speak to your husband, Lady Brougham. There may be more at stake than mere money."

She never looked back, simply pressed onward, all but fleeing Lucifer and his gambling hell.

Outside, she hailed her driver and made her way home, all the while trying to figure out how to fix the mess she was in. Perhaps Lucifer was right? Maybe Cooper would be more willing to help her than not?

Emily sat in her chamber mulling over her interview with Mr. Lucifer. Why had he been so insistent she speak to her husband? It was puzzling, to say the least.

A sharp knock sounded, and then her door opened to reveal one of the men she had been thinking of. "Cooper, what brings you home in the middle of the day?"

"News of my wife's whereabouts." His brows were drawn low over his brown eyes.

She stood and stepped away from her dressing table. "News of my whereabouts? I'm afraid I don't understand."

"I feel much the same. I fail to understand why my wife was seen entering a notorious gambling hell." It was hard to miss the gentle flare of his nostrils every time he breathed out.

Shock rattled her equilibrium as she tried to absorb the notion that someone had reported on her activities to her husband. But who? "How is it that someone saw me enter this establishment and managed to report that information to you so quickly?"

Cooper flushed. His lips pressed together into a thin line of displeasure. Or was it consternation? "I have had my friends following you for some time now. When I first discovered you were visiting Lucifer's, I grew frantic with worry that you were in some kind of trouble."

Emily's stomach flipped and flopped inside. Only one question came to mind. "How long? How long have you been following me?"

He sighed. "It started around the time I discovered you were stealing at balls. I needed to understand why you were sneaking about like a thief. You refused to confide in me, even after we grew closer. I had hoped that would change over time. That you would come to me and share your troubles. But even now, after it seemed we were finding stable ground, you still refused. Then I assumed that with your near exposure as a thief, your need to visit Lucifer would cease. That you would trust me. Yet, that has not proven the case."

Fury swept through her at his admission of having her followed. "So, because I did not choose to trust you, you took the choice from me? You insufferable, high-handed lout."

He strode over to where she stood and grabbed her shoulders. "You left me no choice! You were so busy hiding the truth that you never once considered me as someone to confide in. How could I protect you if you wouldn't trust me?"

"Why would I trust you? As soon as you learned of my theft, you used the information to get me in your bed. And then later, you used our intimate relationship to force me into marriage. Like every other man in my life, you have manipulated me and used me to suit your own needs."

Her chest ached with her anger. Hurt with the knowledge that her husband was every bit as selfish and manipulative as her father and her brother had been.

"I tried to protect you. I begged you to marry me, to let me take care of you and your concerns. But you were too busy being an independent woman to allow anyone to help you, let alone a man." He heaved a breath and cursed softly. "Well, it's too late. I've bought out all your brother's markers and have spoken with him. As long as he stays on the straight and narrow, his debts will be considered absolved. So, there is no more reason for you to sneak about going to Lucifer's or to steal from our peers."

And on that pronouncement, he turned on his heel and stormed off.

Alone in the shattered silence, Emily hunched over as she realized her mistakes. He was right. She had never trusted him, never given him a chance to help her openly. Instead, she had been so determined to solve her own problems that she had refused to accept help, even when she'd needed it.

And now she'd ruined her marriage over her stubborn independence.

Chapter Twenty-Two

Emily took a shuddering breath as she sat in Theo's parlor and faced the women she had come to trust. Could they help her once more?

"I-I was so angry when I found out he'd had me followed. Full of outrage and confidence that I was right and he was wrong." Her shoulders hunched as she suffered the deflated feeling once more. "But then his words sank in. And as he turned to storm away from me, I knew he had the right of it. I had been stubborn and willful. I never trusted him. I never gave him a chance to help me. To be my partner."

Theo hugged her gently as Marie sat forward. "Well now, I wouldn't heap all the responsibility on your own shoulders. The truth is he should have come to you sooner and showed you the trust he so desperately wanted. However, I agree you have certainly made some mistakes. The question is, do you wish to correct them?"

"Of course." Emily smiled tremulously. "I came to you all because I know I wish to make things right with Cooper, but I do not know where or even how to begin."

Theo released her and leaned back. "The first step is to apologize. I know when I have made a mistake, even a well-intentioned one, I always feel better after I own up to the mistake and ask the offended party for forgiveness."

"Very well, I can certainly apologize if he will listen." Emily pushed the uncertainty away. She would *make* him listen. "What else can I do? I fear he is terribly angry with me. I've hurt him."

"Yes, well, we will have to wage a campaign to win back his trust and his heart." Marie grinned. "And while he may be a particularly stubborn male, he does have one particular weakness."

Confusion rolled through Emily. "He does?"

Marie laughed. "*Of course* he does."

Emily looked at Theo, and then her sister, Lizzy. "I don't understand."

Marie took a sip of her tea and then set the cup and saucer down. "His greatest weakness is his desire for you. He may be angry. He might harden his heart to you, even, but there is no way he can escape his desire for you. And we can use that to get him to listen."

"But how? I am no seductress. He had only just begun to open up about his desires. I know so little of what might win him over."

Doubt swelled within her, taking her on yet another emotional dip, like a ship sailing in rough seas.

"I believe we have a friend who can assist us in navigating your husband's desires. But you must be willing to learn through unconventional means." Marie's soothing tone belied the challenge in her words.

Emily smoothed the ruffles on one of her new dresses. The light green color brought out the green in her hazel eyes and made her feel pretty. It was the boost that she had needed once Cooper had stormed out. "I am willing to do whatever it takes to fix things with Cooper. I—" She glanced around the room and finally admitted the truth to herself. She was in love with her husband. "I love him. I'm afraid I was such a fool that I did not realize the truth until he'd stormed out of my room."

"Well, then, it is time you met Madame de Pompadour. She is the person who will be best able to help you learn how to seduce your husband." Marie nodded with confidence.

Emily sat in Lady Heartfield's drawing room and did her best not to fidget. It was not every day that one took tea with a notorious madame. But then again, as she looked at Marie and Theo, who both appeared to be terribly calm, perhaps it happened more often than she realized.

Then Marie's butler opened the door of the drawing room and announced, "Madame de Pompadour."

Emily couldn't stop the gasp that escaped her as the beautiful woman swept into the room. She wore a claret walking dress that was the first stare of fashion. Her blonde hair was swept up into a pile that had a single elegant curl draped from the cluster down her neck. Her blue eyes sparkled with excitement as she took a seat next to Marie. "I do so enjoy these urgent summonses. What intrigue do you plan to entangle me in this time?"

"Oh, Celeste, the best kind of intrigue. Love." Marie smiled fondly at her friend.

"Do tell. Do tell." Madame de Pompadour smiled, her eagerness plain to see.

Marie nodded at Emily. "First, introductions. Lady Brougham, may I introduce Madame de Pompadour?"

Ignoring her sweaty palms, Emily stuck out her hand. "A pleasure to meet you, Madame."

"Likewise, Lady Brougham." She hesitated for a moment. "Is that the Lord Brougham with whom I am acquainted?"

"I believe you are quite familiar with my husband and his circle of friends." Emily smiled, though she was sure the women could see how it wobbled.

Marie waved at Theo. "And you would, of course, remember Lady Stonemere."

"Indeed. How are things with you and Lord Stonemere?" Madame de Pompadour inquired.

Theo blushed a bit—which rather surprised Emily. "We are getting along quite nicely now. I'd say your previous assistance proved to be invaluable."

"Excellent!" The madame smiled in genuine happiness. "So, then who am I here to assist?"

Still nervous, Emily cleared her throat. "That would be me."

"Oh dear, has Lord Brougham gone and cocked things up?" Both her eyebrows lifted as she pressed a hand to her chest.

"Actually, no. I seem to be the culprit...mostly." Emily let her gaze drop as her cheeks warmed. "I need a lesson in how to capture my husband's desires and keep them engaged long enough to get past his ire."

"Hmmm..." The madame paused as though considering her request as Marie poured her a cup of tea. "I should think he will not be so difficult to thwart. He has always been the most easygoing of the Lustful Lords. I shall assume that any tutoring is to be hands-off?"

The warmth in her cheeks flared into full-blown flames. "I-I..." Emily swallowed. "Y-ye-yes."

"Very well." She took a sip of her tea. "Are you able to slip away from your husband for an evening? I believe the tour we provided Lady Stonemere should help enlighten you to your husband's more demanding desires."

Theo grinned at her. "Men can be devilish tricky to sort out. I should warn you, Stonemere discovered my plans when I went about this tour, and then he took over. You should be aware of the risks."

"I doubt he still has his friends following me after our disagreement. I hope I shall be able to keep this one secret until I am ready to reveal what I have learned."

Emily ignored the worry that took root. Would it ruin everything if he discovered her plans? Possibly.

"We should move quickly this time. You'll come tonight at the stroke of midnight. Wear a mask and come to the back entrance so that you will be less conspicuous." Madame de Pompadour nodded decisively.

"Of course," Emily agreed. "And then you'll show me what I need to know."

"Yes, or rather, one of my girls will act as your escort." Madame de Pompadour set her tea down. "Well, if you will excuse me, I have much to arrange before midnight."

Emily rose quickly. "Thank you for your assistance."

"Do not worry, Lady Brougham. We shall get you two on the right track in no time."

Chapter Twenty-Three

Cooper sat brooding in his study. He'd been so angry with Emily when Flint had sent him word that she was at Lucifer's. What must he do to earn her trust? How could he convince her that he only wanted to help her? He'd done his damnedest to protect her at every turn, but each time, he'd failed.

Frustrated by his inability to earn her trust, he slammed his fist on his desk with a low growl. Perhaps he fought a losing battle? Perhaps she would never trust a man? Never trust *him*. Pain seared through his chest, and he welcomed the hurt. Maybe he could dull some of the ache if he burned the emotion from his soul. After all, life had been much simpler before he'd met Emily. Women were lovely companions for an evening, and then he moved on. Rarely did he dally more than once or twice with the same woman, unless she understood that there would be no romance.

But Emily had ensnared him. Captured his interest with her dichotomy—one part wallflower and one part hellion. In his quest to reconcile the two halves of her person, he'd found himself head over heels in love with her. And now, his heart had seized up as he'd realized she would never love him. Never trust him with the truth—let alone her heart.

His only recourse was to distance himself from her emotionally. She would retain the safety of his name, as well as the cloak of marriage to protect her from her problems and the sharp edge of *ton* tongues. But it seemed as if they were destined to live separate lives under the same roof.

The door to his study opened, and Peters stepped inside, carrying a silver salver. When he presented the flat tray bearing a folded piece of cream paper with his wife's familiar scrawl on the front, Cooper sighed. So, it had come to this, an exchange of notes to communicate. He picked it up and dismissed his servant as he opened the correspondence.

Cooper,

I've gone to the Swinton's ball. I shall be home late.

Emily

Perfunctory. His wife had slipped out to attend a ball and had not bothered to request his attendance. Well, he could also get on about his life. Why should he remain at home sulking? So, the woman he'd married had no interest in his heart. He could press on without her, as well. With a determined stride, he left his study behind and went in search of his valet. He needed to change his clothing if he was going out for the evening.

It was near midnight by the time he found himself meandering into The Market in search of his friends. He climbed the stairs and headed to their usual room. It glowed with an enchanting light, with all the gold fabrics and trims. Linc and Wolf were the only two there, each holding a hand of cards.

"Where is everyone?" he asked as he sat at the card table.

Linc shrugged. "Flint is up to his usual business, and I think he dragged Arthur along to see the fights. That leaves just me and Wolf."

Wolf eyed him with concern. "And why are you here?"

Cooper sighed. "I have no reason to be anywhere else." He glanced at the sideboard and saw that his preferred whisky was missing. "I'll be right back. Deal me into the next hand."

Stepping into the hallway, he went in search of one of the upstairs maids. Finding everyone gone, he took the back stairs to see if he could acquire what he needed.

Just off the kitchen, he found the liquor closet, and happily, it was unlocked. He stepped inside and skimmed over the various labels, looking for the bottle he sought. He had just wrapped his fingers around the neck of the bottle when he heard voices.

"Are you ready?" a husky feminine voice asked.

"Yes," a second female answered. Her voice was familiar, but he couldn't reconcile the face his brain paired with the voice with his location. Clearly, he was more upset than he wanted to admit if he was hearing his wife's voice in the back kitchen of The Market.

"Very well, stay close to me, and please ask any questions you may have."

The husky voice sounded even more familiar.

"Of course. Thank you again for helping me."

The second female spoke, and to Cooper's horror, there was no doubt this time. The voice *definitely* belonged to his wife.

Once more, he had turned his back for a moment, and here she was sneaking off and finding more trouble. He listened as the pair of footsteps went up the stairs together. Abandoning his bottle, he found a cloak and mask near the back door and quickly donned both. Quietly, he slipped upstairs in the wake of his wife. As he neared the first landing, he heard her speaking to the other woman.

"You called this the hall of mirrors?"

The other woman chuckled. "Yes. It is a series of our rooms where the occupants can choose to be seen through the mirrors or not. For many, the notion of being watched is exciting."

Cooper wanted to growl as his fury rose once more.

"And my husband, does he enjoy being watched?"

Another growl strangled in his throat. She was asking about him?

"Oh, he was not so interested in being watched, though he did at times seem to enjoy it. He tended to be more focused on the woman he was with, ensuring she enjoyed her time with him."

Emily made a choked sound. "I see."

"Here now, come sit. This man is receiving extra-special attention tonight. Mistress Lash is here to see to his desires. See how he is strapped to the bench? His arse and bollocks are exposed to her tender mercies."

Emily's voice came out in a whisper. "Miranda, is she going to whip him with that crop?"

"Oh, quite so. And he is going to relish every moment of it. He loves the bite of the crop on his pink bits."

Cooper peeked around the curtain that protected the sitting area near the glass. His wife sat staring in rapt attention as she watched the anonymous man's backside being striped. The crop landed over and over again, and his wife's breath seemed to grow more agitated with each blow.

"Oh my," she breathed when the man on the bench had a dildo shoved into his backside as Mistress Lash stroked his cock until he came.

"Come along, we should move to the next window." Miranda ushered his wife along the corridor as he slipped behind a curtain to hide.

Once they were seated at the next window, Cooper crept near so he could see and hear. What was his wife doing at The Market? It took great willpower to resist charging into the alcove to demand answers. Somehow, he managed. For the moment.

Peeking around the curtain, he caught a glimpse of three people entwined. A woman lay on her back with her legs spread as one man feasted on her pussy. Another man was sliding his cock in and out of the woman's mouth as though he were fucking her.

Emily sat for a few moments, taking in the activity. "I find it difficult to believe my husband would welcome such an interaction where I am concerned. May we move on?"

His heart skipped a beat. Could she truly be there for them? For him?

"Very well." Miranda rose, and they moved to the next alcove with Cooper shadowing them. Emily's guide waved a hand toward the next window. "This may be more to your liking."

In this next display, a woman was strapped to a spanking bench with her knees on either side. A man knelt near her bottom, where he proceeded to lick her quim. As they watched, he pushed two fingers into her pussy, swirling them about before he withdrew and lifted them to her anus. There, he impaled her on his fingers. She cried out, her hips bucking as he continued to lap at her clit. After stretching her a bit more, he pulled out and reached down to produce a dildo with a wide, flared base. He used a salve to lubricate it before pushing it into her channel. Then he used the same salve to prepare his cock. As Emily watched, her gaze fixated on the scene, he pushed deep in the woman's arse until his balls rested against her flesh.

A low moan escaped from Emily as she whipped out her fan and put it to good use. Clearly, she was as affected as he was, with his cock standing at full staff as he imagined doing the same thing to his hellion.

The two women lingered over the scene until the man and woman both found their release. Once they moved on, Cooper took a moment to shift his aching shaft. At this rate, Emily would quite possibly be the death of him. How many more scenes did she need to view?

Miranda shuffled them along to the next window, while Cooper contemplated how much longer he would allow this education of his wife to continue. As it appeared she was there of her own volition, the question was: did the erotic scenes excite her? If her breathing was any indication, he would venture to guess she quite liked some of what she'd witnessed. Perhaps he would remain hidden while she viewed a few more scenes...purely in the interest of gauging her response.

Slipping once more into the main hall and then peeking into the next alcove, he found his wife witnessing a woman playing the role of slave to her master. While he enjoyed being in control, he was not so dominant as to need to make a woman crawl to him, though as he imagined Emily doing so, he could not deny the throb of excitement that pulsed within. Interesting.

As they watched, the man laid the woman down and showed her two small balls. He promptly inserted them into her cunny. Next, he leaned over her and sucked on one of her nipples until it grew more prominent. Then he attached a small clamp to the peak from which dangled a gemstone. He repeated the action on her other breast. Cooper quickly found himself imagining his wife with emeralds dangling from her beaded tips, and he damn near lost control.

His body trembling with need for her, he was about to reveal himself when Miranda leaned over and spoke to Emily.

"Those balls are the most pleasurable torture I have ever experienced. Watch her carefully now as she serves him dinner."

As the woman took a few steps across the room to the side-board where a meal stood ready, she paused. Her whole body stilled, yet she quaked like a leaf in the wind. She resumed her path across the room only to stop as she reached the food. Her knees gave a little and she hung on to the furniture as her whole body flushed.

"What has he done to her?" his wife asked her companion.

"Those balls shift within her channel, rubbing against her walls and causing intense pleasure to the point of orgasm. Each time she stops, she is coming." Miranda had turned slightly to answer Emily, giving Cooper a glimpse of the pleasure that she was remembering. Clearly an experience to be savored.

"And the jewels on her nipples? Does that not hurt?" Emily's forehead scrunched up a bit.

"Only at first. Just as some people enjoy the bite of the crop, others enjoy the pinch provided by the small clamps attached to the jewels. These two are exploring the plea-sure-pain dynamics written about by men such as the Marquis de Sade, though to a much lesser extreme." Miranda hesitated. "Would you like to move on?"

Emily shook her head, seemingly unable to reply as she took in the woman in the room coming so hard that her juices had begun to paint her thighs. Cooper found the scene much more erotic than he would have imagined. and considering his wife's reaction, filed it away for future reference.

As the woman delivered dinner to the table and then promptly knelt to suck the man's cock while he dined, Emily shifted on the bench with another low moan.

After a few murmurs, the ladies rose and moved to the next alcove. Cooper trailed behind them; however, this time, Miranda glanced back and gave him a wink. Damn, she'd seen him. Of course, she would also be aware of who he was since they were well acquainted and the fact that his wife was her companion. He girded his loins for one more display and crept up to peek in. To Cooper's great horror, he was looking into the gold room.

Bloody hell! If he had not gone in search of a drink and then been distracted, he might well have been in that room when his wife approached. Though, as he took a gander and realized his friends were deep into their activities, he also realized he likely would have left once they started having sex. It simply would have felt wrong even to be in the room. With a little sigh of relief, he took another look to assess the action. It appeared that Linc and Wolf each had a woman to occupy them, as did Flint, who had arrived after he had departed.

He looked again and was grateful to realize Emily's brother was nowhere in sight. In the room, Wolf had a redheaded woman strung up on a coat hook by a cravat tied around her wrists. He was busy spanking her reddening arse. Linc was on the bed with a brunette who wore a dildo strapped to her pelvis as she plunged the stone phallus deep in his arse. And then there was Flint, who was occupied with another brunette and a blonde. The darker-haired girl was riding his cock as the fair-headed one sat on his face. Every so often, the brunette would slide off his cock and the blonde would bend over and suck his rod into her mouth.

Emily's breathing grew more labored. And damn it, he couldn't be sure which of the scenes excited her. He knew which was his favorite. Which he'd prefer to reenact with her, but did her desires align with his? There was only one way to discover the truth. He slipped into the alcove with his wife and Miranda. The woman rose and quickly departed the niche where his wife sat so enraptured by the small orgy before her that she did not notice when he joined her.

"If I had my choice of the three options, I'd string you up and spank your bottom."

Chapter Twenty-Four

"Cooper?" Emily's breath leached from her chest as she stared at what appeared to be her husband. Except, just a moment ago, Miranda, one of the ladies of The Market, had been sitting right there.

"Good evening, wife." His dark eyes glittered in the low light of the alcove. "Which of the three vignettes would you choose?"

Oh, no. He was there. *Next* to her. And his friends—she had certainly recognized the three handsome men—were just on the other side of the glass. Having sex. A great deal of sex.

"G-good evening." Was her face on fire? Her cheeks burned as though someone had set them alight with a match.

He leaned into her, so close his breath only added to the conflagration that was spreading over her body. "You have yet to answer my question."

Every thought her brain had contained fled as soon as he spoke. "Your question?"

What was her husband doing at The Market? How had he known she would be there?

"Which would you choose?" He waved his hand toward his friends on the other side of the glass.

Slowly, she turned her head and took in the scene. Things had progressed since she'd last looked at them. Wolf was now plunging his cock in and out of the tied-up woman's pussy. With each thrust, she rose up on her toes. Linc was stroking his shaft as he exploded, shooting across the sheets as the woman continued to shuttle in and out of his arse. And then there was Flint, who occupied two ladies. The man had the blonde woman on her knees as he pumped into her from behind while she buried her face between the brunette's thighs.

And her husband wished to know which was her preference? He was not angry? He was not shocked that she was there? Apparently, he simply wished to know which grouping appealed to her.

"Wolf and the redhead."

Cooper reached up and drew a finger across her collarbone and down over her cleavage. Gooseflesh rippled across her skin in his wake as her breath hitched.

"Would you perhaps like to explain how you came to be here this evening?" His voice rumbled in his chest.

What could she say? She wanted to learn about his sexual preferences? Needed to find a way to learn to trust him? To get him to trust her?

"I...you...sex."

He let a wickedly erotic grin stretch his lips. "Oh, my little hellion. Cat got your tongue?"

Annoyance bubbled to the surface, pushing past desire and shock. "I am here trying to understand what it is you desire in bed."

"I'd be happy to show you what I desire." He rose from where they sat and held out his hand to her. "Come with me."

Determined to seize the opportunity to explore what she had seen earlier with her husband, she stood and took his hand. He led her down the hall and then into a room that was a familiar blue.

Emily's mind and heart raced. "Cooper, what if this is someone's room?"

He offered a lazy smile as he stripped off his coat. "The doors here remain locked unless the occupant unlocks it—an invitation of sorts—or a member of the staff does. I assure you, Miranda made sure to leave the door unlocked for us once I joined you."

"Oh." Emily could not hide her surprise. Though when she considered her husband's patronage of The Market and how quickly Miranda had departed upon his arrival, perhaps she should not be astonished in the least.

Cooper sat on the bench at the foot of the bed. "Come and sit with me, Emily. I believe a chat is in order."

Hands trembling, she clasped them together in front of her as she took a seat beside him. He appeared so calm, though she had noticed the rather prominent bulge in his trousers.

"You saw many things this evening. Perhaps even heard a few that you may have questions about." For the first time, she spotted the concern in his gaze. "I am at your disposal and will answer them as best as I am able."

She blinked. Was her husband finally opening up to her? Trusting her with his secrets? Her heart stuttered. "Do you enjoy tying women up?"

He nodded. "I do. I enjoy having you at my mercy and knowing that your pleasure is mine to give."

"And spanking? You enjoy doing that as well?" She bit her lip as she once more imagined Cooper tying her up and spanking her as Wolf had done to the redhead.

"If my partner enjoys it, then yes. I do not enjoy inflicting pain for pain's sake. But a small amount of pain to heighten the pleasure is erotic indeed." He shifted on the seat beside her.

Emily had so many more questions now, very specific ones. "How long were you with Miranda and me?"

"From the first window. I stumbled upon you downstairs." He tugged at his necktie.

From the beginning. So, he had heard everything she'd said. Heat splotched her cheeks once more as she focused on her hands in her lap. "And if there were things I viewed that I wanted to try, you would be willing to try them with me?"

He reached over and tipped her chin up with the edge of his finger until she had no choice but to look him in the eye. "I catalogued every scene that evoked a soft *'oh my.'* Every moment that caused you to squirm where you sat. Every touch that caused your breath to hitch. And I plan to explore every one with you in time. The question you need to answer is: Do you trust me to see to your pleasure?"

With their gazes locked and her heart slamming into her chest as though it needed to break free, she considered his question. She reached deep within and pulled out that small, delicate part of her soul that cried out and shrank away from so much exposure. A tear slipped from her eye as the truth nearly brought her to her knees. Silence stretched as she struggled within, even as she watched his face blanch.

Then she drew a deep breath, his obvious pain pushing her to speak the truth. "I want very much to trust you. I simply don't know how."

Despite the hurt she saw leech into his gaze, he nodded. "I much prefer your honesty to any false words meant to sooth my ego. If you are to learn to trust me, we must be completely honest with each other. If you do not enjoy something we try, you must tell me, and I you. Do you understand?"

A tendril of fear curled through her, but her desire to learn to trust him was far greater than her concern over emotional damage. "I understand."

A small smile curved his lips slightly. "Good. Emily, I want very much to kiss you right now."

Her own lips trembled with want. "Yes, please," she whispered as she leaned toward him.

He swooped in and captured her lips, and drew his tongue along the seam seeking entrance. When she parted for him, he seized her mouth in an erotic tangling of their tongues. All the sexual tension that had built up as they had moved along the hall of mirrors ignited into a flame of desire that burned so hot, she was certain she'd be scorched.

Then her husband hauled her into his arms and continued to kiss her as though his very life depended on it. And for the moment, her heart seemed to agree.

Slowly, he drew away from her mouth to kiss and nibble her sensitive skin as he edged toward her ear. He sucked on the lobe for a moment, causing tingles to spiral down her spine and her nipples to harden beneath her corset. Arms tangled around his neck, all she could do was hang on as he discovered sensitive spots on her body she'd never known existed.

With his lips making a trail back toward her mouth, his clever fingers unhooked the back of her dress before he tugged and pulled at the laces of her corset.

She pressed a hand to his chest. "Cooper, let me."

And then she stood. Her bodice was loose and slid easily down her arms. Then she reached behind and unfastened her skirt as his dark, mesmerizing eyes drank in her movements. Her skirt sagged while she found the ties of her over petticoat, hoop, and then her under petticoat. With everything loose, she pushed the bulk of the material down her legs. Unsure how to step out of the pile of fabric, her dilemma was solved as Cooper scooped her back into his arms and extracted her from the heap. With her pantalets, corset, and chemise all she had on, she stood before him once he set her down.

"So lovely," he murmured as he removed his waistcoat and wasted no time in hauling his shirt over his head.

His chest was trim, though not overly muscled. And while she had seen her husband naked many times, something about the glint in his eye made her heart race as he stepped forward. With economic movements, he stripped her of her corset and chemise. Pausing to heft each breast in his palms, he stroked her puckered nipples with his thumbs. There was no possible way to hide the trembling of her body as she responded to his touch.

And when he leaned over her to suck one tip into his mouth, she moaned at the sheer bliss of his hot mouth engulfing her flesh. "Cooper," she whispered, and slid her hands around his head and neck as though she might not let him go.

He shifted to her other breast, lavishing it with the same attention. With her knees gone soft as aspic, she clung to him to stay upright. He moved her back toward the bench they had recently occupied as he released her breast and untied her pantalets. Naked, she stood before him, both scared and enthralled with all the possibilities that lay ahead.

"Emily, do you remember the scene where the man was strapped down and whipped?" His rich voice had turned into a low rumbling that stoked the dull throb between her legs.

She nodded, her mouth gone dry.

"Speak to me. I need to hear you so I know you are with me in this."

She licked her lips and tried to find what little moisture remained in her mouth. "Yes, I remember."

"Good. Now, before there is more pleasure, we must address your recklessness," he said as he turned her to face the bench.

"My recklessness?" Confusion muddled by need made it difficult for her to follow his intention.

He grunted. "Indeed. You must be punished for worrying me and for allowing yourself to be placed at risk by visiting The Market without me."

Annoyance flared enough to clear the fuzziness of her thinking as she spun back around. "Now just one moment, husband. This is the very same location you had me come alone to in order to conduct our affair. How was that a safe choice and tonight is not?"

"I was here to meet you every time. You were here under my protection, which meant Madame de Pompadour was ensuring your safety." He growled. "Tonight, you were traipsing through the hall of mirrors with naught but Miranda as escort. Any drunken fool could have stumbled across you and mistook you for an available woman."

"Psh. Foolish man. I was here tonight under Madame's protection...as your wife. I was perhaps safer now than I was as an unwed woman walking these halls." Emily glared at him.

Cooper frowned. "Very well, perhaps not so vulnerable as I had thought. However, you did not discuss your visit with me. In fact, you purposefully hid it from me."

She was stymied, because he was right. She *had* hidden her visit from him with the intention of trying to understand his needs and desires so she could better understand the man. "I did hide my intention to visit this establishment. But I had good reason."

One of his brows rose in question or disbelief, she couldn't decide which.

"And that would be?"

She bit her lip. Then, with a sigh, she turned back around to face the bench. "I've already told you why I was here."

"I beg to differ. You told me what you hoped to learn...but not the reason for wanting to learn it." He pressed his chest to her back and reached an arm around her waist. "Why were you here, Emily?"

Her eyes closed as she tried to find some version of the truth to appease him. But since she did not yet trust him by her own admission, she dared not give him her heart. "My reasons are my own."

A small exhale laced with disappointment drifted over her left shoulder as he released her waist. "Then you will bend over and accept your punishment, my hellion."

Her breath caught in her chest. He had spanked her once before, and she had loved it. The notion that she would love it once again both excited and scared her. Everything about her husband scared her, because she knew he could hurt her so deeply. With each new day, as she discovered the depth of her feelings for him, she realized her worst fear had come to pass. She was madly, deeply, irreversibly in love. And now she was married to him.

"I suppose I shall."

"Bend over," he growled as he placed his palm between her shoulder blades.

Doing as he bid, she bent over until her hands were flat on the bench.

"Lower, on your elbows." He tapped her upper arm.

Again, she followed his guidance and found herself with her bottom high in the air. Then he nudged her feet apart until her pussy was exposed to the cool air.

The warmth of his palm settled on her upper back, and then he stroked down her spine and over her left cheek before moving over to the other side. "You will learn very quickly that I cannot abide lies between us. No more subterfuge. No more sneaking around London. Do you understand, wife?"

"I do," she rasped as her nerves jangled in anticipation of the first blow.

"Very good." He smacked her backside.

Heat bloomed along with a sharp pain that quickly dissipated into a dull throb. The second smack landed on the other side, and a matching heat and pain radiated over her flesh. He continued on with the next four spanks. The same as before, the pain fuzzed into pleasure, and all she could register was the heightened sensation that made her quim heat and her channel ache with the need to be filled.

As his palm repeatedly made contact with her backside, she edged deeper and deeper into needy desire. When he landed the final spank against her exposed pussy, she gasped as her body trembled on the verge of orgasm.

"Good God, you are soaked with need." Her husband stroked her drenched pussy and slid a single finger deep inside her.

Her legs shook as she leaned heavily on her arms to keep from collapsing into a puddle of lust. When Cooper rubbed his hand over her heated buttocks and licked her slit, she lost all control. As he lapped at her from behind, she came hard. The room splintered into a thousand pieces, and her body melted into the cracks as bliss swept through her. His hands on her thighs braced her as her knees gave out and she all but collapsed into him. He held her up and continued to lick her until she was floating back to where they were.

Unsure of when he'd moved, she found herself lifted and deposited on the bed. Redolent with the aftermath of orgasm and a fresh wave of desire, she lay there and watched as her husband finished disrobing. She took in the sight of his strong thighs, well-formed calves, and the hard length of his cock as it jutted from his nest of dark curls. And she wondered what he would do to her next.

Chapter Twenty-Five

Cooper stroked his cock as he loomed over his dazed wife. The entire evening had been a shock, but it seemed it was a good one. One that had loosed his inner self, allowing his darker desires to roam free. Turning from the bed, he went to the cabinet on the far wall and opened it. Inside, he found all that he could possibly need for the next part of his wife's introduction to his preferences.

He pulled out a set of leather cuffs and brought them over to the bed. "We'll start slow and explore more next time. For now, I want to restrain you. Tie you to my bed and fuck you until you scream my name in pure ecstasy."

She moaned as she looked up at him. "Please, Cooper. I need you inside me."

Her words nearly broke him in the moment. He wanted to toss the cuffs aside, spread her thighs, and pound into her until he came. But what he wanted even more was to give her an experience similar to what she'd seen earlier. To let her taste what it would mean to be with him like this. To truly be his. "You'll have what you need, when I'm ready to give it."

She whimpered.

Ignoring her obvious need, he wrapped the first cuff around her wrist. Next, he wrapped the second cuff, and then he joined them and linked them to a loop on the bed's headboard. As though the restriction of her movement woke her from her post-climax haze, Emily's eyes widened as she tugged against the restraints. "Cooper?"

The question in her voice excited him, made him want to drive into her. But instead, he brought her face around to meet his, their gazes locked. "Emily, this is where the trust truly begins to grow. You are utterly at my mercy. I can choose to pleasure you, or leave you here. Do you know which I have planned?"

Dark worry flashed through her eyes. "Pleasure?"

The doubt in her voice and on her face stabbed him in his heart, but he had known it would be there. She had told him as much. "Today you say that with a question in your voice. With worry in your beautiful hazel eyes. One day, I won't even need to ask the question."

She sighed softly and nodded. "I want that. I want to trust you without question."

He kept her gaze snared by his. "Then, until then, we will continue to work at it, my sweet hellion."

He crawled on the bed and spread her legs before he knelt between them. Balanced on hands and knees, he leaned down and captured one nipple in his hungry mouth. She arched up into him as he sucked hard on her nipple, and then she cried out. "Ahh!"

Releasing the tip, he repeated the rough play on her other nipple. This time, she moaned low and needy as he sucked. The peak hardened and swelled as he pulled on it. Then he let it go and flicked it with his tongue, once, twice, three times.

Need for her heat and the tight clasp of her channel pushed him lower down her body. He eased over her stomach, licking and tasting her heated flesh as he shifted back toward her hot center.

"Please. Fuck me," she begged.

His cock pulsed, desperately wanting to answer her plea. But he refused to give in just yet. He had more to explore with her. Wedging his shoulders between her thighs, he spread her open and tucked a bolster beneath her ass, lifting her quim up to the perfect height for him to feast on. And so he did. He plunged his tongue deep into her channel, and then pulled out to draw it up over her clit. There, he swirled around the sensitive nub until her hips pumped up to meet each pass. Wanting more. He pushed two fingers inside her, working them in and out, and covering them in her juices. When they were good and wet, he pulled out and drew them down to her rear entrance. He rubbed the tight pucker with his fingers and pressed against the furl.

She gasped and thrashed above him, but with his other arm braced over her pelvis, she had little room to maneuver.

"Hold still, sweetheart. Open for me. Let me inside you," he crooned as he reduced down to a single finger and pushed past the tight ring of muscle. Once his digit was lodged in her rear passage, he leaned up and swiped his tongue over her clit.

She jostled and moaned. "Oh, God."

He slid the finger out and pushed back in. And then he added a second one as he continued to lick her pussy. Once she settled into the sensation and seemed to be enjoying it, he released his forearm from her hips and brought his thumb down to work her clit as he tongued her soaking hole.

She bucked and cried out. "Cooper, please! I-I-I need..." And the rest of her plea was lost as she came hard on his tongue, again. This time, he worked her clit with his thumb as he pumped his fingers in and out of her arse. All the while, he fucked her with his tongue, reveling in her sweetness as she exploded for him. Her climax was so intense, his own hips bucked in sympathy, nearly driving him over the edge as he carried her through her peak and brought her carefully back down.

After withdrawing his fingers from the hot clasp of her bottom, he rose up and drove his shaft into her still-spasming pussy until he bottomed out in her hot core. The grip of her residual orgasm paired with the intense heat of her pussy had him dancing on the edge within a few strokes. Knowing he was close, he pumped into her hard and fast, driving deep with each thrust until his balls drew up tight, and pure unadulterated pleasure exploded from his sac throughout his body. His toes curled, and he shot his load deep inside her until he collapsed on top of her, drained and replete.

After lying still a moment, he pressed up and pulled his softening cock from her searing core. And then he released her wrists, bringing them down to chafe them and rub them to ensure she was well. As she lay there, still in a daze, he realized she must have come again when he plunged into her, and something solid and sure settled in his chest. He'd known he loved her, but he'd never expected to reveal his whole self to her, and this night of sex and sharing was almost more than he could handle. But he refused to scare her by announcing his love for her when he knew she still harbored doubts.

Instead, he carefully scooped her up and tucked her under the covers of the bed and snuggled against her. The swirl of emotions within overwhelmed him as he lay there in the dark and repressed the words he wanted so desperately to say. Would she ever trust him enough to believe him when he said he loved her?

Chapter Twenty-Six

October 1861

Cooper sat in the carriage across from his lady hellion and marveled at the week they had spent together. After waking in The Market, they had dressed, with him acting as her lady's maid, though that had delayed their departure significantly. He had barely laced her corset when his cock had grown hard again, so he bent her over and fucked her against the dressing table.

Once they had arrived home, he had taken her upstairs, and they had locked themselves away for two days. They had opened the door only to allow food and wine to be brought in, and dirty dishes taken away. Finally, they had emerged to find a stack of correspondence awaiting them, as well as his secretary reminding him that he was expected at the Earl of Heathington's house party.

So it was that a week after their rediscovery of each other at The Market, they found themselves locked in a carriage alone, trundling across the English countryside.

Knowing they would have long hours ahead of them, he had planned for their drive. Now he leaned back against the squabs and eyed his delectable wife. "Remove your bodice, Em."

She glanced over at him from where she'd been staring out the window. "Why would...oh."

All week, he'd been surprising her at odd times with various commands. He wanted her to be ready at any time to meet his needs. Only yesterday, he'd demanded she toss up her skirts as he filled her from behind in his study as she'd bent over the desk.

"Do I need to repeat myself?"

"No, sir." She pulled down the shade, sinking them into a shadowy interior, and unfastened the buttons that lined the top of her traveling dress.

The emerald-green wool parted to reveal her corset and chemise. To his pleasure, she wore a traveling corset that offered her more flexibility…and him more access. After carefully setting her bodice aside, she waited for his next instruction. Her hands fidgeted, suggesting she was still nervous with him.

Ignoring the disappointing tic, he held out one of his own. "Give me your hands."

He waited one heartbeat, then two, but she settled her hands in his outstretched palm. Desire sprang up within him, shifting from the gentle, ever-present hum when she was near to a loud roar of need. In his pocket, he had stashed an older necktie that was made from the softest cotton. With steady hands, he wrapped it around her wrists and left a loop exposed to attach to the hook on the back of the carriage wall. He'd had it installed earlier that week. After all, one needed a place to hang one's coat while traveling.

Em said nothing as he raised her arms and slipped the loop over the hook. She smirked at him. "I had wondered why that was there."

Cooper feigned affront. "Why, madam, I cannot imagine what you are suggesting. That is clearly a coat hook."

She chuckled and shook her head. "*Of course* it is."

Now that he had her arranged to his liking, he reached for the front of her corset. This one had more give to it to accommodate a woman sitting for long hours in a carriage while traveling. It also meant that he could easily unhook the front a bit and then later reclose it. With her breasts bared as much as was reasonable, he reached out and cupped one globe. At the same moment her breath hitched, his cock twitched in his trousers.

The earlier surge of need was growing, becoming a low rumble under his tightly held control. He flicked his thumb over her nipple a few times, relishing the way it tightened and furled at his touch. His hellion was as excited as he was at the moment. Shifting downward, he reached for the hem of her skirts.

"Spread your legs for me," he said.

Once she did as he asked, he lifted her petticoats and hoop to find her sweet pussy exposed by the slit in her pantalets. Unsurprisingly, she was wet for him already. His cock jerked at the sight. Taking the underthings and tucking the hems he held into her bound hands, he freed his own for more useful activities.

Hands on her hips, he scooted her closer to the edge of the carriage seat, and then spread her thighs a bit wider. "Very nice, sweetheart."

"Cooper?" Still she sounded concerned.

He stroked her inner thighs with his hands and then planted a kiss on each one. "Shhh. Relax. This will feel good...*better* than good."

And then he bent over and stroked his tongue over her pink, glistening pussy. The sweetness of her excitement tantalized his tongue, reminding him how much he loved tasting his wife. As he licked with more pressure a second time, her gasp above was muffled by her skirts.

Determined to take his time, he settled on the floor of the carriage and leisurely set to licking and sucking on her swelling flesh. Then he went in search of her clit, flicking the sensitive nub with a ruthlessly slow cadence that had her hips bucking in an attempt to achieve more contact. Savoring the moment, he swirled over the bud and then shifted down to her core. As he changed positions, she moaned, a low throaty sound that stirred the need inside his own body.

But he refused to rush. They had hours to go before they arrived at the house party.

After tucking his hands under her arse, he lifted her slightly and pushed his tongue deep inside her. She groaned, a languid sound full of need and impatience.

"Cooper, please," she whimpered.

"In time, my hellion," he said, and then returned to working his tongue in and out of her body.

As he fucked her like that for long minutes, she wiggled and flexed her hips, trying to gain more contact, to find the release she was beginning to so desperately seek.

He wanted her to beg. Wanted to hear her need his cock so badly that she pleaded with him in the most filthy and direct terms to fuck her. Only then would he let her come. So he shoved his tongue inside her again before drawing it out to trace a path up one side of her cunny and down the other, never touching her engorged clit. He continued to tease her, pushing into her hole before sweeping up and around her tingling flesh.

She wiggled and jerked, panting heavily above him.

"Oh God! Please, Cooper. I need…" Her voice trailed off in an anguished cry.

"What do you *need*, my little hellion? Tell me. Tell me every filthy detail," he demanded.

She writhed and moaned, her hands still suspended above her head, helpless to help herself. Instead, his little hellion needed him. Needed him to bring her the pleasure she sought. And he would do that for her…very soon.

Returning to his labors, he continued the slow, slippery torture of her sweet pussy, all the while relishing her taste and her reactions. Though he'd prefer to be able to see her face, some things had to be sacrificed in the name of adventure. Her hips bucked sharply, nearly breaking his hold. But he hung on, certain she would break soon. It was important she be able to tell him what she wanted in bed. Tell him anything, really. So, he remained a supplicant to her cunny, licking, lapping, stroking, and filling her with his tongue.

And then she broke. "Please…" she wailed loudly, her pussy dampening her petticoats with the sweetness he had not caught with his tongue. "Please, let me come. Fill me with your cock, shove it deep in my pussy or my arse—I care not—but please make me come hard all over you."

With those dirty demands ringing in his ears, he growled as he sat back on the bench, opened his trousers, and waved her over. "Come slide down on my shaft. Fill yourself with me as you wish."

Her cheeks turned a bright magenta as she rose from the opposite bench and lifted her skirts, pushing them back behind her so she could straddle him on her knees.

As she settled into position, he grabbed her waist. "Mmmm. Hold a moment."

And then he sucked one peaked nipple into his mouth and rolled the tip with his tongue. He loved sucking her tits, since she was neither too small nor overly ripe, making them a perfect mouthful. Then he switched to her other nipple and thoroughly serviced it, as well. By the time he was done, she sat on his lap with his cock nestled in the vee of her legs.

With her hands resting on his shoulders, she rose up, dragging her soaking folds along his stiff shaft until she found his tip. Then she centered herself over him and pressed down.

Cooper wanted to shove her to the floor of the carriage and pound into her, but somehow, he dug deep and found enough restraint to allow her this small bit of control.

Slowly, inch by inch, she lowered herself onto his throbbing erection until her arse was pressed against his rather swollen sac and her mons pressed against his pubic bone. "Oh, God, you feel so good. So long and thick, like you fit me perfectly."

He managed a grunt as she sat there, her pussy occasionally clamping down on his cock. "Em, I need you to move. Need you to ride my cock—now!"

His command rang out in the carriage and she immediately took action. Rising on her knees, she slid up and then pushed back down his length. The hot, wet slide of her quim was a delicious torture. But one he could take only so much of. Lifting his hand, he slapped her thigh. "Faster, Em. Ride me."

And she did. She worked herself up to a bruising pace that had his eyes crossing and his toes curling as he prayed he could hold off long enough to see her come. Then she slammed down on his cock and started grinding against him, a new and different sensation that lit up his nerves and had his balls drawing tight. With her no longer bouncing so violently, he leaned into her and captured one breast in his greedy mouth, sucking hard on her swollen nipple.

She cried out and seemed to grow more frantic as she gyrated on top of him, until a resounding *yes* broke from her lips as she wailed her pleasure. He was quite certain his coachman and outriders had heard her, if not the nearest village. Assured of her ecstasy, he took hold of her hips and lifted her slightly so he could pound out his own release. He slammed up into her once, twice, three times, and then exploded into her as she continued to come all over his cock, as she had requested. Finally, she slumped over him as they both heaved for breath.

As his awareness of their surroundings returned—he'd never come so close to passing out during a climax—he nudged his wife. "Em, are you well?"

With a groan, she nestled deeper into his shoulder, as though she would burrow inside him if she could. Then a light snore sounded from his exhausted wife. Cooper couldn't contain the grin that split his lips as he wrapped his arms around her and let the rocking of the carriage lull him into a light doze.

A few hours later, Cooper and Emily had greeted Lord and Lady Heathington and were busy saying hello to many of the other house guests. All of their immediate circle were in attendance; Wolf, Flint, and Linc were there, as were Stone and Theo, Lord and Lady Carlisle, and even Lord and Lady Heartfield. The house party promised to be a lively one. Other guests were mixed in as well, some Cooper recognized, but a few he did not.

He and Stone were chatting when Cooper felt his wife stiffen beside him. "Is all well with you, dear?" he asked, concern drawing him from his conversation with Stone.

Emily smiled, though it failed to reach her beautiful hazel eyes. "I am fine."

Not wishing to cause a scene, he let his concern go, and after a bit, she seemed to relax. Eventually, the ladies drifted away to join the other women that had gathered near the fireplace. A man joined him and Stone, and his friend made the introductions. "Lord Brougham, may I introduce Lord Fredericks?"

"Delighted." Cooper greeted the man, shaking hands, and then the three of them settled in to talk of parliament.

A short while later, a fourth man stopped to greet Lord Fredericks, who then introduced Lord Wilton to them.

Cooper was sure he should know the man. His name was very familiar, but he was having trouble placing it. Then, as Stone and Lord Fredericks fell into conversation, Wilton turned to Cooper and grinned. "I heard you managed to snare the Winterburn chit. A fine play, if I may say so."

Cooper stared at the man for a moment. "I'm not sure what you mean, my lord."

"Oh, you know, I took a run at her once. Found her a bit of a cold fish, if you catch my meaning. But there were rumors about her dowry that made it worth a try," the man confided as though Cooper were not the cold fish's husband, or worse, as though he expected him to commiserate.

"My lord, I find my wife to be a wonderfully passionate woman. Perhaps *she* was not the problem? If you will excuse me."

And then Cooper turned on his heel and stalked away before he punched the wilted fop in the face.

Chapter Twenty-Seven

It was the second full day of the Heathingtons' house party, and Emily finally ventured downstairs alone. The first evening, when she'd seen Lord Wilton was among the guests, all the memories of her first season slammed into her like a herd of runaway horses. After that, she had carefully avoided being alone except for in the chambers she and Cooper had been given. That morning, he had tried to entice her to join him for a morning ride, but she had preferred to remain in bed a bit longer. After all, her husband had kept her up quite late with his amorous attentions.

Thinking it still early for most of the guests to be up and about, she had slipped down to the library to find something to read while she nibbled on a roll and sipped her morning tea. Book in hand, she turned from the shelves only to find Lord Wilton closing the door of the room. When he turned the lock, the snick of the tumblers falling into place made her jump and squeeze the book she held tightly to her chest.

"At last, Lady Emmaline. I have been seeking a moment of your time, but you seem always to be surrounded by friends," he said as he crossed the space between them.

Objectively, Emily knew Lord Wilton was a handsome man. But after his poor treatment of her during her first season, which in truth ruined her following seasons, she could only think of the man as ugly. "I cannot imagine what you might desire, but I am sure it is of little consequence."

She lifted her chin and strode forward, making to pass him and depart the room. But he reached out and grabbed her upper arm in a bruising grip.

"Oh, do be a good girl and stay a moment." His tone was pleasant on the surface, but the words were intended to demean.

She jerked away from him, though she was unable to break his surprisingly strong grip. "I am a woman, my lord. And I refuse to stay and be further mistreated by you. I suggest you release my arm at once."

"Oh-ho! You are a lively one. How was it I missed this fire in you before?" His words were more a spoken thought than a conversational sally.

Without further discussion, he hauled her into his arms and plucked the book from her protective hold. Her stomach dropped and then did a slow nauseating roll as he lowered his mouth toward hers in an attempt to kiss her. Images from her first season assailed her. Unlike then, as a naïve debutant with little feminine guidance, when she merely turned her cheek, this time she pulled back and pressed her now-free hands to his chest to ensure he could not close the distance.

"What is this? Certainly you are not refusing my attentions?" He seemed shocked by her reluctance.

They struggled for a moment, her efforts to extract herself causing his clothes to be disordered. "My lord, unhand me this minute. I am a married woman. A *happily* married woman."

Despite her best efforts, he held on tight.

"I see, you like it forceful, do you?" He leered but did not release her. Instead, he tossed her down on the nearby settee and then landed on top of her, crushing her skirts.

When he started to tug them up, hoops and all, she knew she had to do something, or things would get much, much worse than they currently were.

As he lifted his weight once more to yank at her skirts, she waited until her leg was free enough, and then she jerked her knee up toward his groin. To her dismay, she missed her particular target; however, she did hit close enough to it to send him scurrying away in some pain while trying to protect his jewels.

She leapt to her feet, her dress falling back into place despite being wrinkled beyond repair. "If you know what is good for you, my lord, you will leave this house party at once. Should I tell my husband of what you tried, I am certain he will exact his own retribution. I cannot say for certain that you would survive such an occurrence."

With that, she spun on her heel and stormed for the door. Forgetting in her haste that it was locked, she grabbed the handle and wrestled with it for a moment. Finally, she remembered the lock and released it, letting her open the door. She calmly walked down the hallway, waiting to turn the corner before she broke into a run, desperate to get back to her rooms before she bumped into anyone.

Cooper watched his wife leave the library. He'd started to call out to her, but something seemed off about her demeanor. By the time he thought to check on her, she was around the corner.

He was about to make haste after her when Lord Wilton strolled out of the library. He looked up from his personal disarray and winked at Cooper. "Quite the hellion, that one."

Fury sparked in his belly as he imagined what that bastard might have done to his wife. How the philandering popinjay might have attempted to take liberties with her person. Because *his* hellion was loyal and steadfast, she would never betray him with another man. But what he could believe was that something was not right. Something untoward had occurred, and he planned to get to the bottom of it.

With a growl born of pure anger, Cooper grabbed Wilton and shoved him against the nearest wall. "What did you do to my wife?"

Fear and uncertainty replaced the cockiness that had resided in Wilton's gaze only moments before. "I... I don't know what you mean."

Cooper pulled the coward forward and then slammed him back against the wall. "My wife did not look well as she left the library. I can only imagine that has everything to do with you."

Wilton's gaze darted over Cooper's shoulder before a sly look came into his eyes. "Lord Brougham, I do not know the meaning off this outrageous display, but you will remove your hands at once."

Cooper stiffened. The man had shifted from cowardly to confident too quickly. A glance over his shoulder proved his reasoning was sound. Wolf and Lord Heathington stood staring at them. Cooper growled once more. "If I find out you have done something to upset my wife, I can promise you I will not stop next time."

He banged the man against the wall one last time, but by then, Wolf had stepped up and was pulling his hands off Wilton's lapels. "Cooper, I don't know what has occurred, but you need to release him unless he has done something to you or Emily."

As Cooper did as directed, the smarmy fop stumbled away toward Lord Heathington. "My lord, certainly you do not condone such behavior?"

Heathington stared at Wilton, a single brow lifted. "I do not, unless of course you have in some way insulted Lord Brougham or his wife?"

Wilton tugged on his clothes. "Absolutely not."

"Very well, then. Lord Brougham, unless Lord Wilton has caused harm to you or your wife, I will ask you to refrain from laying hands upon the man while you are guests in my home."

Lord Heathington waited for a reply.

Cooper growled, frustration riding him hard. "My wife exited the library just before him, looking upset. He then came out and insinuated he had intimate knowledge of her. And since we arrived, the man has made other inappropriate comments about Lady Brougham."

Wilton's chest puffed up. "I merely called the woman a hellion. She certainly does not carry herself as a lady should." The dandy sniffed as though *he* were the offended party.

Cooper took a threatening step forward, his hands aching to wrap around the man's neck.

"You will refrain from provoking Lord Brougham." Heathington glared at Wilton before looking back at Cooper. "I apologize, but unless you have evidence he has been untoward with your wife, I simply cannot allow you to harm another guest. Should new information come to light, please do make me aware."

Then the two men turned and departed the hallway.

Cooper cursed as he watched them leave, certain that if he'd had but a few more moments alone, he could have convinced Lord Wilton to reveal what he'd done. He was less certain of his wife's pliability, particularly if she thought she was protecting him in some way.

"What did he do to provoke you?" Wolf's forehead wrinkled.

Cooper turned to go in search of his wife, but said over his shoulder, "I don't precisely know, but I plan to get to the bottom of it before the day is out."

Chapter Twenty-Eight

E mily paced her chamber restlessly. What time was it? She glanced at a clock and saw that it was close to midday. Surely the rest of the house party would be up by such a late hour? Determined not to hide and cower, she smoothed the fresh dress she wore over her hoops and crossed to the closed door of her room.

Not long after her encounter with Lord Wilton, Cooper had appeared in their room, back from his ride. With a quiet greeting from where she lay on the bed and merely a glance in his direction, she'd drawn his notice. Heavy footsteps had alerted her that he was drawing near, and then he'd taken one look at her pale face and cursed. With a gentle touch, he'd caressed her cheek and asked her what was wrong. Terrified of telling him what had happened, she pleaded female troubles and assured him she would be down later when she was feeling better. He had relented, though she was sure it was with great reluctance.

Two hours later, she still wasn't truly ready to face him again, but she knew she could not hide in their rooms for the remainder of the house party. So, with her usual determination, she opened the chamber door and stepped out into the hall.

Her hands shook, and bile rose in her throat as she imagined seeing Lord Winton again. Having to encounter such a monster and behave as though he had not pawed her person and attempted to defile her was almost beyond her. She'd traveled only a few doors when the urge to retch took hold and had her turning around to flee back to their rooms.

But then Theo opened the door to her chamber, just next door to her own rooms, stepped into the hallway, and called out to Emily. "Good morning."

Instantly, Theo could see all was not well, she quickly ushered Emily into her and Stone's chamber and delivered a chamber pot in the nick of time.

Emily cast up her accounts, what little there was, and collapsed onto the nearest chair, still gripping the porcelain basin, as though it might save her somehow.

Theo knelt and tried to remove the pot from her friend's hands. "What is wrong, dearest?"

Emily sat there, certain that if she opened her mouth, more of her stomach contents would appear.

A maid bustled about the room and handed something to Theo that her friend then pressed to Emily's forehead. The cool dampness of the cloth soothed her as little else could have.

Theo turned to her maid. "Bethany, please go downstairs and search out some soda bread, or perhaps some other very dry bread for Lady Brougham."

"Yes, my lady." The woman curtsied and hustled out the door, leaving the two alone.

Theo returned to blotting Emily's forehead with the cool rag. "Perhaps I should send for Cooper?"

Panic sent Emily's stomach into a tailspin. "No! Please—" And then she expelled the last of the tea and toast she had consumed earlier as she'd tried to settle her nerves.

As she sat up from bending over the chamber pot, Emily saw the concern etched on Theo's normally happy features. She needed to tell someone what had happened. If not her husband, then perhaps her friend could offer good counsel. Feeling empty and listless, she handed Theo the basin and took hold of the cool rag. She pressed the cloth to her forehead and cheeks as she tried to gather her thoughts.

Finally, she blurted out the crux of things. "This morning, Lord Wilton attacked me."

"What?" Theo exclaimed. "What happened?"

Emily collected the frayed ends of her thoughts and tried to piece her tale together. She quickly summarized what had occurred with Lord Wilton as her cheeks flamed with a mix of embarrassment and anger.

Theo, still on her knees, wrapped her arms around Emily, who was not beyond enjoying the comfort her friend offered. Tears finally escaped as she was able to lean on someone else for a few moments. As she sat there crying, she realized that this was what it was like to have friends. And the realization only made her cry harder for all the time she'd lost striving to be so independent, when she'd believed she didn't require anyone.

After she finally wept all the tears she'd pent up, she sat back and used the cloth in her hand to dab at her eyes. "My apologies for crying all over you."

Her friend made a pishing sound. "This is what friends are for. Certainly, it's nice to have tea and gossip and whatnot. But it is when your load is so heavy that you can no longer bear it alone that friends are truly a blessing."

Emily matched Theo's smile and then leaned in for a hug. "Thank you for being a true friend."

When they parted, Theo sat back and looked carefully at Emily. "Considering how distraught you were, I am assuming you have yet to inform your husband of this morning's events."

Emily started worrying the cloth between her fingers and couldn't bring herself to look Theo in the eye. "He tried to convince me to tell him what was wrong, but I was afraid of what he might do if I told him."

Theo gasped. "Emily! You cannot mean you thought Cooper would take retribution on you?"

Looking up, shocked by her friend's suggestion, Emily shook her head. "No! I merely meant that I worried he might do bodily harm to Lord Wilton and end up in no little amount of trouble. One simply can't go about hitting other peers of the realm, and there is little doubt in my mind that Cooper would do just that."

Theo sighed. "Yes, I do see your point. It is a very Cooper-like thing to do. Honestly, any one of those Lustful Lords would behave the same under those circumstances." She hesitated. "However, I do believe you need to tell your husband what has occurred."

Emily chewed her lower lip, still unsure. "I-I don't know."

Theo took hold of her hands and squeezed them gently. "He needs to know. If he found out from some other source, or worse, some other version of the story, he would be furious. Furious, and very hurt that you did not trust him enough to tell him."

Emily's doubt faded as she thought about their growing trust. It was like a delicate bud, waiting, hoping to burst free and flower into something beautiful. If she went to him, trusted him to act in their—not merely her—best interests, that bud could find its full potential.

She wanted to experience that beauty. She'd tasted moments of it when she let Cooper have his way with her body. When she trusted her pleasure to his care—be it tender or rough. The warmth that suffused her body and seeped into her soul was fast becoming a craving—no, a basic need—for her well-being.

And with that, she was decided. "You're right. I need to tell him. When I do, could you and Stonemere be nearby? I still fear that he may give in to his temper and do something regrettable. I know he trusts and respects your husband, and would listen to him in the heat of the moment."

Theo gave her hands another squeeze. "Of course. Let us go find our husbands and deal with this directly. You will feel better once this is done."

Emily stood and nodded. Theo was right. Even making the decision to tell him had settled the turmoil in her stomach.

Cooper stood talking with Stone and Linc by the fire. Wolf and Flint had gone out shooting, claiming they felt cooped up in the house.

Linc suddenly excused himself, and Cooper and Stone turned to see him head into the hall. A moment later, a soft, feminine giggle sounded from the same direction Linc had gone.

Stone shook his head and turned back to Cooper. "And how are things with your wife? Have you made progress?"

Doubt swelled where only hours before had been a small flame of hope. The carriage ride to the house party had made him sure he and Emily would sort things out. That she was coming to trust him. But then he'd seen her scurrying from the library, followed by that overdecorated lothario, and the man had had the nerve to make that comment about his wife...a comment that reeked of sexual overtones. Not to mention her refusal to speak with him when he saw her in their chamber. She had seemed unwell, and the mystery combined with her obvious distress had him on edge.

"I thought things were going well. She was responding so well when we were alone. I had even begun to think I was truly earning her trust, but then this morning after our ride, I saw her leave the library followed by Wilton, who had the gall to straighten his clothing and insinuate something untoward had occurred. My wife has far too much integrity for me to believe what that man attempted to imply, but for a moment there, I wavered. I wanted to storm after her and demand an explanation. Now I merely feel as though I am standing on a precipice, waiting for something to push me over the edge. And the hell of it is I am not sure of what waits for me on the other side. Is it the happiness of a warm marital bed? Or the dark misery of loneliness?"

Stone grunted. "Welcome to the fold, my friend. Being in love can be a scary thing until you are assured of its return."

"There you two are." Theo walked in with Emily trailing just behind her.

His wife still looked as though she might be ill, and Theo seemed to have an overly bright smile on her face, as though she were trying to distract them from Emily's wan countenance. The worry he'd been fighting to keep in check surged free of his restraints. He crossed to her and took hold of her shoulders. "Emily, are you still feeling unwell?"

"I am, but I hope I shall improve soon." She offered him a small smile.

Stone and Theo moved closer to them. "Excuse us. My wife wishes to take a walk in the gardens."

Cooper nodded to them as they moved into the hall. Then Theo stopped and slid the double panel doors closed. He turned to look at his wife, one eyebrow creeping high. Clearly, his wife wished to speak to him in private, and Theo was aiding her in that endeavor. Had she spoken to Theo about what was upsetting her? The idea both soothed and irritated him. He wanted to be her confidant, and yet he trusted Theo to give his wife good counsel when it came to marriage and womanly things. Stone's wife was headstrong, but loyal and honest to a fault.

"Cooper, I need to tell you something…upsetting." She hesitated as though gauging his reaction. "Perhaps we should sit?"

He considered her suggestion, but somehow, he felt certain that whatever she was going to tell him would negate sitting almost immediately. "Why don't you simply tell me what it is you need to share. I doubt sitting will make the news better or worse."

She placed her palms against his chest and met his gaze with her own. "This morning, there was an incident."

He couldn't control the reflexive tensing of his muscles. His whole body went rigid as he waited for what she was going to say. "An incident?"

"Yes. I was in the library when Lord Wilton slipped in behind me and locked the door. He accosted me…attempted to take liberties." Her voice trailed off as her hands slid from his chest and she spun around, giving him her back.

Fury pounded through his frame, making his flesh and bones vibrate with the need to kill the man who had the nerve to lay hands on his wife. "He dared touch you?"

Emily hunched over herself, and a light tremor seemed to shimmy through her. His own hands still shaking, he turned her back around and hauled her into his arms. "Did he…"

He swallowed past the lump in his throat. Past the fear of what she may have suffered. And he had simply stood there and watched the bastard stroll away. "Did he…hurt you?"

She slipped her arms around him and burrowed closer to him, as though seeking comfort. "No. I managed to injure him enough to affect my release, and then I left the study as quickly as I could manage. Other than that night at the Landstones' ball, I don't think I've ever been so scared." She pressed her face against his chest.

"Why did you not say something sooner?" He palmed the back of her head with one hand as he stroked along her spine with the other.

She sniffled softly. "I was worried you would do something drastic. Something that might cause more trouble for you than it would right what happened."

He leaned back and tipped her face up to meet his. "Thank you for telling me. For trusting me with this."

"But I didn't—" She bit her lip and tried to look away.

He refused to let her avoid him.

"But I *didn't* trust you. Didn't tell you when you came into our room." A tear slipped down her cheek, leaving a wet trail.

"And I could see you were upset, yet I did nothing. I didn't press you. I simply walked away." He felt ashamed that he'd left her alone to grapple with something so awful. "But you came to me and have told me now. That is what is important."

Confusion creased her brow. "It is?"

"Of course." He smiled softly at her, his heart bursting with love. "Trust is not blind, and it can take time to develop. You may have hesitated, but in the end, you did trust me." He ached to kiss her. To show her how much this meant to him. But first, he needed to address the matter of his wife's honor with the cad who had thought he had some claim upon her person. "Now, I need to go speak with Lord Wilton about this matter."

"But Cooper, you cannot assault him. What if he presses charges?" She clutched at his coat, fear making her hazel eyes huge.

"I merely said I would speak with the man. I shall not lay hands upon him...without provocation." He tried to reassure her with a smile, but it felt more like a grimace.

"Please, Cooper. No more spectacles. I only wish to leave, and if we never attend another house party or ball, it will be too soon." She sniffled again, but her eyes were bright with determination.

"Go upstairs and see to the packing. We shall return home at once." He rubbed her back but then stepped away.

He opened the drawing room doors and found Stone and Theo sitting on a bench nearby. He hesitated and then looked at Theo. "Garden too chilly?"

Stone stood. "Don't do anything rash."

Cooper sighed and pinched the bridge of his nose. "I merely intend to have a word with him."

"Very good." Stone slapped him on the back. "Then you won't mind a witness."

Cooper bared his teeth briefly. "If it's you, certainly not."

The two men went in search of Lord Wilton.

Chapter Twenty-Nine

C ooper and Stone found Lord Wilton in the stables, fresh off a ride. Typical of the entitled, he handed his sweating and heaving mount off to a groom and didn't think twice about the poor beast's condition. His obvious rough handling of such prime horseflesh only added to Cooper's desire to kill the man. But his little hellion was right. If he wasn't careful, he would land himself in more trouble than Wilton was worth.

"A word, Lord Wilton." Cooper stopped the man by blocking his exit.

Even when engaging in outdoor sports, the man was overly adorned. He wore tan riding breeches, tasseled Hessians, and a red velvet riding jacket that sported gold braid trim in a military style that was all affectation. "Perhaps later, Lord Brougham. I am due to clean up, and then I am scheduled to meet with a certain pretty lady in the greenhouse."

"I think not, my lord." Cooper all but snarled. "There is the little matter of your morning interlude with my wife to discuss."

Wilton's eyebrows rose. "My lord, I assure you anything that occurred was of mutual design."

Cooper clenched his fists at his sides and resisted the desire to punch the man. "In a different time and place, I would call you out for such an aspersion to my wife's honor. Be that as it may, I am given to understand your advances were unwelcome. My wife, I was told, made her disinterest quite clear. I warned you earlier that if I discovered you had done anything to upset my wife, I would not hesitate to find you. She is most decidedly upset."

Wilton placed a hand to his chest. "Why, that sounds remarkably like a threat, my lord."

Stone took a step closer to Cooper, who merely grunted before returning his focus to his prey. "Not a threat, my lord. A reminder of an earlier promise."

He shifted out of Lord Wilton's path as the man tried to barrel past him. Respect for Lord Heathington made him hesitate.

Wilton muttered as he started past, but then he stopped and turned to look at Cooper. "You know, women are fickle creatures. It's really not your fault if they choose to share their charms with others. And I must say, your wife is rather charming."

Cooper lunged forward with no warning and punched the taunting fop square in the face. The satisfying crunch of bone and cartilage filled the stable as the nearby horses grew restless. "You bloody bastard!"

Lord Wilton landed on his arse and rolled to his side, clutching his face. "Hell and damnation, you hit me," he said, somehow surprised that Cooper had followed through on his promise. The words came out muffled and nasally as blood dribbled from between his fingers and onto the hay-strewn floor.

"You're bloody lucky that is all I've done." With Stone's urging, Cooper stalked past the bleeding cad and back toward the main house.

Inside, he and Stone went in search of Lord Heathington. It was time to take their leave.

Emily snuggled closer to Cooper as the carriage rumbled along the lane. The heat of his solid body seeped into her clothes and down to her bones. She'd noticed his right hand was swollen and the knuckles mottled as though he'd hit something—or, more aptly, someone. "Thank you for taking me away from there. I did not wish to run into that man again."

"He will not bother you again, I am quite certain," Cooper said, and pressed her closer to him with his left arm.

Her stomach dipped a little, but she wanted to tell him what had happened. Wanted to share her story with him. "Lord Wilton paid particular attention to me my first season."

Cooper stilled next to her, his body strung as tight as the reins of a runaway team of horses.

"For a brief period, I felt like the belle of the ball. It was all so new, and Arthur and I were just out of mourning for our parents." She took a breath and continued. "I was ignorant of Society's ways and had no notion that something might not be on the level."

"Society can be petty and mean to those who do not know its ways," he agreed.

"Yes, I discovered that." She sighed but pressed on with her tale. "It had been weeks of him dancing with me and fetching me punch, and then he convinced me to go for a garden stroll during the Stantons' annual ball. I was nervous, but felt sure he was seeking a private word with me to ask for my hand. I fancied myself in love with him. But then all that happened, as you might expect, is that he pawed at me and tried to steal a kiss. I was so naïve. I rebuffed him but did not believe that would deter his suit."

Her husband turned his head and pressed a sweet kiss to her temple. "I wonder what the sweet, tenderhearted Emily was like?"

She swatted his chest. "Do be serious. And I am still sweet and tenderhearted, I'll have you know."

He tipped her face up to meet his. "I know you are, my sweet hellion," he said, and then he gently kissed her.

After a few precious moments, he pulled back. With a thoughtful look on his face, he reached up with his injured hand and caressed her cheek.

Her heart fluttered in her chest, and she let the love she had been fighting to suppress to bubble up. "At the next ball, another girl pulled me aside and tried to warn me. She told me of her mistreatment at his hands, but I was too arrogant to listen."

He leaned in again and kissed her once on each cheek. "Too stubborn and starry-eyed, perhaps, but never arrogant."

Mayhap her husband was right. Was she being too hard on herself? But she continued her tale. "Shortly after, on a night I expected once more for him to declare himself—if not in words, then perhaps with multiple dances—I was utterly crushed. He walked right past me without even a tip of his head in acknowledgment, and approached an American heiress who was visiting. It might as well have been the cut direct. Very few men danced with me after that."

"A ballroom full of fools." He tut-tutted.

"Emotionally distraught, I retreated to the ladies' retiring room and hid behind one of the changing screens. I happened to overhear a group of other debutantes gossiping about Lord Wilton and the apparent bet in White's betting book concerning his ability to relieve me of my virtue. They also made a point to make some disparaging remarks on my clothing and general appearance. It was the night I learned that I could trust no one in Society."

"And then I come along and ruin you at the Landstones' ball." He grunted and muttered a curse. "How you were able to forgive me, I'll never understand."

She bit her lip and admitted both to him and herself the truth she'd always known. "That night was not your fault, and had you not ruined me, I most certainly would have been hauled off and questioned, which would have ruined me anyway. You merely gave me the protection of your name and a safe place to land in the midst of the chaos I had created. While I likely would have survived a questioning and ruination, undoubtedly I would not be as content sitting alone in a house with my brother as I am with you."

He pulled her into his arms and kissed her fiercely as the carriage continued to roll along. They kissed and reveled in their freshly renewed closeness, neither making a move to escalate the intimacy, nor to part.

Emily would have happily ridden in the carriage forever, cuddled with her husband, but it seemed he had other plans.

Chapter Thirty

It was late when they arrived home. Emily yawned, having just woken up from a nap. It had proven hard to fight the pull of sleep as the carriage gently swayed and her husband's warmth seeped into her clothing.

Cooper exited the vehicle and then turned to her and offered his hand. She lifted her skirts, perhaps more than was truly required, to alight from the carriage. Her two feet had barely hit the ground when he bent over and tucked his shoulder into her stomach. The next thing she knew, she was tossed over said shoulder and being hauled into the house like a sack of grain.

"Cooper! What are you doing? Put me down this instant." She pounded a fist lightly on his back.

"To the victor go the spoils. I am the victor, and you, my little hellion, are the spoils!" he announced gleefully as he took the stairs to his bedroom two at a time.

"Robert Cooper, you put me down before I break my neck," she said again, but ruined her demand with wild laughter.

He ignored her feeble demands and carried her past the housekeeper and at least two upstairs maids before he replaced her on her feet inside his bedroom. She smoothed her skirts out and attempted to readjust her corset, which had not appreciated his theatrics. An awkward moment of hesitation stretched as she tried to decide what she should do.

Her husband stood a foot away, watching her closely.

She flicked her gaze from him to his large, velvet-draped bed, and then to the door that separated their chambers. The desperate urge to sleep in his bed, to lie next to him, skin to skin all night long, surged deep within. But propriety, for once—and at the most inconvenient moment she might add—pushed her to retreat to her own room to prepare for bed. She bit her lower lip and turned toward the door to her room. "Good night, Cooper."

"What? Where are you going?" He looked confused.

She stopped walking. "To my chamber to prepare for bed."

He straightened up and eyed her with a sense of dark command. "You will do no such thing. Spoils remain with the victor. They do not have a room of their own."

Her breath caught in her chest. Was he playing a game with her? Was he serious?

He walked over to a wingback chair near the fire and sat as regally as any king. "Come."

The dominance in his tone moved her with little thought to compliance. She was drawn to him like the needle of a compass to true north. A sense of rightness bloomed in her chest as she waited for further direction from him. While separating to go to her own room had seemed logical, it had felt empty and wrong. *This* felt right.

"Turn around." His voice rumbled, a deeper tone than normal, that sounded almost gravelly.

Her husband served as lady's maid and unhooked her dress, then her skirts, and then the rest of the layers, working steadily to free her from her clothes until she stood before him naked. The warmth from the fire licked over one side of her body while the other remained chilled by the shadows.

His gaze stayed steady, unwavering. "Kneel before me."

Emily did as directed, dropping to her knees. That was the moment she noticed the solid length of his erection in his trousers. How had she missed such an obvious display? Perhaps it had only grown to such a state while her back was turned? Could undressing her excite him so greatly?

He opened his trousers and freed his hard cock, taking a moment to stroke it. "I plan on using that pretty mouth until I come all over your breasts."

She inhaled sharply, and her nipples pebbled to tight little peaks. She was utterly excited by the idea of him using her in such a way.

"Come, my little hellion. Suck my cock."

His raw demand would have made her weak in the knees had she not already been on them. So she leaned forward and gripped the base of his shaft. The tip was mottled with need, a drop of precome seeping from the slit. She licked her lips as she leaned forward and then swiped her tongue over the drop of moisture. His male essence burst over her tongue, a slightly sweeter version of what was to come. Eager to get to the heart of his command, she took the head of his cock in her mouth and then slid more in behind it. She wanted as much of him as she could take, all of him, if she could. When she drew back, he growled low in his belly, a primitive sound that egged her on. She reversed directions, taking him back in and swallowing until she had his entire length engulfed. Quickly, she retreated, only to repeat the action again.

He groaned, low and needy. "Yes, take it all."

And she did. She continued to work the length of his shaft in and out of her mouth, relishing the power she wielded over him as he moaned and shook with pleasure.

Then he threaded his fingers into her hair, destroying her coiffure as he urged her on. "Faster." His breath hitched. "Bloody hell."

Emily's entire body tingled with want. Her nipples were so tight and achy, and her pussy throbbed between her clenched thighs. Oh, how she wanted him inside her, but she trusted him to see to her needs. To take care of her pleasure and satisfy the hungry desire that simmered within.

"Off!" His grunted words were accompanied by a firm pull on her hair.

The tugging on her scalp tingled and buzzed over her body, adding more fuel to the fire. Dear God, she burned for him. Panting, partially from sucking his cock and partially from the overwhelming need that seethed within, she knelt there, back bowed as he held her by her hair and pumped his cock.

And then the first warm spurt of his seed landed on her chest. As he continued to come with a low growl, he worked his hand up and down his slick shaft, drawing his cum out and aiming it at her breasts. A few drops landed on her cheek, not far from her mouth. Snaking her tongue out of her mouth, she managed to scoop the stray fluid up and swallow it. Something dark and primitive seemed to flash in his gaze as he watched her tongue. Then his cock finally softened, an apparent prompt for him to release it—but not her.

No, his hand remained fisted in her hair as he loomed over her. "You belong to me, Emily. You will always be mine, as I will always be yours."

And then he reached out and rubbed his load into her skin. Massaged the creamy fluid into her breasts, swirling it over her nipples and up to her collarbones. Apparently satisfied with the mess he'd made, he held his fingers up to her mouth. "Lick them clean, love."

And she did, eager to please him. But equally eager to please herself.

"Such a lovely pink tongue," he murmured as she swept away the last dollop of seed from his fingers.

Hand still holding her hair, he leaned in closer and kissed her. She surrendered to his possession, meeting his tongue and tangling hers with it until she was certain she would burst into flame. Her skin felt ablaze and her body ached with her desire to be touched by him, to be filled. And as he pulled back from their kiss, his smile suggested he was well aware of how desperately needy she felt in that moment.

With the cascade of emotions and desire pummeling her, something deep within broke free. An inner glow illuminated the dark shadows inside and warmed her from within.

"Go arrange yourself on the bed for me. Arms and legs splayed wide." He motioned toward the imposing tester bed that dominated the room.

Emily did his bidding, even as her body demanded his touch. She knew if she did as he asked, he would give her all that she needed. Her husband was not a stingy lover. Crawling on the massive bed—it could have easily accommodated four large adults—she lay on her back and spread her arms and legs as requested.

Cooper rose from where he'd sat and crossed to his dresser. There, he withdrew four neck ties and a wood box. When he returned to the bed, he set the box and two of the ties by her feet and then moved to one side. She watched with only a little trepidation as her husband bound each wrist to the nearest spindle of the headboard. Then he moved to her feet, repeating the same action using the more widely set posts of the bed frame. She felt impossibly open, exposed. Of course, that was likely the purpose behind his positioning her in such a way.

He remained between her legs, still standing at the foot of the bed, and slid a hand along the inside of her leg until he reached just above her knee. Then he stroked back toward her bound ankle. "You might have the prettiest pussy I have ever seen."

He crawled on the bed, set the box off to the side of her legs, and then moved closer. Unsure if his comment required a reply, she remained silent. Watchful. What was he planning? Because clearly, he planned something.

"I have been dying to play with your sweet cunny. I don't mean simply lick it—heaven knows I've done plenty of that. But really play with it. See just how far we can push you." He stroked higher up her thigh, his fingers teasing the crease where her thigh met her torso.

Her breath hitched as she imagined the things he might do to her pussy. Having visited the hall of mirrors at The Market, she knew there were myriad ways he might tease her. Torture her until she exploded with pleasure.

He opened the box and pulled out an elaborately carved dildo. Ever the gentleman, he held the stone up for her inspection. It was a lovely pink-and-white color, polished to a high shine. All along the length of the cylinder were raised carvings in swoops and swirls that created a series of ridges. "Mmmm...do you like the rose quartz? I acquired this set a few years ago from an unusual merchant."

She licked her lips, seeking the moisture she needed to speak. Her mouth had gone dry at the notion of him inserting the dildo inside her. "It's lovely," she managed to rasp out.

Cooper set it down and then raised another item of the same stone. It was a squatter shape with a slight flare at the base. Her brows rose to her hairline as she tried to imagine how he might use such an implement.

"This is a rectal plug. I've heard there was a time when doctors believed sperm could escape from a woman's womb through the rectum. This was a fertility aid to stop such a thing. Quite a silly notion; however, I think you may discover a more pleasurable purpose for it." He grinned and set the item aside as well.

Last but not least, he withdrew an interestingly sized circlet of the same stone. It was too large to be worn as a ring on his hand and too small to be a bracelet. Instead of telling her what it was, this time he demonstrated the item. He reached down and slid the item down over his semisoft shaft. He pushed it down his length until it reached his balls. Then he worked both sacs through the ring.

"What is that?" Curiosity drew the breathless question from her.

"This is a cock ring. It is intended to help delay orgasm, extending our amorous activities." The hungry look on his face suggested to her that he may need just such assistance, despite the fact she had so recently drained him of his seed.

The last item he retrieved from the box was a small glass pot. He removed the lid and carefully set it aside, though she couldn't see where. Finally, he grabbed a bolster that sat nearby. "Lift your arse."

She did as bid, and he slid the pillow beneath her bottom, which tilted her hips upward, exposing her pussy even more. It also seemed to make her backside more accessible, which made sense considering the various implements he had shown to her in the last few minutes.

No longer able to glance down her body and see what he was doing, she bit her lower lip and waited. The sharp edge of desire that had her burning for him had eased as she lay there. But it had not dissipated. Like a well-banked fire, it would take little stoking to bring her body roaring back to life.

"Emily, do you trust me with your pleasure?"

Cooper's voice had deepened, grown rough with desire. Or perhaps it was anticipation?

Chapter Thirty-One

Regardless, little shivers of need sparked all along her body. "Yes. I trust you, Cooper."

His gaze shimmered for a moment as desire and something gentle flickered through his bottomless brown eyes. Then the softness leeched away, and the commanding glint returned. Her body melted in response, heated in welcome for whatever pleasurable torture he had planned.

"We have discussed the things you are interested in trying. Tonight, you will experience something more than my fingers filling your arse."

He didn't hesitate as he reached for the pot of what she assumed was salve, and then a cool, wet substance pressed against her rear hole.

A gentle brush over the tight ring had her clenching in surprise, but then he leaned down and pressed a kiss to her inner thigh. "Relax, my little hellion. Let me inside you," he urged, as a fingertip—or so she guessed—pressed firmly against her opening.

He eased inside, slowly sinking into her heat. With a slow, steady pace, he worked in and out of her body until she relaxed around him. Then he added a second digit. The fullness returned with a slight pinch that quickly settled into a pleasurable feeling. After a few minutes of him filling her and then gently stretching his fingers open, he withdrew.

With her pussy back to aching and now her arse sharing in the wantonness, she moaned and shifted her hips restlessly. A few moments later, something cold and very hard pressed against her rear entrance. She tensed for a moment when he leaned over and sucked hard on her clit, but relaxed as he shifted to a gentle lapping that sent delicious shivers up and down her body. At the same time, he'd eased the tip of the rectal plug inside her. He continued to lick her pussy as he slid the piece of stone deeper into her passage. The thing widened, and she groaned as the pleasure bled into pain. "Cooper!"

His hand stilled, and he looked up at her. "Breathe, sweetheart. Just breathe through it, and soon, the pain will feel so good."

He eased the plug out and then back in, fucking her with it slowly until she relaxed again. Then he returned to lapping at her pussy, yet now he avoided her clit. Her body throbbed with the need to be filled even as he popped the last part of the plug in place.

He retreated from her pussy but remained between her thighs, his hands pressing her legs wide open. "My God, you are an arousing woman. The base of the plug looks like a beautiful gemstone lodged between your cheeks. Just above it, your pussy is wet and swollen, your channel clenching in need. I want nothing more than to sink my cock into you, but not yet. Not until you're begging me to fill you."

His words sizzled through her, feeding the flames of her desire until she was certain she would be consumed by the inferno. "Please."

"Not yet, my hellion. I promise, when I am done with you, you will be incoherent with pleasure, drunk on the bliss I've given you. Just a little longer." He pressed a kiss to her inner thigh.

Out of her mind with the pulsing lust that owned her body, she lay there bound to his bed and at his mercy. Having been given no other choice, she waited to see what would come next.

The next sensation was again one of cold stone, considering her body was on fire. The blunted tip rubbed gently over her needy flesh, skating up one side and down the other. Again, he refused to touch her sensitive nub that seemed to throb with every beat of her heart. Then he swirled the tip around her pussy hole, and her hips bucked, greedy to take it in. He chuckled at her body's uncontrolled movement.

As she looked up at him where he knelt between her spread thighs, her breath caught in her chest. He was beautiful, like a fallen angel with his hair aglow in the firelight and his dark eyes as fathomless as a bottomless well. But there was a glow about him that captivated her and made her realize that perhaps for the first time, she was seeing the real Cooper. The man carefully hidden behind the façade of a peer of the realm.

He was breathtaking, and he was all hers.

And then he was filling her with the pink-and-white stone. At first, it was simply a new sensation to add to all the others, but then as he withdrew it, the ridges in the sides stroked over that special spot inside her and she cried out with the intensity of her pleasure. "Oh, God!"

But he pulled the shaft out of her body and returned to rubbing it over her swollen pussy lips and tender tissues. Then, with no warning, he shoved the dildo back inside her pussy. The sense of fullness between that and the plug swamped her senses and had her panting for air. And then he withdrew it again and hit *that* spot. She clamped down on the stone piece, reluctant to let it leave her body again. "Please, Cooper. Fuck me with it."

He groaned. "Mmmm... Such a filthy girl. Beg me, sweetheart. Beg me to ram the stone dildo into your pussy."

Oh, God, she wanted to say the words, but she couldn't. She'd never said such dirty things, couldn't bring herself to say it, despite how desperately she wished to.

He waited a moment, but when she failed to speak, he withdrew the stone and returned to teasing her outer folds. But this time, he grazed her clit, sending bolts of pleasure through her stretched-out frame.

A second graze of her sensitive clit set her to trembling uncontrollably. Need rolled through her like a wave rolling a boat in a vicious storm. Her arse clenched around the plug as her pussy clenched around nothing. And then he leaned over, and as he shoved the dildo inside her once more, he flicked her clit with his tongue.

She balanced precariously on the edge of orgasm, her body aching with the need to release. The pain was exquisite, a lovely pressure that would give way to unbearable pleasure as soon as he allowed it. As soon as she said the filthy words.

Clearly set on torturing her, he started pulsing the tip of the dildo in and out of her pussy, a shallow fucking that merely teased and tormented. Then he added the gentlest of tongue lashings against her clit, again barely enough pressure to feel the touch let alone take her over the edge. Need sliced through her sharp and desperate. "Pleeaassee!" she wailed. "Fuck me with the dildo. Ram it into my pussy and suck my clit. Make me come *hard*."

He growled, a low guttural sound that made her nipples pucker tighter. And then he shoved the dildo inside her, filling her as he sucked on her clit. He stroked once, twice, and she exploded. Screaming his name, she gripped the ties at her wrists and hung on as her body heaved, seeking more of the stone, more pleasure, simply more.

Her eyes closed, and stars danced across the field of black as her body seemed to come apart from the quaking of her muscles as her pussy gripped the stone lodged deep within. He continued to lap at her clit, driving her through wave after wave of orgasm until the pleasure ebbed and focused on the gentle swipe of his tongue between her legs. Over. And over. And over again.

She lay there, twitching and breathing, unable to do more than simply exist for the moment. But then his gentle swipes grew more determined, and soon he was pushing her back up the hill. She wanted to say no, but all she could manage was a soft whimper as he pulled the dildo out of her pussy and shoved his tongue inside her. He swirled it around and then returned to her clit. As her hips flexed a bit, her body seeking more of what he offered, he pushed the dildo back into her cunny. He kept it deep and fucked her with it, all the while working her clit with his tongue in long lapping strokes that made her toes curl and her breath hitch. Then he pushed the dildo inside her and left it there. Curious, yet unable to do more than accept his lusty torture, she gasped when he moved the plug in her arse.

"Yes, sweetheart. I plan to fuck you back here. I'll fill your sweet pussy with this dildo while I slide my cock in your arse and let your heat envelop me." His gravelly voice told her how close to the edge he was.

"Yes. Whatever you want. My body is yours." She whispered the words, incapable of speaking louder as he slid the plug out completely while he flicked her swollen clit one last time.

Something cool and moist coated her rear hole once more. Then he was pushing inside her, stretching her tight opening until she pressed back against him. As he was slightly bigger than the stone plug he'd used, she took a deep breath as her bottom burned with his intrusion.

"Fuck, Emily. You're so tight, so hot wrapped around me." He groaned as he pressed his balls against her bottom.

Then he withdrew, sliding back until just the tip stretched her opening, and then he pushed into her in a single strong stroke. Sensations that she had only recently discovered fired through her body, making her pussy ache as he filled her arse. Then he pulled back and paused for a moment before she felt the pink-and-white dildo sliding into her pussy. With the stone lodged deep in her channel, he resumed plunging into her backside.

Swamped by the fullness of the dildo and his cock, she moaned low. "Oh, God, yes."

And then he reached down and dragged the pad of his thumb over her swollen clit. Suddenly, her body was aflame, racing toward another explosive orgasm as he worked in and out of her body at a frantic rhythm that matched perfectly with the way he rubbed his thumb over her clit. Her orgasm slammed into her out of nowhere. She screamed, an incoherent sound of utter bliss as he worked her hard through the crest and down the other side.

Then, with a haste she could barely track, he pulled the dildo from her sheath and pushed his cock deep into her arse. He pulled out and slammed inside her again, and she shuddered with an aftershock of orgasm. Without pause, he set a pounding pace as his cock filled her bottom. She'd never felt so complete as she did in that moment. Cooper was everything she'd never known she'd needed, and more. As he fucked her hard, sweat dripped down his nose and dropped on her breasts. All the while, he rutted into her, cursing and swearing in a litany of sorts.

Eventually, he ceased muttering and drew a breath. "I want you to come again for me."

"What?" She couldn't imagine surviving another climax.

"Come for me, sweetheart. You're so full of my cock right now. It's so tight in your bottom, I want to feel you grip me hard as you come again." The demand came as he reached between them and teased her clit with his thumb.

The fullness of his cock in her rear passage and the continued stimulation of her throbbing nub coalesced into an utterly earth-shattering orgasm that had her screaming once more. He worked her hard, fucking her as she came.

"Fuck, yes!" he cried out as she gripped his shaft with her muscles, squeezing him and releasing him in a quickening rhythm as she lost all control.

She came and came as he continued to pound into her. Her body soaked his, the wetness seeping out around them and down onto the sheets below. "I'm coming! Yes, Em. Fuck, yes!" Cooper joined her orgasm with a curse as he continued to shuttle in and out of her.

Slowly, his hips eased their pace and then tapered to a stop. He collapsed on top of her, his weight a delicious addition to her oversensitive body. Still he filled her with his cock, and she lay there, bound to the bed, relishing the utter freedom he'd shown her. The total abandon of trusting him with her pleasure. Maybe even with her heart?

After a few minutes, he peeled himself off her and slid free of her backside, and she shivered at the gentle friction. Once more kneeling between her spread thighs, he looked down at her display. "I love seeing how pink and wet you are from me filling you."

She nodded, still feeling a bit tongue-tied from the emotional intensity of what they'd shared. He reached down and dragged the tip of his finger over her sensitive folds until little jolts of pleasure had her pussy clutching with spasms, though she was certain she couldn't actually come again if her life depended on it. Then her husband untied each ankle before he pressed a kiss to her pussy and then another to her clit. Eventually, he worked his way up to her lips for one last gentle caress. Lastly, he released her two wrists and then rubbed each until the feeling she hadn't realized she'd lost returned.

Gently, he tucked her under the covers and settled in next to her.

Chapter Thirty-Two

A fortnight after he and Emily had returned from the Heathingtons' house party, Cooper found himself walking into his club with a spring in his step. Life was settling into a comfortable routine where he went about his business during the day, and by night he dined with and made love to his wife. The more they chatted and the more they explored in bed, the more his delight in her grew. They had certainly been friends before the wedding, and he had no doubt he had feelings for her, or he'd not have cared about protecting her. But slowly, the idea of love was taking over. Growing. Filling his chest until he walked about like a puffed-up dandy.

After entering White's, he found his friends in their usual corner near the fireplace. Linc, Flint, Wolf, even Stone was in attendance, as well as Emily's brother, Arthur. The fivesome sat sipping whisky and discussing whatever the topic of the moment was in the comfort of the wood-paneled, all-male enclave. It was a cozy spot their group had claimed, and it beckoned to him.

He approached the group. "Good afternoon, gentlemen."

"Cooper!" Stone greeted him with delight as the others joined in with jovial welcomes and hellos.

"Stone, however did you escape to join us this afternoon?" Cooper ribbed his friend.

Stone snorted. "A far cry more easily than you, my newly-wed friend."

Cooper pulled up a chair and settled in with his friends. "No, doubt. But I fear not for the reasons you imagine. My hellion countess keeps me busy."

The group chuckled, except for Arthur. "Good God, man! She's my sister."

Which only made the rest of them laugh harder than before. Clearly perturbed, Arthur rose, grabbed the fire poker, and jabbed at the logs burning merrily in the fireplace.

After the mirth ebbed, Cooper leaned toward Arthur as he retook his seat. "Fear not, my friend. I'd say no more were you here or not."

Emily's brother nodded and resettled in his chair, clearly flustered by the conversation.

"Besides," Cooper continued, "I want to hear how things are going on your bride hunt."

Arthur paled as the rest of the group looked at him. "Yes, I promised my sister I would look for a bride."

"But we've only just found you, Dunmere!" Linc's face became a rictus of horror.

"Indeed, and I have no intentions of finding one so quickly. However, I plan to thoroughly enjoy the looking." Arthur grinned at his compatriots.

Cooper shook his head, knowing his wife would not be pleased once she figured out her brother's ploy.

Stone sat back in his chair and stretched his long legs out before him as close to the fire as he could manage. "I plan to thoroughly enjoy watching the lot of you crumble before the women that claim you. If Cooper and I are any indication, you will all be rather entertaining to watch."

Wolf sat quietly next to Arthur, his face set in a grim countenance that far outpaced his normal glower. Cooper wondered what was troubling his friend. Curious, he nudged Stone and leaned close to him. "Any notion what is troubling Wolf?"

"None at all, though I have noticed he has been extraordinarily dour of late. As affable as the man is in temperament, he looks positively fierce. I heard there once was a woman he cared for, but some tangle occurred. She must have truly done him in." Stone sighed. "I fear he will have the most difficult time finding love."

Cooper reached up and tugged at the collar of his shirt. His necktie suddenly seemed uncomfortably tight. "Sometimes love can be hard to spot."

Stone cast a startled glance at him. "Don't tell me you've had issues with Lady Emily. You two seemed to be in accord of late."

"More aptly stated, we had established a cease-fire. I believe we have only just reached a truce. I'm still waiting to see if it will result in a lasting peace." Cooper tucked his chin slightly and let his eyebrows rise.

"Well, I wish you well on that front. It took Theo and me a bit of time to sort ourselves out, but now that we have, I believe all will be smooth sailing from here." Stone nodded with far more confidence than Cooper had.

"I cannot fathom any circumstances under which anything surrounding Theo would be smooth sailing." Cooper knew—perhaps more than anyone except Stone—just how trouble-prone Stone's wife could be.

"Perhaps you're right. I have been rather overbearing lately, according to her. She even threatened violence if I did not settle down." Stone leaned closer to Cooper. "You know she's positively dangerous with a dinner fork."

Cooper laughed as he imagined some poor unsuspecting dinner partner of Lady Stonemere's finding himself at the business end of an eating utensil.

Settling back into his chair, he turned his ear to what the single men were planning for entertainment later that evening.

Flint grinned. "I'll meet up with you blokes after my evening rounds."

Arthur turned to him. "Your rounds?"

"Oh, yes. I plan to head down to the docks for a few rounds with some of the hands who like to bareknuckle fight. It's all quite a lark."

Flint was so jovial, Cooper knew Arthur wasn't understanding.

"Oh, that sounds entertaining. May I tag along?" Arthur's eyes sparkled with excitement.

Cooper knew he had to interject. "Arthur, your sister would positively trounce me if I let you run off to some of Flint's amusements. The man has no sense of self-preservation...or pain."

Arthur's eyebrows shot up. "You don't feel pain?"

Flint laughed uproariously. "Don't let old man Brougham over there pull the wool over your eyes. I feel pain well enough. I just enjoy it a bit more than the average man."

Arthur grew a bit pale at that announcement, as he should in Cooper's mind. Whatever it took to keep the man whole, hale, and on the bride hunt. Copping a mouse would neither endear Arthur to the ladies nor Cooper to Emily.

"I'm sure Linc and Wolf can show you plenty of other entertainments until you all join up at The Market later. Save the rough stuff for those who know what they're doing."

Arthur nodded. "I might tag along sometime to watch, but I'd have to pass on taking a facer."

Stone rose at that point. "Well, it seems I should be heading home. Promised the wife I'd be home for an extra early dinner so she could retire. The baby wears her out, and it's not even here yet."

Cooper rose and joined his friend. "I've a stop to make on the way home. I'll join you in leaving these unfettered gents to their amusements."

After dinner, Emily found a note in her husband's familiar scrawl waiting for her on her dressing table. Curious, she unfolded the paper and read the message.

My Dearest Emily,

The past weeks have brought a welcome closeness in our relationship. In the interest of helping both of us with our growth, I have arranged for a special interlude tonight. Once you are ready for bed, if you will join me in my chambers, I shall reveal my plan.

Your Doting Husband,

Cooper

The past weeks had been a revelation for her. Slowly, with each meal, each conversation, each time they'd had sex, a bridge had been built between them. Before her marriage, she had been enjoying the physical pleasure, thrilled at the adventure of exploring her sexual needs with a man. For a short time after, she'd wanted to exact retribution—punish the man who believed he knew better than her, the man who had had ruined her. But over time, if she was honest with herself, she had come to see that perhaps he had not so much commandeered her life as he was trying to protect her.

As her maid helped her disrobe, she pondered what she might wear for her husband's surprise. Not knowing what he had planned both excited her and made her nervous. Would he try and bring another man into their bed? No, she discarded that idea immediately.

Perhaps he'd bought her new lingerie? That was a possibility, and if it were the case, wearing just a robe might make sense so she could easily slip into the new garment.

Another idea popped into her head, and she blushed at the thought. Had he acquired another device like the ones they'd used recently? Little shivers of excitement raced through her limbs as she decided to don a silky robe—one meant to cover a nightgown—and nothing else.

Dressed, she sent her maid away for the night and then tended to her own hair. After brushing the golden-brown locks until they shone, she approached the door that separated Cooper's chamber from hers.

Butterflies swirled through her belly—which logically was ridiculous—but she persevered and knocked. A rustling noise could be heard, and then, after what seemed an eternity, he called out, "Come in."

Emily opened the door and stepped inside the chamber. For a moment, she just stood there, frozen by the tableau. Every flat surface she could see held a candle, to the point she wondered how the servants would manage overnight without light. Her husband stood next to the bed wearing a robe and, if his bare calves and feet were an indication, nothing else.

Cooper smiled at her. "Come to me, Emily."

"Yes, sir." She responded to his command, both in voice and movement.

"Sir is not required. In fact, it would rather ruin tonight's festivities." He still stood next to the bed as he waited for her.

After a few more steps, for his was a rather large chamber, she stood before him. Every muscle on her frame vibrated with energy. Something peculiar was afoot, and she could not puzzle it out, so she followed his lead for the moment. She *trusted* him.

Cooper shook his head. "No specific event. More a celebration of us."

"Very well." She glanced about the room once more. "What did you have planned?"

He took her hand and led her over to the sitting chairs by the windows. "Please, sit. May I pour you something to drink?"

Emily considered her taut nerves and nodded. "Please."

Her husband presented his back to her as he poured something into a glass. She studied the breadth of his shoulders, the way they tapered down to his trim waist, and how even under his brocade robe, the play of muscles could be detected with his every move. She thought about how it felt to run her hands over his back as he made love to her. And she realized that he had been making love to her. They hadn't simply had sex in a long time if she considered how things had evolved. When he turned back around, he handed her a glass of wine.

"It's the same red we had at dinner. You seemed to enjoy it." He took a sip from his glass.

She couldn't stop the smile from stretching her lips. She had enjoyed it, and he had noticed. "Thank you."

The ruby-red wine had a light, fruity sweetness that made it far more palatable than some of the dry reds she'd tasted. But more importantly, the fortification helped to settle her nerves as she waited to discover what her husband had in store for the evening.

Cooper took the seat next to hers and canted the chair so they could speak comfortably. He fidgeted a bit as he settled in, which drove her to gulp her wine in lieu of sipping. If he was nervous, she was unsure what to expect. They had done all manner of things in the bedroom. From spankings to him fucking her backside, they'd truly run the gamut. What might cause him to appear at all discomfited?

"In order to help this relationship to not only grow but flourish, we need to experience the ultimate in trust. Whether you recognized it at the time or not, you have in the past trusted me implicitly in the bedroom. We need to grow that connection, but in a new capacity." He took a sip of his wine and set it down. Then he reached around to a small table on his right that had drawers and opened one.

When he faced her once more, Emily was surprised to see him holding cuffs similar to the ones they had used the other night. Her belly flip-flopped like a landed fish as she considered letting him restrain her in such a way. Could she trust him like that? He was correct in that she once had trusted him implicitly, letting him bind her, blindfold her.

Instantly, she thought back to those intimate moments. Remembered her fear but also the sense of certainty that Cooper would never do her harm. And she knew, despite all that had come between them, she would allow him to restrain her and do as he wished with her body. It was her heart that she still fiercely protected.

"I am willing to let you do this again. I-I—" She tried to find the words to express her nervousness while showing him she was making progress. It had been much easier in the heat of the moment rather than making a clearheaded decision.

Cooper shook his head. "These are not for you. They are for me. I would like you to cuff me to the bed and do with me what you will."

She inhaled sharply, letting out a small gasp of surprise as a plethora of images flitted through her head. She could tease him until he was hard and then suck him until he came for her. Over and over again. Or she could ride him to orgasm after teasing him unmercifully, drawing out the pleasure for them both. So many possibilities.

"You would trust me...with your pleasure?" Her heart beat so hard, it felt as though it were battering against her chest.

"I would." He took a breath. "If you are to understand what trust is, I must demonstrate it, give *you* the very thing I desire most. And if I am to learn to be more forthcoming, then I must learn to tell you what pleases me. What I need from you. My hope is this bridge will carry beyond these walls into our daily lives."

Emily was so deeply moved by the moment, she wasn't sure she could respond. After a long silence where she grappled with her chaotic emotions, she drew a slow breath and released it. "Thank you. I, too, hope we can continue to establish an accord that carries beyond this room."

That familiar, wolfish smile of his appeared. "Then, my lady, would you like to strap your husband to the bed and have your wicked way with him?"

Laughter bubbled up from within as the intensity of the moment dissipated. The import remained, but with a lighter, more adventurous quality. Excited by the prospect of taking control of the evening, she rose and took hold of the cuffs. "Come along, Cooper. We have much to attend to."

His brows rose a bit as she assumed command as easily as any field marshal. "Of course." He stood beside her.

"Of course, *my lady*." She looked back at him over one shoulder and lifted one brow.

He bowed slightly. "As you wish, my lady."

With a roguish wink, she ruined the moment, but turned and headed to the bed, confident he would follow. Once there, she pointed to the middle of the space. "Please remove your robe and lie down."

He did as she asked, baring his body to her. She took in the width of his shoulders, the taper of his torso down to a trim waist, and then down over his lean but well-muscled thighs and calves. As directed, he settled in the middle of the bed and waited.

Emily reached down and wrapped one of the cuffs around his wrist, buckling it into place. Then she took his arm and raised it toward the corner of the bed where a hook was embedded in the wood of the headboard. It was tucked off to the side, where drapery could hide it from prying eyes, but it was still easily accessible. She approved of his attention to detail.

Then she walked around the bed to the other side and repeated the process.

Once Cooper was strapped to the bed, she stepped back and admired the tableau. He brought to mind a mythological god or fallen angel trapped by an earthly lover. His golden hair glinted in the candlelight, the shadows sculpting his face as he waited for her direction. Now that she could do anything she wanted with him, what would she choose?

Chapter Thirty-Three

Cooper lay on the bed with his arms cuffed to either corner of the bed and wondered what his hellion might do to him. Were it up to him, he would ask that she press her luscious breasts to his face. But it wasn't his decision to make. He'd handed the reins to his wife, and now waited to see what she might do with absolute control.

A naughty smile flitted across her shapely lips, and the first kernel of doubt flickered through his brain. Could he withstand whatever she conjured up to torment him? Certainly, it would all feel good, but one could take only so much pleasure at once.

"You should know, I have a mental list of all the things I have ever wanted to do to you. We could be here well past dawn," she said, her tone full of mock warning as she untied the belt of her robe.

Beneath the silky fabric, she wore nothing, and the notion pleased him immensely. In just a few short weeks, they had come further than he ever could have hoped. But then, they had come so far prior to the schism, it made sense that they both had rebounded with alacrity.

He struggled to maintain a sufficiently solemn expression. "As you see fit, my lady. I am at your disposal." He wiggled his arms a bit to draw attention to his cuffs.

"Mmmm...you are. I must say, I do like this arrangement." She crawled on the bed and perched by his feet.

All over his body, his skin prickled with awareness. Her every small shift sent a new wave of sensation rolling over him, exciting him. It took every ounce of control he possessed to hold still in anticipation of what was to come.

Emily leaned over his foot. Every sinew in his body tensed, waited.

And then he felt it. A mere wisp of sensation. It was so faint, if he hadn't watched, he wasn't certain it would have registered. A breath of a kiss on the top of his foot. Another on the matching appendage. Then her lips caressed each ankle in turn, each shin—in two places.

Between kisses, she said, "There was a night not so long ago when you promised me—and delivered—endless delights and slow, agonizing pleasure." She looked up at him, a wicked smile slowly curving her mouth. "Tonight, I return that promise to you."

She slowly made her way up his thighs, past his groin. His cock throbbed with need. Ached to feel her soft, sweet lips. If it had been a sentient thing, he knew it would feel utter jealousy of the kisses she rained on every other spot on his body.

More kisses came as she worked over his hip bones, up his stomach, and then she teased his belly button with a flick of her tongue. Hands cuffed, he had no choice in the matter, no ability to simply take what he wanted. To take her as he had the night they'd reconciled. Certainly, she had started out riding him slowly, but his restraint had snapped, and he had taken control long before she could fully execute her intention. He should have guessed with him cuffed, she would follow through on her original plan.

Instead, he watched, fascinated by her deliberate pace and attention to every detail. As she moved up his torso, she skirted his nipples, again ignoring the obvious places where one is assured to receive pleasure. When her tongue slipped out to stroke along his collarbones, his cock bumped against his stomach as though attempting to draw such attention to itself. He was hard, possibly harder than he'd ever been, and ached with the need for release.

His breath grew choppy, and it became a Herculean effort to draw each one. To fill his lungs during her bliss-filled assault.

But his hellion countess continued to defy convention and do as she pleased. And as a result, she pleased him very much.

Next came his shoulders, and with them, the added torture of feeling her heat and her presence against his chest as she leaned over to minister to his opposite side. Added to the heat was her scent. A soft, indecipherable floral smell that was as wild and free as Emily herself. He would forever associate her with that perfume.

Finally, she placed her lips on his neck. Tickled his skin with the moist heat of her tongue. And then she nibbled his ear closest to her, her breath an added layer of sensation to his overly stimulated nerves. When she sucked his earlobe into his mouth, his body commenced shaking. Need gripped his balls like a vise and forced a low, agonized groan from deep within.

Emily released his flesh and sat up on her knees. She gazed at him, visibly trembling with desire, and pursed her lips together. "Cooper, are you well?"

He blew out a steady breath and tried to regain control of his galloping lust. She certainly appeared satisfied with the results of her efforts, despite her feigned concern. "I am, my lady," he said, knowing he could not hide the ragged note in his voice.

"My, you don't sound well. Perhaps there is something I can do to alleviate your distress." She batted her lashes coquettishly.

He refused to play her game, even as adorable as she was when she attempted to appear innocent. "Anything you chose to do would be welcome, my lady. I am at your disposal." His cock perked up, flopping up against his stomach.

Though not entirely in his control, he could have minimized the movement some. However, doing so seemed counterproductive at the moment.

"Oh, well then, I suppose I shall do as I please." She winked and leaned back over to baldly swipe her tongue across his nearest nipple.

A faint tingle of sensation swirled about the point, but unlike her nipples, he did not experience great pleasure. It was almost as stimulating as having her lick or kiss his bicep. She treated the other nipple the same, but quickly moved on.

The feel of her lips caressing his flesh as she moved lower, and then lower still, drove his need higher. Then she pressed a kiss to the underside of his cock.

His hips thrust, and his balls tightened, sending pulses of lust ripping through him. She took his base in her hand, lifted him up, and wrapped those very same lips around his tip.

Fuck, he wanted to push deep within her mouth, sink into her until the tight grip of her throat tried to strangle his shaft. Instead he held back, checked the beastly urges within, and waited to see what she would do next.

Emily did not disappoint. She drew a breath, relaxed her jaw, and sank down on him until her throat blocked her progress. Then she swallowed and relaxed the muscles, allowing her to continue forward until her nose pressed against the wiry hairs at the root of his erection. The incredible tightness squeezed his tip, causing his balls to draw up. The intense gratification had him teetering on the edge of climax, but then she withdrew, and the burning need for release retreated a bit.

The respite did not last long as she sank back down on his shaft without hesitation, taking all of him once more. He groaned, arching up against his restraints as he sought more contact, more depth. She choked, but remained steadfast in seeing to his pleasure.

She once more pulled back and then returned, sliding down his length. Over and over, she repeated the slow shuttling of his cock in and out of her mouth. Every so often, she paused at the deepest point and encouraged him to pump his hips, creating an even more intense pleasure that sizzled through his trembling frame.

The need to come, to explode, crept over him with each pass until black spots danced in his vision as he tried to refrain. "Please, my lady," he said as his voice cracked on the last word. "You must stop, or I shall come."

Instead of heeding his plea, she glanced up at him and moaned as she cupped his sac and squeezed ever so gently. Cooper was lost as the pressure on his balls twined around the vibrations of her moan and caused his release to rip through him. Despite his hands not being free, he pumped furiously into her mouth, fucking her as pleasure slid up and then down his limbs. When his toes curled, he shouted his bliss.

All the while, his hellion sucked his cock, swallowing his seed until his orgasm subsided to a dull pulsing within. Apparently satisfied with her efforts, she lapped at him as she slipped off his cock and sat up.

Tremors still shuddered through him; he was utterly wiped out.

Emily considered her husband as he lay there, spent and all but unconscious. Between her thighs, her cunny throbbed with need as she reviewed her options. She could return to sucking him until he grew hard again, she could touch herself until he was ready, or she could sit on his face and have him service her. Hmm...that last idea sounded delightfully naughty.

Determined to give him a smidgen of recovery time, she began kissing her way up his torso again. As she neared his neck, he seemed to revive enough to utter a whispered curse. "Bloody hell, woman, you will be the death of me."

She stopped and looked at him for a moment. "I suspect there is no other way you would wish to go." Then she scooted closer to him and leaned over his prone form. "And the French do call it *la petite mort* for a reason, do they not?"

Cooper chuckled and then grinned wickedly, "Indeed they do. It sounds as though my lady has been doing a spot of research."

"Perhaps. I also seem to have a set of very knowledgeable friends. In particular, Lady Heartfield has been a font of information."

Cooper jerked against the restraints as he attempted to sit up, but found he was unable. "I somehow thought that hoyden would be a good influence on you." He shook his head, obviously ruing such thoughts. "I should have known that Theo would introduce you to Lady Heartfield."

"Tsk. Tsk. Lady Heartfield is a perfectly lovely woman, and I can assure you she has not violated your privacy in the least.

Even when Theo begs her for stories about you and Stone, the lady is nothing if not circumspect." Emily pursed her lips together for a moment. "Now, I believe there has been enough chatter."

She rose to her feet on the mattress, used the headboard for balance, and looked down at him. He lay flat on his back, hands stretched out toward the corners of the bed. Then she stepped between his arms so that a foot was planted on either side of his head.

"I believe I have a far better use for your mouth at the moment."

And then she lowered herself onto her knees until her pussy hovered over his face. She wavered, feeling out of her depth at the forward nature of the moment. Cooper had always given her pleasure, but she had never, in all their interludes, taken pleasure for herself without his guidance. She wanted this, needed to feel in control of her destiny in some small measure. So she pushed past her doubts and unfounded concerns and sank until she was almost sitting, though not quite making contact. "Lick me."

A newly obedient husband, Cooper complied without delay, dragging his tongue along her dewy slit. Her legs quaked as he moaned. His breath twined with the sound and caressed her swollen flesh almost as though he had physically touched her.

"Again," she said, her tone firm and commanding.

He did as requested, swirling his tongue over her wet center and dragging it up her pussy until he reached her clit and continued with firm pressure. He continued until her hips jerked.

"Please, my lady, sit. Let me pleasure you." Cooper's voice sounded raspy, as though he'd been carousing all night.

A thrill shot through her, but she hesitated. Could she be so bold? Determination welled up from within, pushing her to take action until she did as she had originally wanted and sat on his mouth.

He feasted on her. There was no other way to describe the enthusiasm with which he licked and nibbled her quim. The way he devoured her pussy. Using his tongue, he penetrated her over and over and then swirled up to her nub and over it until her hips lobbed against him. But as good as his mouth felt, she needed more. Needed something to help push her over the edge. So as she ground her cunny against his mouth, she reached up and tweaked her nipples. A light pinch with her fingers that sent a flash of pleasure straight to her core to mix and mingle with the wondrous sensations he was creating with his mouth.

"Yes, Cooper!" She cried out as need churned and grew within until it buzzed through her as though a living thing.

Pinching her nipples harder, for longer, she tipped her hips and demanded, "Lick my clit. Make me come."

And so he did. As he focused on her bundle of nerves and she played with her nipples, the living thing within her exploded, shattering into a million pieces. "Yes!"

Her cry rang out through the room while her body spasmed and jerked, overwhelmed with the bliss of orgasm.

As the room came back into focus, she extricated herself from her husband and melted onto the mattress next to him. With his arms still stretched wide by the restraints, she simply nestled into his side. Cooper lifted his head enough to kiss the top of hers, and then they both lay there for a few moments.

Finally—it could have been moments or it could have been an hour; she'd lost all sense of time—she sat up. "Let me release you."

"I'd stay here, tied to this bed forever, if it made you happy." The low rumble of his voice sent shivers up and down her spine.

She laughed as she unfastened the first restraint. "*You* make me happy. And right now, I very much wish to feel your arms wrapped around me."

She released his other wrist, and he was able to rub at the slightly chaffed skin. "As you command, my lady."

She placed a hand on his chest. "Let me take care of you." And then she jumped up and ran into her room. Grabbing her pot of best skin cream, she plopped down on the bed next to a sated but rumpled Cooper. "Here." She took one of his wrists and quickly applied the cream with a gentle touch. Then she did the same for the other one. When she was done, she found him looking at her with a world of emotions swirling through his deep brown eyes.

"Emily, I—"

Panic had her interrupting what she worried would be a declaration. She was not ready to say the words she felt pulsing within. Soon, but not yet. She yawned mightily. "I am terribly tired after all that activity."

Cooper merely nodded and laid back down. "Come, snuggle with me, *wife*."

"I'd like that, *husband*." She sighed a little and settled in with him. To her great satisfaction, this time, he wrapped her in his arms as they drifted off to sleep.

In the dark hours before dawn, Emily awoke as Cooper rained kisses over her shoulders and down across her breasts. Need erupted within her like gooseflesh rippling over one's skin after a chill. A light, sensuous teasing of sensation that was a strange mix of pleasure and discomfort. Then he swept her lips into a kiss that stole her breath and her few scattered thoughts as he slid deep within her body.

With a steady yet determined pace, he thrust into her over and over, until a desire-filled moan escaped her lungs while she arched into the searing touch of his lips on her skin. Flames licked over her as he lapped at one furled nipple and then the other, without ceasing his deep penetration. And, greedy wench that she was, she wanted more. "Cooper, please."

"Please what? Tell me what you want." His rough demand seared through her haze of desire.

"You. I want you." She moaned again and wrapped her legs around his hips as he pumped into her again and again.

"You have me," he huffed out. And then she swore she heard him whisper, "I'm yours forever."

But as he thrust one last time, she shattered around his cock, screaming his name as pleasure swamped her like an inexorable tide taking the beach. With each new crashing wave of pleasure, her certainty that she loved him grew stronger. The new fresh sprout of hope sparkled and shimmered in welcome.

And as Cooper joined her in bliss, pumping into her until he collapsed on top, she knew she had nothing to fear from

her husband; that once they declared their love, all would be
right in their world.

Chapter Thirty-Four

E mily sat in her front salon sipping tea as she waited for Arthur to arrive. It had been two months since her wedding, and she had not seen him with the same woman twice. While she was greatly pleased with her marriage and no longer bitter about the union, she was—as always—a woman of principle. Her brother had used his desire to marry as leverage to get her to agree to a wedding. He would make good on his promise to search for a wife.

That said, she allowed her thoughts to stray back to the night a week earlier. When she had strapped Cooper to his—no, *their*—bed, everything had changed. The way he had trusted her, had made himself vulnerable to her, helped her open up to him. It had allowed her to reveal her true self to him in ways she had not until then. Taking control of their lovemaking empowered her and reinforced that they were equals in their relationship. They had fallen asleep wrapped around each other, only to wake in the night and continue where they had left off. As he had slid deep inside her and filled her, she had finally allowed the love she felt for him to come forth. Though she had not said the words yet, every movement, every touch had been imbued with the surfeit of emotion immersed within her heart.

And then later, as they lay in bed, he had asked her to stay with him. To sleep next to him that night and every other night. His shy request had only reinforced her new and wondrous feelings. And every night since had been glorious, whether they made love, or he growled and dominated her, or they spent it simply snuggling together as they discussed the day's trials and tribulations.

Soon she would tell him how she felt. She simply needed a bit more time to adjust to the truth of how powerful her feelings were.

The sound of footsteps alerted her to her brother's arrival.

"I see my beautiful sister is loitering about the house today. Where is your husband? I received his note requesting I come for a visit. It has been a few weeks since I last saw him." Arthur crossed the room to where she sat and bussed her on the cheek.

"Sit, Arthur. Cooper sent that note at my request." Emily sat up straight and allowed her commanding tone to reinforce her words.

Her brother's gaze narrowed as her statement hung in the air. Then, without much resistance, he took the offered seat. Casting his gaze over to the tea service, he said, "A spot of refreshment would be welcome before you browbeat me about whatever transgression I have committed."

She nodded. "Of course."

After a few moments of pouring tea, Arthur selecting a few nibbles, and the requisite first sip, she launched her attack. Head-on. "So, tell me how the bridal hunt goes."

Her brother rolled his eyes and set down his saucer of tea. "As these things often do, it goes slowly. Truly, I fear I shall not have an opportunity to truly engage in a thorough search until next season."

Emily huffed. "The little season is fast upon us. There is no reason you need wait until next season to hunt a wife. Arthur, you claimed this was important to you, and now I fear you merely did so in order to force me into marriage."

He paused for a long moment, his gaze searching hers. "Is marriage to Cooper so awful?"

Cooper had walked into the house and was on his way to his study when he heard the question asked by Arthur. He knew eavesdropping was wrong, yet he could do nothing but tarry outside the door of the salon and listen. As he waited, his heart beat wildly in his chest. What would he do if she said yes? Could he let his hellion go if being married to him was so horrible? It felt like a stab to his heart, but he knew he would release her if that was what she wanted.

"Of course not." Emily hesitated. "I care for my husband a great deal."

Her brother replied, "Merely care? If I know nothing else about you, dear sister, it is that you rarely feel such tepid emotions. If you are not wildly in love with him, then I have done you a disservice."

"Oh bother." His wife huffed. "This was to be a conversation about *you*."

He could picture his little hellion pinching the bridge of her nose in annoyance that her plan had gone astray. Again.

"Yes, I adore him. I am utterly in love with the man, and I plan to tell him soon. But that does not absolve you of your promise to me. I agreed to marry Cooper, but you are required to search for a bride in earnest. I do not see the diligent hunt I was guaranteed."

Cooper couldn't have wiped the ridiculous grin off his face at having heard his wife's declaration if doing so might save his life. She loved him!

"I am glad to hear it. I would not have encouraged the match if I thought it would make you miserable. I've only ever wanted your happiness, Em. So I promise to take the search for a wife more seriously. But I shall not be rushed, either. I hope to be as in love with my wife as you seem to be with your husband."

Cooper heard the rustling of clothes and the creak of furniture. Assuming the visit was coming to a close, he resumed his path to his study with a spring in his step. His wife loved him.

He'd tried to say the words, to tell her how he felt the night she'd tied him to the bed. But before he could get the words out, he'd seen the panic in her eyes. As a result, when she'd yawned and claimed tiredness, he'd let the moment pass. Since then, there hadn't been what seemed an opportune time to make his declaration. Of course, now, he could perhaps admit some trepidation at possibly saying the words and not hearing them returned.

Considering this and his newfound knowledge of his wife's feelings, he knew he needed to do something to show her how he felt. Merely saying the words would be wonderful, but he wanted to eradicate any doubt in Emily's mind. Taking a seat behind his desk, he thought about what he knew of his wife. The root of her doubts and fears always lay in the security of her future. As a woman, she generally was reliant on men for that security, and the truth was most had failed her in some way. Even himself.

The question was, how could he secure her future in such a way that she would feel safe no matter what might come? She had fought hard to save her family home, had even been willing to take criminal action in order to do so. For his own peace of mind, he wanted her never to feel that need again. He smiled grandly as he realized the best way to show her his love. And it would make the perfect Christmas gift, to boot.

Chapter Thirty-Five

December 1861

E mily woke up on Christmas morning, certain that all her plans for the day would unfold perfectly. She'd personally overseen the menu, handwritten each invitation to family and friends herself, and had shopped for weeks for the perfect gift for Cooper. Though it would have to be a private gift exchange, neither of them would wish to share the item with their guests.

She got out of bed, stretched, and went to select a dress for the day's festivities. She settled on a simple hunter-green day dress and set out the red gown with the green trim she had had specially made for dinner.

Half an hour later, dressed, coiffed for the day, and feeling very positive about what lay ahead, she went to the breakfast room. The house had holly and pine boughs strewn throughout, permeating the air with a refreshing wintery scent. The fire crackled merrily in the fireplace, and the servants were bustling about. She paused for a moment. Perhaps they bustled about a little too much?

"Mrs. Pedigrew, is something amiss?" Emily experienced a sudden sinking feeling in her stomach.

The kindly old lady with her blue-gray hair and soft, faded green eyes tried to muster a smile. "I'm afraid the cook has come down with a terrible cold. She is bedridden, unable to even come sit in the kitchen. Unfortunately, this was discovered only a short while ago. The kitchen maid is attempting to step in, but quite honestly, I fear for your breakfast. Christmas dinner is likely ruined as well." The woman hung her head and tsked.

Disappointed, though not defeated, Emily did as she always did. She took charge. "Well then, let us go see about breakfast, and we can sort out dinner arrangements, as well."

Half an hour later, she finally sat down to a plate of runny eggs, burnt toast, and a rather charred shape she suspected was meant to be meat. Cooper walked in just as she had begun to scrape the burnt parts off the bread.

"Good morning, my lovely wife, and Merry Christmas." He stopped as he took in the pathetic-looking meal on her plate. "Oh my, that looks rather unpleasant."

She huffed but kept rasping her knife across the toast. "It seems the cook is sick in bed, and the kitchen maid, who has ostensibly been learning from the cook, is rather inept at actually cooking. This meager effort was what I managed to accomplish without burning down the house."

Cooper eyed her plate suspiciously, not that she could blame him. Were she not starving herself, she would pass on the questionable fare. "I have sent round to Theo's house to see if she has anyone on her staff that might be capable of stepping in to assist us. I'd send to the employment agency, but it's Christmas. I can't imagine anyone being in the office, nor any help available."

He looked at everything once more, a little forlorn crease between his brows. "I suppose there is nothing for it. I'm sure I have had worse in my life."

She couldn't hide her grimace. "Perhaps you should taste the food before making any pronouncements on its fitness for consumption."

His brows rose nearly to his hairline. "Very well."

And so he made a plate and settled across from her. She waited for his first bite with a sense of impending doom hanging over her. He shoved the eggs in, chewed a moment, stopped, and then swallowed. And coughed.

Emily wanted to die. Of course, no noble woman of her acquaintance knew how to cook. They all had servants. But to have her deficiency so openly exposed on the day she had planned to profess her love to her husband seemed a cruel twist of fate.

She shoved another bite of gloppy eggs in her mouth before she could start crying. To his rather inestimable credit, Cooper choked down the food on his plate. For that alone, Emily would have declared her love. But she had a plan, and she refused to deviate.

Around midmorning, as Emily was seeing to those details she could at least do something about, a note arrived from Theo in the hands of her cook. Emily read through the short missive, then looked up at the apparently happy woman. "I cannot tell you how grateful I am for your assistance."

"It is my pleasure, my lady. I was sore disappointed when Lady Stonemere told me she wouldn't need me to cook Christmas dinner." The pleasantly plump woman was all smiles. "I had best get started if you are to eat at a decent hour."

"Thank you again. The guests will not arrive for a few hours, and there were a few items my cook had prepared in advance. Please let me know if you need anything at all."

"Very good, my lady." The woman curtsied and headed toward the kitchens behind the footman, who acted as her guide.

A sense of calm settled in now that the most urgent matter had been addressed. Emily went to her room, which she used as a private sitting room now that she slept next to Cooper every night, and pulled out her gift for him. She looked at the sheer pale green trousers that would billow a bit and then tighten at the ankles. Then she pulled out the small green velvet vest that had no fastenings and would come down just below her breasts. And finally, she admired the accompanying jewelry, a pair of peridot stones that dangled from a set of gold rings. The ensemble was completed by a pair of matching slippers that turned up slightly at the toes.

She pictured Cooper's face when he saw her in the outfit. Imagined how he would touch her, love her.

Excited to give him the gift, she wrapped everything up, tucking it all into a beautiful red box covered in silvered snowflakes. Then she looped a silver ribbon around it and tied a sweet bow.

By early evening, Emily was dressed and ready for their dinner guests. Despite the day's challenges, she was excited to give Cooper his gift. With the red-and-silver box in hand, she knocked on the door of their room.

He swung the portal open. "Why are you knocking? This is our room now."

"I did not wish to walk in on you unawares." She smiled shyly and stepped through the opening. "I have your gift, and I'd like to give it to you now."

He eyed the beribboned box she held out. "An excellent idea. Let me fetch yours."

She sat on one of the two chairs nestled near the window and waited for her husband to return. A few moments later, he appeared, holding a simple green box with a red velvet ribbon wrapped around it. Too excited to wait, she held her gift out to Cooper. "You should go first."

He laughed at her obvious excitement and handed her the other box as he took hers. He held the larger box, shook it a bit as he listened, and then tried to predict its contents. "A new robe for your lord and master." He waggled his eyebrows comically.

Emily laughed. "Open it, silly man."

So he did. As was Cooper's wont, he made a large production of pulling the ribbon to untie the bow, then slowly easing the lid off, and finally pushing aside the thin paper protecting the delicate garments. As he took in the sheer material and jewelry, his merriment fell away and confusion took hold.

He held up the small velvet vest and admired it. "While it is beautifully crafted, I fear you may have purchased the wrong size for me."

Emily laughed again, a full belly laugh. "It's not for you to wear. It's for me to wear...*for* you."

He looked at the garment again, then over at Emily, and back at the vest. He cleared his throat. "I fear you may still have the wrong size, sweetheart."

"It certainly fits. It is designed not to cover certain bits very much. Take a look at the rest of the box," she said, still smiling despite the warmth in her cheeks.

He delved back into the box and pulled out the pants. He looked at the trousers and then back at her, and the wicked smile she had come to love appeared. Then he held up the dangling jewels, looked at her ears and then back at the glittery items.

Realizing they would be there all night as he tried to puzzle out their purpose, she took one from him and held it against one breast. "They're jewelry for my nipples."

His confusion cleared, but then he groaned. "As we are soon to receive dinner guests, I take it you are not planning to don this outfit now."

"I am not." She smiled, letting her excitement and desire shine through. "But I shall put it on later when I give you the rest of your gift."

"The rest?" His interest was obviously piqued.

She nodded and leaned into where he sat. "Your very own slave girl."

He groaned again. "You are a wicked, wanton woman, and I adore you."

She bit her lip, bursting to tell him how she felt. It had been hard not blurting the words out over the past weeks, but she knew it would be worth it once she told him. And while she wanted to tell him then, he had his own agenda.

"Now, my gift to you." Cooper pointed at the box sitting in her lap.

She picked it up, pulled the ribbon, and carefully lifted the lid. Inside lay a rolled-up piece of paper with a small ribbon around it.

Curious, she looked up at her husband, her own confusion as to what he could possibly be giving her writ plain on her face. "I don't understand."

"Open it," he said, urging her to take action.

Carefully, she lifted the paper from the box and untied the ribbon. When she unrolled the sheet, all she saw was the neat scrawl of whoever had penned the document. The very top of the page identified it as a Title Deed. As she continued to read, she realized what he had given her, what he had done.

All the blood drained from her face as she took in the fact she was now the owner of a dower house. That regardless of what happened in her life, she would never again be without a home. Tears filled her eyes, making it difficult to read beyond that point. As she looked up at the man she knew she loved and the full force of her emotions swelled within, the first tear slipped down her cheek. "Cooper, I can't tell you how much this means to me. I know I was not the heiress you may have desired—"

"You are everything I could have wished for in a wife, had I been intelligent enough to know what I truly needed." He reached out and cupped her cheek, wiping some of the tears away.

Emily drew a deep breath and said the words she had feared for too long but now ached to say. "I love you, Cooper. I love how thoughtful and considerate you are. I love that you make me laugh, and I love that you know me well enough to have found the perfect gift for me."

She stood up, still clutching the precious paper in her hand. The moment he rose, she flew the short distance into his arms and claimed his lips in a passionate kiss. She reveled in the strength and heat of him, the faint taste of eggnog, and the hint of sweetness from the rum. She explored him, savoring the control he once more surrendered to her as she commandeered his mouth—and this time his heart—if she had any say in the matter.

After long minutes of kissing, tasting, and being close to one another, they pulled apart, both shaking from such an intense moment. Cooper cupped her face and looked her in the eyes, allowing all the passion she'd just stirred to heat his gaze. "I love you, too. I think I fell in love the moment I pulled that necklace from your bosom."

She laughed. "I believe our dinner guests should be arriving soon. I had better check on Theo's cook to see if all is well."

"Dinner and our friends can go hang."

Then he hauled her into his arms and simply held her as his heat sank into her body. They clung together, absorbed in such a powerful moment. Despite all the fiascos of the day—runny eggs, burnt toast, a sick cook, and the Christmas dinner that almost wasn't—she wouldn't have changed a thing about standing there enfolded in his arms. She might have been the thief, sneaking about in the shadows of ballrooms, but in the end, Cooper had stolen *her* heart.

The End

Chapter 1 - February, 1862

"Gather round, ladies and gentlemen. Tonight, we have a most unique entertainment."

Madame de Pompadour's voice quivered with excitement as Grayson Powell, Viscount Wolfington, walked into The Market. He was late, but the unusual announcement grabbed his attention.

Despite the frustration that pulsed beneath his skin—not uncommon after a confrontation with his father—curiosity had Wolf veering away from the stairs and edging into the back of the half-filled salon.

The attractive madame continued her pitch, exciting the men, and a few of the women. "In a rare occurrence for an establishment such as The Market, tonight we shall have...an auction!"

Murmurs ran through the crowd. Moving closer, Wolf couldn't help but find himself intrigued. Auctions occurred all over London, but most of them were of a questionable nature, typically featuring a virgin prize. He found the practice disturbing for multiple reasons, primarily because if the woman being auctioned *was* in fact a virgin, it was doubtful she was participating of her own free will.

Most of the time, the woman in question was not a virgin at all, which meant the buyer was being duped. Toss in the notion that buying and selling human beings smacked of slavery—a practice he could not condone, and England had outlawed in 1833—and all around it made the auctions an objectionable practice.

All of which made The Market holding one entirely outside the norm.

"The woman up for bid this evening is *not* a virgin." Madame paused, drawing out the moment. "In fact, she is a woman of experience, who has been a wife to a peer of the realm and lover to a desert sheik. Tonight, she seeks an enthusiastic lover—or two—for a night of unrestrained passion."

Wolf spotted his friends, Flint, Linc, and Arthur, milling about toward the back of the crowd. He stepped up and greeted them with a quiet nod.

"Interested in the auction, Wolf?" Linc grinned, a clear indication that he was most certainly intrigued by what Madame might have on offer.

"Not particularly. I have my doubts about these spectacles. Honestly, I would have thought The Market above such practices," Wolf said and returned his focus to the front of the room as Madame raised her hands to quiet the murmuring crowd.

"Ladies and gentlemen, I give you Lady Eatifi 'Ahmar."

Wolf's heart suddenly leapt from his chest, only to lodge in his throat. A woman had appeared next to Madame de Pompadour, her hair a deep, fiery red that seemed to ignite in the gaslight. She might call herself Lady Eatifi 'Ahmar now, but Wolf would know Julia Fairchild—or more aptly, Lady Wallthorpe—even if she were covered in robes from head to toe. And covered, she was not.

Next to him, Linc murmured, "Bloody hell, that woman is brazen. Wanton *and* brazen."

And she was. Julia stood before a room full of mostly men wearing a puffy-sleeved chemise that ended far short of where such a garment should. Just below her breasts, the material banded and stopped, leaving her torso uncovered and exposed to all and sundry. The rest of the garment reappeared at her waist, creating a full-skirted look that swished about her ankles, offering suggestive peeks at her lower legs. Around her hips, she had wrapped a brightly colored scarf and a coin-draped belt, which tinkled as she paraded around the makeshift stage in her bare feet.

When she stopped at one end, she turned and flicked her hips, causing the coins to jangle and the material to swirl about her legs. Wolf's mouth felt as though he'd ridden across the dells, only to be rewarded with cotton in lieu of water.

Finally, Lady Eatifi 'Ahmar returned to Madame's side and finished her tempting display with a shimmy of her shoulders that set *everything* to jiggling in the most enticing manner.

And with that, the bidding commenced.

"One hundred pounds from Lord Glennmore," Madame announced.

It took mere moments for the bidding to reach a thousand pounds. With each subsequent raise in price, Wolf's fury swelled.

How could Julia do such a thing? What of the scandal this would mire her in?

Had she no care for her reputation?

He listened to the lascivious men call out ridiculous sums of money for the privilege of slipping between her long legs, all the while watching for the point when the bidding slowed.

Wolf leaned over to Linc and nudged his friend. "How much blunt do you have on you?"

"Not interested?" Linc jabbed an elbow in his ribs. "I've got seven thousand pounds. Hit a run of luck at the tables tonight."

"Can I borrow it? I'll write you a draft on my bank."

Linc grunted and handed him the wad of cash. "I don't want the money. Share her with me."

Wolf's gut churned. *Could he do such a thing?* There was a time when he had been deeply in love with Julia. But he'd long ago closed off that part of himself, and willed it to wither and die. His intervention tonight was nothing more than common decency, a way to ensure she didn't suffer at the hands of some pompous, overblown lord who wouldn't take no for an answer.

"I plan to release her from any obligation to us."

Linc sighed. "I rather figured. Go on, then."

As the offers reached the five-thousand-pound mark, Wolf made his move. "Ten thousand pounds. *Ready.*"

The room grew quiet, except for a few mutters of annoyance from the previous highest bidders. Madame looked fit to burst, she was so pleased. Julia appeared surprised, almost as if she couldn't fathom such a large bid.

Or perchance it was because it had come from him?

"Sold to Lord Wolfington!"

Madame's excitement bubbled over, even as Julia leaned over and whispered in her ear. The enigmatic owner of The Market merely held up her hands, as if to say it was already done, and Julia frowned in response.

A few men grumbled, but it was clear Madame had achieved whatever her goal was, and she would not continue the auction.

Wolf pressed through the now-dispersing crowd until he reached the raised platform. Stepping up, he towered over the petite Madame de Pompadour, as usual, but the statuesque Julia still all but looked him in the eye. Years ago, when they had been young, her height and her refusal to appear of lesser stature was one of the many things he'd loved about her.

Wolf bowed over the proprietress's hand. "Good evening, Madame." And then he turned toward Julia, who automatically lifted her hand. Good manners always won out—even hers, so it seemed. "Ju—Lady 'Ahmar, such a lovely surprise to see you again."

Madame waggled her eyebrows. "Ah-ha! Now I understand. You know each other already."

"Yes, we were acquainted many years ago," Wolf replied. "But alas, she left me behind and gallivanted off to tour the world with her new husband."

The bitterness over that turn of events was hard to squash down again, since it currently felt as though someone had ripped the bandage off the wound, causing it to seep anew.

"Well, that is what one does when they are deserted on a London street corner and left to be married off."

Julia's green eyes flashed sparks he'd never seen from her before. When he'd known her, she had been strong-willed, but soft-spoken

"And I suppose one also stays away from England for nearly ten years after his death?" Wolf let one of his brows rise, his anger refusing to be quelled.

"Such passion between you two, it gives me chills." Madame's eyes appeared glassy, and her cheeks flushed. "Alas, we must conduct business before pleasure."

"Of course, Madame." Wolf looked about and spotted his friend standing nearby. "Linc, can you take Lady...uh, 'Ahmar, upstairs? I'll be along in a moment."

"My pleasure." Linc held out his hand and assisted Julia down from the platform. Leaving Wolf to quickly follow Madame into her office to settle their business.

When he finally headed upstairs to find Julia and Linc, he tried to tamp down his more hedonistic instincts. He'd told Linc he planned to let her leave unmolested, which he fully intended to follow through with. But images of her standing on the dais with her torso exposed kept flashing through his brain. All that smooth, creamy flesh bared, and then the small peeks of her ankles as she'd stood barefoot.

Next his dastardly mind retrieved images that took him up her calves, over her thighs, and presented him with the notion of feasting on her sweet pussy. His cock flexed in his trousers, rising to the occasion, regardless of it being all in his mind.

Determined to be a gentleman, he willed his lusty thoughts to retreat and his shaft to soften as he steeled himself to see the woman he had once wanted more than his next breath.

Julia sat beside the man Grayson—no, Wolf—had called Linc.

Wolf? She tested the name out in her head, and thought about the man who had strode onto the makeshift stage to claim her. There had been a predatory quality to him that had not been part of the young man she had once known and loved. The moniker suited him far more than Grayson.

Linc eyed her speculatively as she sat across from him in the growing quiet. "Lady 'Ahmar, it appears you have already met Lord Wolfington."

Julia tried not to sigh as she thought of the idyllic young man she'd once known. "We were neighbors, many years ago."

The blond man seemed to ponder that notion for a moment. "You must have been quite young."

She couldn't repress the smile that came to her lips as she remembered their youthful romps across the countryside near Marribone Manor, and then later, when they'd met again after he finished school and she had been launched into Society. He had acted the earnest, doting suitor during her first seasons, and made her believe in fate and fairytales.

While not the daughter of a peer, Julia's father had been very successful in his business endeavors, which had afforded them the ability to move amongst the *ton*. Of course, as she later learned, that had all been done with a very *precise* purpose. Specifically, for her to marry into the peerage, thereby making her parents related to that upper echelon of Society versus the fringe dwellers they had been relegated to as nouveau riche upstarts.

"We were young and blissfully ignorant of gender and class expectations at the time." Not to mention naïve about how unreliable love could be. Following her heart again was *not* a mistake she would make anytime soon. Memories of her past tasted bitter on her tongue, even as she waited for the source of all her heartache to reappear.

The door suddenly swung open, and she peered at two men and the ladies that accompanied them. However, Wolf was not among the small party.

"Hello!" One of the men, whose short-cropped hair fell in a soft wave of golden brown across his forehead, lifted a glass of amber liquid in a salute. "Where has Wolf gotten off to? I figured you two would be relishing your spoils by now."

Julia's cheeks heated at the obvious reference to their having won her in the auction. She drew a deep breath. She had known what would occur. Had even arranged for the event downstairs, but that knowledge didn't mitigate the fact she had all but been forced into the event. Nevertheless, she had intended to make the most of an untenable situation.

Why shouldn't I have the opportunity to explore a new sexual experience while holding the jackals of Society at bay?

Linc glared at the friendly man. "Hold your tongue, Dunmere. Lady 'Ahmar is our guest."

Dunmere's eyebrows rose, but he ceased asking uncomfortable questions, which Julia was grateful for.

Then the door of the room swung open once again, and this time Wolf strode through, looking fiercely determined. About what, she had no idea. However, she hoped it had something to do with having hot, sweaty sex with her. And if that happened to include the boyishly handsome Linc, all the better. The man *owed* her a little pleasure after all the pain he'd caused.

"Julia—uh, Lady 'Ahmar."

Wolf seemed unsure for a moment as he pulled up short and stopped.

She rose to her feet. "Please, Julia is fine. My identity is no great secret, despite the nom de guerre."

"Very well." He nodded sharply. "I came to escort you home."

"Home?" She was confused by his words, as images of the two men wrapped around her still teased her brain.

"Yes. Shall we?" He indicted the door, which he held open.

She crossed her arms under her breasts. "I believe we have some business to attend to first."

Wolf's golden-brown brows drew down over his clear blue eyes. "We do not."

Her spine stiffened in indignation. "On the contrary, you won a night of sexual adventure with me, and I have no plans to renege on that promise."

Just then, a group of noisy men and women stampeded past the open door of their room.

She let one brow rise. "Perhaps we could have this argument with less of an audience than the one both currently in the room with us, and the one passing by?"

Wolf grunted and waited until the man called Dunmere and the rest of his party departed. Then he closed the door with an imperious thud. "I bid on you with the full intention of releasing you from your obligation."

Julia drew a deep breath. The man was going to be impossible about this. With no warning, she turned and wiggled onto Linc's lap as he sat in a wing chair. Completely caught off guard, he had no chance to block her maneuver.

"Unfortunately, I have no such good intention on my part," she continued. "You bid on me and won, and I fully intend to extract my night of pleasure from you *and* your friend. I believe you won together, did you not?"

Linc looked distinctly uncomfortable as she wrapped an arm around his shoulders and pressed her breasts closer to his chest and face. He coughed, then answered. "Yes, I provided some blunt."

"Excellent. It was my preference that *two* men would win the night with me. Wolf, will you be joining us, or am I to be disappointed by you once again?"

She winced inside at her reference to their past, but she needed to move him off the mark. She needed to know what having Wolf as a lover might be like, just this once. Because despite her lingering anger with him, her body still responded to his mere presence.

To her excitement, Linc appeared to be game for her plan. His cock grew harder by the moment beneath her thighs. She turned her face so she was close to his ear and could whisper to him. "What will it take to get him to join us, do you think?"

"This secret conversation alone might do the trick," Linc whispered back. "But if not, then maybe you could kiss me. That ought to get him moving...though hopefully not to punch me in the face."

She chuckled and then leaned in and captured Linc's lips with her own. Pushing past his teeth, she swept in to taste the whisky on his tongue and explore his mouth. He met her with a vigorous twist of tongues that reminded her of what it was to have a man touch her again. It had been nearly a year since she'd last felt the touch of a desirable man in his prime. And Linc fully met both requirements.

Though Wolf might easily obliterate the competition if he would remove himself from hovering near the door like a clucking hen.

And then his presence suddenly loomed over them, casting a shadow from the gas lamps along the wall. Rough hands, like those of a laborer, cupped her face and pulled her mouth from Linc's. As she turned to look up at Wolf, their gazes met. His expressive blue eyes had shifted to a more stormy gray, and he slammed his mouth down on hers in a move that was pure declaration.

Julia's senses reeled as Wolf kissed her. He tasted of man, and the faint hint of mint, which triggered the echo of a memory as their tongues tangled and twined. The wet slide was an erotic caress that had her nipples hardening and her pussy dampening in immediate response. Then one big hand slipped around to the back of her neck and hauled her up and off Linc's lap. Once she was standing, Wolf pressed closer to her, deepening the kiss, as though he wanted to crawl inside her.

Behind her, Linc rose and pressed closer to her back, sandwiching her between them. He unfastened her belt, letting it fall to the floor with a muffled tinkle. Then he loosened the scarf at her waist and slipped it free from her hips.

Wolf broke the kiss, finally retreating for a much-needed breath. Julia's head spun as she tried to take in the truth of the matter. The man she'd dreamed about for a decade was here in her arms, if only for one night.

How could she let the opportunity to bring every fantasy she'd had to life pass?

Wolf's tumultuous blue gaze bore into her, demanding the truth. "Do you truly want this, Jules?"

About the Author

Sorcha Mowbray is a mild mannered office worker by day...okay, so she is actually a mouthy, opinionated, take charge kind of gal who bosses everyone around; but she definitely works in an office. At night she writes romance so hot she sets the sheets on fire! Just ask her slightly singed husband.

She is a longtime lover of historical romance, having grown up reading Johanna Lindsey and Judith McNaught. Then she discovered Thea Devine and Susan Johnson. Holy cow! Heroes and heroines could do THAT? From there, things devolved into trying her hand at writing a little smexy. Needless to say, she liked it and she hopes you do too!

Find all of Sorcha's social media links at
link.sorchamowbray.com/bio
~
or scan the QR Code

His Hand-Me-Down Countess
Lustful Lords, Book 1

His brother's untimely death leaves him with an Earldom and a fiancée. Too bad he wants neither of them...

Theodora Lawton has no need of a husband. As an independent woman, she wants to own property, make investments and be the master of her destiny. Unfortunately, her father signed her life away in a marriage contract to the future Earl of Stonemere. But then the cad upped and died, leaving her fate in the hands of his brother, one of the renowned Lustful Lords.

Achilles Denton, the Earl of Stonemere, is far more prepared to be a soldier than a peer. Deeply scarred by his last tour of duty, he knows he will never be a proper, upstanding pillar of the empire. Balanced on the edge of madness, he finds respite by keeping a tight rein on his life, both in and out of the bedroom. His brother's death has left him with responsibilities he never wanted and isn't prepared to handle in the respectable manner expected of a peer.

Further complicating his new life is an unwanted fiancée who comes with his equally unwanted title. Saddled with a hand-me-down countess, he soon discovers the woman is a force unto herself. As he grapples with the burden of his new responsibilities, he discovers someone wants him dead. The question is, can he stay alive long enough to figure out who's trying to kill him while he tries to tame his headstrong wife?

His Hellion Countess
Lustful Lords, Book 2

A duty bound earl and a jewel thief might find forever if he can steal her heart...

Robert Cooper, the Earl of Brougham must marry in order to fulfill his duty to the title. He's decided on a rather mild mannered, biddable woman who most considered firmly on the shelf. But, her family is on solid financial ground and has no scandals attached to their name.

Lady Emily Winterburn, sister of the Earl of Dunmere, is not what she seems. With a heart as big as her wild streak she finds herself prepared to protect her brother from his bad choices, even if it means committing highway robbery. But marrying their way out of trouble is simply out of the question. What woman in her right mind would shackle herself to a man, let alone one of the notorious Lustful Lords?

Cooper's carefully laid plans are ruined once he must decide between courting his unwilling bride-to-be and taming the wild woman who tried to rob him—until he discovers they are one and the same. And when love sinks its relentless talons into his heart? He'll do anything to possess the wanton who fires his blood and touches his soul.

His Scandalous Viscountess
Lustful Lords, Book 3

Once upon a time, a boy and a girl fell in love...but prestige, power, and a shameful secret drove them apart.

Julia fled abroad after the death of her husband, Lord Wallthorpe. She has finally returned to England, but little has changed.

Except for her.

As a dowager marchioness, Julia lives and loves where she pleases. And the obnoxious son of her dead husband does not please. But what can an independent woman do? Why, create a scandal, of course!

Viscount Wolfington is no stranger to the wagging tongues of the ton. Between being a Lustful Lord and the scandal of his birth, he learned long ago that society had little use for him. So when he walks into The Market and finds the woman who once stole his heart being auctioned for a night of debauchery, he jumps at another chance to hold her—even for just a single night.

As Julia and Wolf unravel their pasts, will villainy win again, or will love finally conquer all?

His Not-So-Sweet Marchioness
Lustful Lords, Book 4

He's shrouded in shame, fighting with his demons in the shadows. Until she sets her sights on him...

Mrs. Rosalind Smith once followed her heart and love to the battlefield and left a widow. Spending the remainder of her life alone is enough... until she meets a man who's need for pain sparks an answering flame deep within her soul.

Matthew Derby, the Marquess of Flintshire is a fighter, it is all he's known since childhood. Throwing his fists is the only way to keep his need for pain at bay, and a certain gentle woman off his mind. She deserves a better man than him—Lord or not. Though when faced with the prospect of losing Ros, Flint realizes he has found something to fight for...something to live for.

To Ros' dismay, everyone around her believes her demeanor too sweet for someone like Flint. When his world begins to unravel and his dockside violence bleeds into the drawing room, a shocking family secret won't be the key to all the answers. Questions remain, can he solve the mystery, tame his dark needs, and still win Ros' heart?

His Reluctant Marchioness
Lustful Lords, Book 5

A notorious woman must rely on the devil himself for help. Too bad she learned long ago never to trust anyone...

Frank Lucifer is having one hell of a week. His gambling hell is short staffed after firing his floor manager, and his half-brother has offered him a title—one he doesn't need or want. Then the woman he's obsessed with dismisses him from her bed, and the problem is he doesn't know who the hell she is.

Mistress Lash has her hands full. Her apprentice is missing under sinister circumstances, and Scotland Yard refuses to lift a finger. A liaison with Frank Lucifer—however attractive she finds him—is something she no longer has time for. Besides, someone should take the arrogant rake down a peg or two.

She sets out to find her apprentice on her own, but everywhere she turns, up pops Lucifer. He's following her, and she's growing suspicious about why that is. When he suggests they join forces, she reluctantly agrees. After all, one should keep their friends close and their enemies closer... she's just not sure which he is. Yet.

Working together to find her missing apprentice, she worries about her ability to protect both her heart and her own secrets from the perceptive man. And as events play out, she must decide if Lucifer is the villain she is searching for... or just the devil who haunts her scorching hot dreams?

Other Books by Sorcha

The Market Series
Discover the series that started it all...

In this sizzling series The Market becomes the setting for Londoners of all walks of life to discover pleasure, lust, and even love. But can they do what is required to claim the ones they've fallen for?

Love Revealed (The Market, Book 1)
Love Redeemed (The Market, Book 2)
Love Reclaimed (The Market, Book 3)
The Market Series Books 1-3 (Boxed Set)
Love Requited (The Market, A Short Story)

One Night With A Cowboy

The One Night With A Cowboy series is a set of short stories linked by cowboys and Soul Mates Dating Service, a dating service with an uncanny ability to match up soul mates. These sizzling little treats are perfect for a quick hot read.

Claiming His Cowgirl (Book 1)
Taking Her Chance (Book 2)
A Cowboy's Christmas Wish (Book 3)
Roping His Cowboy (Book 4)
One Night With A Cowboy Books 1-4 (Boxed Set)

Stealing His Cowgirl's Heart (Book 5)